NIGHTFALL

TSEZAR BRATVA DUET (BOOK ONE)

NICOLE FOX

Copyright © 2019 by Nicole Fox

All rights reserved.

No part of this book may be reproduced in any form or by any electronic or mechanical means, including information storage and retrieval systems, without written permission from the author, except for the use of brief quotations in a book review.

✿ Created with Vellum

MAILING LIST

Sign up to my mailing list!
New subscribers receive a FREE steamy bad boy romance novel.

Click the link below to join.
https://readerlinks.com/l/1057996

ALSO BY NICOLE FOX

Kornilov Bratva Duet

Married to the Don (Book 1)

Til Death Do Us Part (Book 2)

Volkov Bratva

Broken Vows (Book 1)

Broken Hope (Book 2)

Broken Sins *(standalone)*

Heirs to the Bratva Empire

Can be read in any order

Kostya

Maksim

Andrei

Tsezar Bratva

Nightfall (Book 1)

Daybreak (Book 2)

Russian Crime Brotherhood

Can be read in any order

Owned by the Mob Boss

Unprotected with the Mob Boss

Knocked Up by the Mob Boss

Sold to the Mob Boss

Stolen by the Mob Boss

Trapped with the Mob Boss

Other Standalones

Vin: A Mafia Romance

Box Sets

Bratva Mob Bosses (Russian Crime Brotherhood Books 1-6)

Tsezar Bratva (Tsezar Bratva Duet Books 1-2)

NIGHTFALL

TSEZAR BRATVA

By Nicole Fox

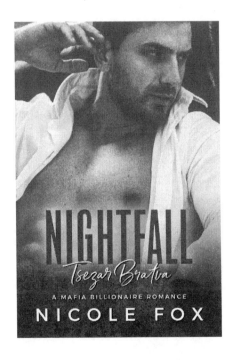

I just discovered the don's darkest secret. Wait 'til he finds out mine...

The Bratva don and I made a deal:

Spare my father. Take me instead.

But Dmitry Tsezar wasn't satisfied with my body.

He wanted everything else, too.

My obedience. My submission.

My heart. My soul.

And when that still wasn't enough, he came to take my life.

But then I found something.

Something twisted. Something wrong.

Something hidden in a locked room of his mansion, in a wing he warned me never, ever to wander near.

When I opened the door and discovered Dmitry's secret...

Everything changed forever.

1

DMITRY

The footage is grainy. Dots and whirls of gray and white flutter around the screen as though I'm seeing the scene through a snowstorm.

Still, it isn't enough to disguise his face.

"It's Sevastian," someone says.

I don't respond. I already know. Plus, I don't want to look as surprised as I feel.

Sevastian Nikitin has been one of my closest friends since I was a kid. We practically grew up together. The Bratva is a family, but within that family, I considered Sevastian a brother.

And now, I'm watching him spill his guts to the FBI.

"Who knows what he told them," someone whispers. "We could all be fucked."

I glance down at the stack of papers on my desk—pictures, dates, and locations. All of it proof of Sevastian's meetings with federal agents.

When I first got word that he might be a rat, I didn't want to believe it.

So, I had him tailed. For weeks, he was monitored and followed, and I hoped it would turn out to be nothing more than a Bratva rumor. Maybe even a case of jealousy. Another member wishing they had Sevastian's close connection to the boss.

But now I know the truth.

"We can't let this stand."

I look over my shoulder and see Rurik Zaytsev standing behind me. He's leaning back against the wall, arms crossed over his chest. His face is half hidden in shadow, but he stands tall when he sees me looking.

Next to Sevastian, Rurik is my second most trusted lieutenant. Though, with Sevastian's betrayal still fresh, I wonder whether I can truly trust anyone.

"Obviously," I say, sharp enough that the rest of the men in the room straighten their spines. "Do I strike any of you as a forgiving man?"

The question is rhetorical, but a few men shake their heads.

"A good leader is merciless to those who betray him and his family. You're my family and Sevastian has betrayed us all. So, he must die."

There's no room for emotions in the Bratva, especially for the leader. There are relationships, but they're founded on trust. When that trust is broken, the relationship breaks with it. If I want my men to respect me, I have no choice but to kill Sevastian.

I can't give him an opportunity to defend himself—because there is no defense. There is nothing he could say that would excuse the fact that he met with federal agents on numerous occasions without once telling me.

My father before me, and my grandfather before him, led the Tsezar Bratva with an iron fist. Ruthless. Unforgiving. They had no time for regret or disappointment. There was only anger and a sense of satisfaction when justice was dealt.

I intend to lead in the same way.

I pause the video, my office plunging into silence except for the nervous breathing of my men.

I point to Rurik. "Send for Sevastian."

Rurik answers with a sharp nod. "Should I tell him to meet you at headquarters?"

I think on it for a moment and shake my head. "My house."

I don't often conduct business from my home, especially when it will require a cleanup, but Sevastian will be nervous if I tell him to meet me at my office. He may guess I know something and dive into the rat's nest prepared for him by the FBI. I have to make him believe things are just as they should be. As they always have been.

"Actually," I say as Rurik is leaving. "Take two men with you and pick him up. If he asks any questions, tell him I told you it's an emergency. I don't want to give him the chance to run."

Rurik grabs two other lieutenants and the rest of the room follows them out, leaving me behind with the paused video showing Sevastian taking an envelope from the undercover agent he met at the restaurant.

I study the screen for another moment, assuring myself that the blurry man there is really Sevastian. The camera work is sloppy, but I see the tattoo peeking out from the collar of his sweater as he reaches across the table. It's the brown bear he had tattooed on his back the day he turned eighteen. A symbol of his love and loyalty for our family. Our organization. Our purpose.

A symbol that, in the end, meant nothing to him at all.

I turn off the television and leave. I have to be at the house when Sevastian arrives, so there is no time to linger.

Sevastian has always had pitch-black hair. As a child, even into his teen years, his face peeked out from under the mop like a friendly ghost, smiling and laughing.

While I followed the example set for me by my father and grandfather, greeting people with a stoic nod and burying my laughter behind a clenched jaw, Sevastian was jovial. He pulled pranks on maids, told dirty jokes loud enough for my grandmother to hear, and followed me blindly through every bad decision I ever made.

When I see Sevastian walking up my stone driveway, flanked on either side by lieutenants, it's that pale, smiling boy I see. Not a traitor —my friend.

Weakness. That's what my father would call this emotion.

Sevastian turned his back on our family. He considered himself stronger alone, better without the Bratva at his side. So now, he has to know exactly what it would feel like to be on his own.

There can be no mercy, no holding back.

Starting now, Sevastian is not my friend or my brother. He is my enemy, and I would do well to remember that.

By the time the front door opens, I'm sitting down in an armchair in the den, one leg crossed over the other, hands folded in my lap. I'm at ease. Visibly, at least.

Sevastian appears in the doorway first. "Dmitry."

The lieutenants fall away beside him, hanging back, and I see Sevastian glance around. His brow furrows, and I know he is suspicious. As he should be. Sevastian has always been a smart man, and I have no intention of fooling him tonight. Surely, he has to suspect what is coming for him.

"Sevastian," I say warmly, beckoning him into the sitting room. "Come, sit."

He hesitates. "I was told there's some kind of emergency?"

"Did they say that?" I ask, eyebrow raised, looking around him to where my lieutenants are lurking in the shadows of the entryway. They won't interrupt the proceedings unless they have to. Unless Sevastian puts up more of a fight than I expect. "Very dramatic. It's hardly an emergency."

"Okay," he says, his tone somewhere between a statement and a question. "So, what's up?"

I gesture for him to sit on the sofa next to me. "You missed our meeting tonight."

Sevastian's forehead wrinkles as he sits. "I didn't know there was a meeting."

"I sent a message to everyone in the Bratva. Did you not get one?"

He pulls out his phone and scrolls through it. "No. Strange. This piece of shit phone is always acting up on me."

He scrolls to the top and then looks through his messages a second time. I wonder if he's worried about any messages he may have missed from the FBI. Though, if he's smart, he'll have a second phone to communicate with them. He won't use the same phone he uses for Bratva work. It's too big of a risk.

"It wasn't anything too important," I say, waving my hand. "I just wanted to call you in here and make sure you were still alive. It's been a long time since we've hung out the way we used to."

"It has," he agrees. Sevastian runs a hand through his spiked black hair, the gelled strands returning to their previous spikiness the moment his hand moves past them. "I've let myself get a little busy."

"I'm not giving you too much work, am I?" I ask, leaning in.

Sevastian swallows. "No, no. Anything for the Bratva, you know that."

He smiles, but his eyes are wide and alert. Everything about his body language tells me he's uncomfortable. Probably because I'm being kind to him. Sevastian knows me well enough to know that, if I'm being kind, there is an ulterior motive.

He plants his palms on his knees and sits forward on the couch. "So, you just brought me here to check up on me? I'm flattered to hear you care so much about me."

"I care about those who care about me," I say, reaching out and clapping a hand on his shoulder. "And I'm loyal to those who are loyal to me."

I see him process the words, and his smile slips. Sevastian goes pale, and he swallows a lump in his throat before taking a deep breath. "Why am I here, Dmitry?"

"Because I sent for you," I say simply.

He nods, his hands lacing together in front of him. "What for?"

I sit back in my chair and stretch. Then, I turn and grab the crystal globe sitting on the side table. It's a trinket from my father's office. Something given to him as a gift from another boss, maybe a past leader of the Japanese Yakuza. It means nothing to me, but I've kept it around. I spin the globe with my finger, watching it turn slowly.

"Why?" Sevastian repeats, his voice shaking. "What is going on? And why is everyone waiting in the other room? What is this about? Have I done something?"

"Have you?" I ask quietly, tilting my head towards him.

He licks his lips, and I can see his fingers shaking. Slowly, the tremor moves up his body, claiming him inch by inch. He can't stop it. Soon, his head is twitching back and forth, too.

Sevastian is terrified.

"Who told you?" he asks.

I appreciate his not trying to lie his way out of things, even if it's not like he stood a chance if he made the attempt.

"Does it matter?"

He bites the inside of his cheek.

"What did you tell them?" I ask calmly, letting my duty to the Bratva wash away everything else.

There are men waiting in the other room, expecting me to look out for them. To take care of them.

Who knows what Sevastian told the FBI? Who he turned over? Any one of my men could be hauled in for questioning and it's entirely Sevastian's fault.

And ultimately, my fault.

For trusting a traitor. For being loyal to a man who wasn't loyal to me.

Now, I have to rectify it.

"Does it matter?" Sevastian asks, repeating my own question back to me. "You're going to kill me regardless of what I say."

I nod. He isn't wrong. "I would respect you more if you confessed. It might lessen the severity of your punishment."

"Bullshit," he spits. "I'm dying tonight regardless. So, go ahead, Dmitry. Do what you brought me here to do."

When I don't move, Sevastian leans forward, his top lip pulled back in a snarl. "What? Are you afraid to hurt your best friend? Because that's what we are, right? *Best friends*. You know I only did what I did to save my own ass. It had nothing to do with you or the Bratva. I wouldn't have gone to the FBI if they hadn't found me first. That's why you didn't kill me the moment I walked through the door. Because you know I have an explanation. You know I only did what I had to do—what anyone would have done. You know—"

Before he can finish the sentence, I rear back and smash the crystal globe against the side of his head.

Sevastian drops to the floor without so much as a groan, knocked out cold.

I study the globe, and aside from a smear of blood over Europe, it's as if nothing happened at all. I replace it on the side table and stand up, stepping over Sevastian's body on my way out of the room.

I nod to Rurik as I pass. "Take him to the basement. Chain him up."

My men get to work without hesitation.

The room is silent as I enter.

Sevastian is in the middle of the room—my personal gym—chained to the bench press. He can lift his arms a few inches, but otherwise, he's immobilized.

"I'm not going to tell you anything," he says, flinching away from me as I near him. "So you might as well kill—"

The wooden paddle cracks across his face before he can finish.

There's already a lump where I hit him with the globe, and now I've added a split across his cheekbone. Blood pours from the wound.

"Who did you turn over?" I ask. "Which stash houses did you reveal?"

Sevastian spits blood at my feet and glares up at me. I bring my knee up hard and fast into his chin. I hear his teeth smash together.

"Which of your brothers did you rat on?" I growl.

"*Brothers*," Sevastian laughs. "You were my brother once, too, Dmitry. What are we now?"

I bend down until we're nose to nose and growl, "Whatever we are is your doing. Remember with every flash of pain that *you* are the one who turned your back on *me*."

Sevastian looks away, and I see shame cross his face before he hides it with a scowl. He clenches his jaw and winces. I wouldn't be surprised if I cracked one of his teeth. "I'm not going to talk."

"You're loyal to the feds now?" I hiss. "Remember when you said you only did what you had to do to survive? Well, your life is on the line again. Suddenly you aren't so interested in begging?"

"Because it won't do any good," he said, lifting his chin like a petulant child. "You'll kill me, either way. At least this way, I'll take some of you down with me."

The lieutenants around me bristle with anger. I know they want to tear into Sevastian. They want a piece of him. They want revenge.

I try to imagine stepping back and giving them free rein, but no matter how much Sevastian has changed, I still see the pale boy peeking out from the dark black hair. I see the friendly little ghost who existed next to me for most of my life. My best friend. My brother-in-arms.

The paddle clatters across the floor when I toss it aside and trade it for the gun at my hip. I lift my arm, the muzzle pointed at Sevastian's mouth.

"Do you have anything left to say?" I ask.

Sevastian looks up at me, his eyes narrowed. "Yeah. Fuck—"

I pull the trigger and he slumps forward.

My ears are still ringing when I tell my men to clean up the mess. I don't look at his body before I leave. I've shown my family I don't stand for traitors, and I've maintained my authority. There is no need to carry the image of Sevastian's dead body with me. My job here is done.

Up in my office, I make a few calls, announcing Sevastian's actions and my sentencing, ensuring the news spreads quickly to the rest of the Bratva. When I'm done, I look down and realize there is blood spattered on my shirt.

The maid has washed enough of my bloody clothes that I know she could get the stains out, but I take it off and stuff it into my trash can. I have more than enough shirts that I don't need to worry about saving this one. Plus, I'm not sure I'd ever want to wear it again.

I pull a new shirt from the closet behind my desk and slip into it just as my phone rings. I recognize the number as Amanda's and answer.

"Any change?" I ask without saying so much as 'hello.'

"Nothing," she says.

I nod and take a deep breath.

"I'm sorry," Amanda says quickly. "I was told you wanted nightly reports on Tati. Is that still true?"

"Yes. I want to know the second there is any change. No matter what time."

Amanda agrees, and we hang up.

I stare in the mirror hanging behind the closet door and button my shirt with slow fingers. It's late, and I should go to bed, but I can't imagine sleeping. So, instead, I sit down at my desk and go through the list of collections I have to make the next day.

Usually, Sevastian and I collected together.

But tomorrow I will go alone.

2

COURTNEY

I stare at the page and widen my eyes, trying to keep my vision from going blurry. At this point, I can't tell if it's because I'm wired with caffeine or because I haven't slept more than a few hours at a time for the last three days.

My highlighter has become a permanent fixture in my hand, and I'm not sure I'll be able to put it down come test time.

Which is in one hour.

"Shit," I whisper, hunching down over my textbook. My professor told us over and over again throughout the semester that the best thing any of us could do would be to study the material periodically throughout the semester rather than cramming right before tests, but what did she know?

Well, probably a lot, considering she teaches behavioral neuroscience.

That's what I want to do. Not teach, but work in the behavioral neuroscience field. I want to be a clinical psychologist and help people.

But that won't happen if I fail this test.

I close my eyes, focusing my mind for a moment, and then begin reading again. Half of the page is highlighted. Hell, half of the book is highlighted. There isn't enough time for me to memorize all of this before the test. I'm going to fail. I'm going to have to drop out of school, and then what?

In the midst of my downward spiral, my phone rings.

I groan and dismiss the call without looking to see who it is. Everyone in my life knows I have this test today. I told my dad I would be coming home tonight and not to bother me until then since I'll be staying with him for the entire winter break. And Sadie is going to pick me up after the test to take me home, so she knows not to call. Whoever it was—probably a telemarketer—is not worth the energy it would take to read the number.

I sigh and focus on the page again.

When my phone buzzes a second time, I actually let out a scream, which my roommate—a Chinese exchange student who has been in a perpetual state of jet lag since she arrived four months ago—does not appreciate. She glares at me and then rolls over, pulling the blankets over her head. I have no idea if she has any finals, but based on her sleep schedule, I'd have to guess that she has missed them all.

I don't recognize the number, so I dismiss it with a quick flick of my wrist and go back to studying.

I'm in the middle of highlighting an important sentence I missed the first ten times I read through the chapter when my phone buzzes once more.

"Goddammit," I mutter, grabbing my phone off the charger and answering it. "What?"

"Courtney?"

I frown and pull back to look at the number on the screen.

My heart drops.

Then, I bring it back to my ear. "Mom?"

"Hey, baby girl," she croons in the sickly sweet voice she uses when it has been way too long since we've spoken. "How are you?"

"Did you get a new phone?"

"Oh yeah," she says. "A couple months ago. Did I not give you the number?"

"No, but I guess I have it now."

She laughs. "That's right. You sure do. Now you have no excuse not to call me."

"What was *your* excuse?" I say before I can think better of it.

I don't have time to fight with my mom right now, and when she sighs on the other end of the phone, I try to backpedal.

"I was just joking."

"I know I promised I'd see you over fall break, but time got away from me," she said. "I was traveling and lost my phone and had to get a new one."

I make a noncommittal noise to let her know I get it. Even though I completely don't—and I don't really care to, either.

"Things just got crazy," she says. "But I wanted to call and make plans for winter break. I thought I could come to town for a few days. Maybe see your dorm room and you could show me the campus and—"

"Actually," I say, interrupting her. "I'm in the middle of studying for a final."

"This will only take a second," she says, her sweet voice disappearing. "Just a 'yes' or 'no.'"

"The dorms are closed over winter break. I won't be in town."

"Oh," she says, disappointed. "Where are you staying? You could come stay with me. I'm in a one-bedroom studio and Markus stays over a lot these days, but we have a futon, and I'm sure we could rig up a partition so—"

"I'm staying with Dad," I say. "We arranged it weeks ago."

Weeks ago. When my mom was traveling and too busy to talk to me. Like always.

She tries to sound offended, but even if I did come visit her for the break, she'd find a reason why I needed to leave early or why I should maybe get a hotel room instead. Her boyfriend doesn't like kids and refuses to acknowledge that I'm a grown woman and not a child who's going to get Pringles crumbs on his leather La-Z-Boy.

"Well, if your father gets time with you, then I should, too."

"I'm not a brownie you're splitting in half," I snap. "I'm a person. I choose where I spend my time. Dad doesn't *get* time with me. He's earned it by being there. Like a parent is supposed to be."

I really don't have time for this argument right now, but I can't help myself when it comes to my mom. She gets under my skin.

She huffs. "That's not fair, and you know it. When your father and I split up, I couldn't take you with me, and you resent me for it."

"I resent you for acting like you can waltz back into my life at any time you want," I say. "Like I said before, I'm busy studying. I have to go."

"Call me later. This isn't over."

It is over. I won't be calling her later. I have no intention of seeing her over the break.

"Bye," I say shortly, disconnecting the call.

My heart is racing the way it does every time I get in a fight with my mom. There's something instinctually wrong with having this kind of a relationship with your own parent, and my body knows it. I'm always jittery for a while after we argue. I shake my arms to dispel the weird feeling and pull my book towards me.

I've only read three words when another phone starts to ring. I don't recognize the song and then realize it's Dandan's alarm, chirping from the other side of the room.

She groans and shoves the phone under her pillow, stifling the noise but not stopping it.

"Dan." I lean around my desk. "Dan!"

Nothing. No movement or rustle. Just the slightly muted sounds of bells chiming.

Forty-five minutes until my test.

There's no point in trying to study anymore. It'll take me fifteen minutes to walk to the exam room anyway.

I sigh and pack up my books. I won't be able to use them during the test, but maybe their knowledge will leach into me like osmosis if I carry them.

That feels like my only hope at the moment.

The sun is high in the sky when I walk out of my test, and I swear there are more birds singing than normal. If this was a musical, I'd skip down the sidewalk, twirl a stranger into a dance, and click my heels.

I passed.

I don't know that for sure, but I can feel it. I crushed that test.

I don't know if it was my relentless cramming or the osmosis technique, but it worked. I didn't have to skip any questions and come back to them. I didn't have to make any guesses. I made it through the multiple choice, true/false, and essay questions like a boss, and now I'm free.

Winter break awaits.

I'm walking past the rec center, heading back towards my dorm, when I stop and look through the large wall of windows into the dance studio.

I've passed it every day, multiple times per day, all semester, but I've never gone in. There were always classes in there, ranging from beginners to longtime dancers, that I didn't want to interrupt. Or I had studying to do. But now, the room is empty and the semester is over.

I'm free.

Before I can second-guess myself, I cut across the grass and test the studio door. Despite no one being inside, it's unlocked.

As soon as I walk in, the automatic lights flicker on, and I'm home.

The smell of wood greets me, and I drop my backpack in the corner and kick off my shoes on the rug.

I haven't been in a dance studio since the summer. I haven't danced since summer, either. Not even in my dorm room. There isn't enough space, and Dandan would definitely give me judgy eyes if I woke her up. So, tiptoeing across the floor and spinning feels like dipping my feet in a cool lake on a hot day. It feels refreshing, like my body is awake for the first time in months.

I've always enjoyed school and exercising my mind, but after months of studying and bending hunchbacked over my schoolbooks, it feels incredible to exercise my body.

There's a small CD player in the corner, and I hit play, hoping something is already loaded up, and immediately pop music begins to play through the speakers in the corners of the room.

I slide to the center of the room and easily transition from ballet to a more contemporary style. As I lose myself in the music, the two begin to blend until I'm alternating from fluid movements to a grand jeté and back again.

I'm completely lost in the movement when the music turns off.

Stuttering to a stop, I turn to see a middle-aged woman standing near the stereo. "You're great, but I have a class in here in five minutes."

I blanch, blushing a deep red. "Sorry," I mumble.

I jog the rest of the way to the dorms barefoot, my sneakers in my backpack, and dance into my room. In a startling turn of events, Dandan isn't there, so I turn up the music on my laptop and dance to and fro as I clean the room and pack for winter break.

When I'm done cleaning, I watch a few bootleg episodes of a reality TV show someone has uploaded to the internet and then make my way down to the dining hall for lunch. Everyone is gone by this point in finals week, so the offering is just some stale sandwiches and a cereal bar. I opt for two bowls of marshmallow cereal, assuming my dad will have made a big dinner to welcome me home.

By the time I get back to my room, I only have a few minutes until Sadie will be there to pick me up. She lives in a suburb just outside the city that's only fifteen minutes from my dad's house, so she's going to give me a ride since I don't have a car. My dad tried to convince me he could afford to get me a car, but I told him that between the cost of textbooks and my meal plan, I wouldn't have any money for gas and zero time for a job. So, he dropped it. Thankfully, Sadie has been an accommodating chauffeur.

She arrives just as I finish packing, and I turn off the lights, lock my door, and race down the back stairwell to meet her.

I expected her to be alone, but there's a large man with dark red hair sitting in the front seat. He climbs out as soon as he sees me, offering the front seat to me, and climbs in the back.

"Thanks," I say, pinching my brows together in a question as I slide into the seat.

"This is Devon," Sadie says in answer. She smiles in the rearview mirror at him. "His car is at the shop, so I offered him a ride as well."

"Sadie girl is our very own taxi service," Devon says, reaching up and laying a hand on Sadie's shoulder. Her cheeks blush.

Sadie girl? I want to tease her about the nickname and the behemoth in her backseat, but based on the way she keeps glancing in the rearview mirror, Sadie is in love with this guy.

"I haven't seen you in months, it feels like," I say.

She nods, the messy blonde bun on top of her head bouncing around. "I know. Work has been crazy, and I'm sure school has been busy for you, too, Miss Neuroscientist."

"Whoa," Devon says, leaning forward between the front seats. His cologne is strong enough that it tickles the back of my throat, and I have to clear my throat. "I didn't expect Sadie to be friends with a brainiac."

I frown. "Sadie is smart too."

Sadie smiles at me but doesn't say anything. She went into cosmetology school right after high school, and while I know she loves what she does, her parents make her feel bad about not going to college. Devon doesn't need to pile on.

"Of course she is," he says, pinching Sadie's side and making her jerk the steering wheel, nearly sending us into the gutter. "All of her other friends are just hairdressers like she is. I didn't know she was friends with any scientists."

Just hairdressers. I don't even begin to unpack that statement.

"I want to be a clinical psychologist," I say to change the subject, turning around to study him as if I'm peering into his very thoughts.

Devon smiles back at me, eyes vacant. Somehow, I don't think he has many scientist friends, either.

Sadie must be able to sense my dislike towards Devon because she turns on the radio and manages the conversation for most of the drive. Devon seems incapable of not making at least one sexual innuendo or flirtatious comment for every normal sentence he utters, and Sadie doesn't mind at all.

The drive is only thirty minutes, but I still thought it would be a great time to chat with Sadie and catch up. I wanted to hear how work was going and her family. Instead, I'm trying not to vomit while Devon suggests we all hang out together in a "threesome." I wonder whether it didn't just come out wrong, but when I turn around, he's wagging his eyebrows, and I knew he meant it exactly the way it sounded.

"You two would totally get along," Sadie insists, nudging me in the arm.

"Would we?" I ask disinterestedly.

"Totally," she says.

"I can tell already," Devon says. "Maybe some time over winter break we can all get together."

"I'm actually going to be pretty busy hanging out with my dad." I shrug. "We don't get to see each other very often."

Sadie glances over. "You can spare an afternoon, can't you?"

"Maybe," I say noncommittally. "I'll have to check."

"You can't be busy every single day," Sadie pushes.

I sigh. "Like I said, I'll have to check."

"Courtney," she complains. "You don't really want to spend every single day with your dad. It's winter break. Have some fun."

"Just because you don't like your parents doesn't mean I don't like mine," I snap.

Sadie jerks back like I've slapped her, and then stares straight ahead at the road. "Yeah, I guess so."

"Sorry," I whisper. "I'm sorry. I'm just tired from finals."

She nods but doesn't say anything. And for the first time, Devon sits back in his seat and stops breathing in my ear.

There's only another five minutes left in the drive, but the car feels like it's running short on air, and I'm desperate to get out. We're driving down Main Street, and I see my dad's repair shop up ahead. The window in the back is illuminated, meaning he's in his office.

"Pull over," I say, pointing to the shop. "My dad is here. He must not have gone home yet."

Sadie pulls into the gravel drive along the side of the shop and parks. "I'll see you around?"

I grab my duffel bag from between my feet and crawl out of the car. I turn around and smile back at her. "Definitely."

"Great," Devon says, as if I was talking to him.

I refrain from rolling my eyes and wave at Sadie. "Thanks for the ride."

I watch them pull away and then walk around to the back and pull out my key. My dad gave it to me years ago, but I've only used it a handful of times. Even now I could just knock, but I want to surprise him.

As soon as I open the door, however, I freeze.

There are voices coming from the front of the shop.

Usually, I would just assume it was a customer and walk on in, but something about the mood in the shop feels different. The voices are loud and angry.

I close the door silently and tiptoe down the hallway, sticking close to the cinderblock wall.

"Have I not been generous with you?" a deep voice says. "Have I not held up my end of our bargain?"

"You have," my dad says quickly. "You absolutely have."

He doesn't sound like himself. His voice is high-pitched and frantic. I can feel the fear in it.

"And yet," the deeper voice says, "you don't have my money."

"Not today," my dad corrects. "I will have it—"

"Not. Today." I hear slow footsteps, and I can imagine the person pacing around the room, hands folded behind his back. "And when was the money due?"

"Today," my father says. "I know it was due today, but—"

"So, where is it?"

My dad tries to answer but before he can even get a word out, there's a loud bang.

I throw my hands over my ears and wince. For a moment, I think it might have been a gunshot, but I creep forward and am able to see a fist pressing against the metal top of my father's shop counter. Whoever the person is, he has big hands and is strong enough to dent a stainless-steel countertop.

Not good.

"Your dues ensure our protection," the man says. "Without them, you're left to fend for yourself. Is that what you want?"

"No, no," my father says. "Please. I just need a bit more time."

The unfamiliar man sighs. "We all want more time. Unfortunately, we don't always get it."

I don't understand exactly what is going on, but I know I don't like where the conversation is headed. My father is a good-sized man who has spent his life working with his hands, but he isn't a fighter. He doesn't even own a gun. Whoever this person is, I suspect they don't have exactly the same background.

I inch forward down the hallway with no plan or thought in my head aside from helping my dad.

That's the only thing that matters.

3

DMITRY

Shitty day.

Beyond shitty.

Collection day is always a mixed bag. Some trips are dull and routine—knock, collect, leave. Others take an unexpected turn. People don't have their payments or they try to run or fight.

Regardless of the outcome, Sevastian and I, along with a few other lieutenants, always handled it. We worked well together.

Now, he isn't here, because I killed him. And Lawrence, one of the people I can always count on for a drama-free collection, is short on his money.

He's a small white man with a balding scalp and a soft chin. He wears a blue jumpsuit with grease stains around the wrists and oil splatters across the front. He's unassuming; clearly not the kind of man to challenge me to a fight. When I walk towards him, he holds up his hands in surrender.

"What are we going to do?" I ask, shaking my head.

My men shift behind me like starving dogs tracking an injured animal. Everyone has been on edge since the news about Sevastian was confirmed. I know I'm not the only one feeling pent-up. They want to beat Lawrence bloody—maybe even kill him. It really wouldn't be anything personal. They just need the release.

The trouble is that I like Lawrence.

Like with stray dogs, it's best not to get attached to our customers. They can come and go so quickly. Some don't pay or fight and need to be taken out. Others try to go to the police and come to the same gruesome end. Others simply move away, disappearing into the night, never to be seen again.

Lawrence always pays, never fights, and never runs. He's not a large man, but he faces me with courage I've rarely seen before and it's hard not to respect him.

Once, Sevastian and I came to collect alone, and Lawrence offered us a sucker from the cup on his desk. I refused, of course, because I'm not a child, but no one had ever offered us anything other than the money we came to collect.

Lawrence lowered his head and shrugged. "Do what you have to do, but if you could wait, just this once, I know I can get the money."

One of my lieutenants chuckles low under his breath. They have no suspicion that I'm going to be merciful, but Lawrence has never been late on a payment before. So, I'm going to reward his past timeliness with threats instead of a beating.

Power is important, but so is fairness.

A good leader knows when to show strength and when to offer encouragement. Lawrence just needs a little motivation. If he screws up again, then I'll pummel him.

"Twenty-four hours," I say finally. "That's how long you have to get what you owe me, do you understand?"

I can still see the panic in Lawrence's eyes. He blinks and opens his mouth but no words come out.

"Do you understand?" I growl, leaning down to get into his face.

He flinches away from me and nods. "Yes. Yes, I understand."

"You know I like you, Lawrence," I say, stepping back and twisting my neck to one side and then the other, a flurry of pops releasing the tension in my upper back. "But I don't often mix business and pleasure. If you fuck me over, I'll fuck you up. No second chances."

Lawrence pinches his mouth together and nods. "I understand."

I take another step backwards and shrug. "I just killed my best friend yesterday. So, if you somehow think you can sweet-talk your way out of this, I'd urge you to reconsider. Get the money. Hand it over. Make it easy on yourself."

His eyes flare when he hears my confession, and he looks around at my men. I see recognition flood his face. Sevastian isn't here with me. He isn't standing behind me like he usually is.

"He must have done something horrible," Lawrence says.

"He made his choice."

Lawrence looks up at me, his brown eyes wide and glassy. They crinkle in a sad smile. "We all make choices."

Me. He's talking about me.

I made a choice, and Lawrence doesn't agree with it.

But Lawrence doesn't know shit.

The anger that has been building inside of me since last night, the anger that I've kept quietly contained, breaks its mold for a second, flashing out. Before I can think about it, I've reared back and hurled a fist into Lawrence's stomach.

At the last second, I pull the punch slightly, but the force of it is still enough to make Lawrence groan and double over.

My men press forward, ready to act the second Lawrence tries to fight, but he just stumbles back and grips at the counter to keep standing.

I flex my fingers and am about to turn to leave when a flash of shadow catches my attention. I don't even have time to recognize what it is before I hear a high-pitched scream and then a person is on top of me.

Hands scratch at my face and chest, and I wobble, trying to find my balance with this new weight affixed to my side.

"Courtney!" Lawrence yells.

Suddenly, I remember Lawrence has a daughter. I've never seen her before, but he has mentioned her briefly. Never by name or anything identifying, just enough that I know she exists.

I suspect the woman pounding her fists against my chest is her. She's too small to be much of a threat to me with just her bare hands.

I grab for her flailing limbs, trying to peel her off me. My men are so surprised by her sudden appearance that it takes them a few seconds to recognize what's happening and step in to help. When they do, they manage to extract her from me easily, grabbing her arms and legs and pulling her back.

Her black hair is hanging over her face, wild and frizzy, and her chest is heaving from exertion.

"Courtney," Lawrence sobs, his first genuine show of emotion. "Please, let her go."

I hold up a hand to silence Lawrence and then direct my men to release her. They do it at once.

Courtney yanks her arms to her sides and then flips her hair back with an annoyed huff.

Now that I can see her face, I see the rage written there. Her top lip is pulled back in a snarl, her eyes narrowed and focused directly on me.

Still, even as angry as she is, she is beautiful.

I wouldn't have guessed she was Lawrence's daughter. He's pale and round, whereas Courtney has beautiful brown skin and a tight, lithe body. Her nose is pert and, presently, wrinkled in distaste.

"You son of a bitch," she spits, stomping forward like she's going to attack me again.

My men follow her movements, but she doesn't touch me.

I know I should be angry. Annoyed, even.

But I can't find it within me. I'm simply curious.

"Were you trying to attack me?" I ask.

Her eyes narrow further. "Only because you attacked my father."

"One punch," I say, holding up a finger. "That hardly constitutes an attack."

"He's a hardworking man, and you are a fucking leech."

"Courtney, baby," Lawrence warns. "I'm okay. I'm fine."

I wave another hand to silence him. It's hard to believe such a strong-willed woman could come from such a docile man.

"Don't speak again until I give the okay," I bark over my shoulder to him. "I'd like to have a word with your daughter."

I hear Lawrence's breathing pick up. My fists didn't scare him. But my merely looking at his daughter has him terrified.

"He isn't your slave," Courtney snaps. "He can do whatever he likes."

"True," I admit. "And so can you. Unfortunately, whatever you do, I'll take out on him."

Her eyes widen. I can see the words burning at the end of her tongue, but she doesn't speak them. She bites them back.

Good girl.

I walk towards her, enjoying the way she stiffens with every step. Just before we're chest to chest, I turn and walk around her, admiring every inch.

She has on a pair of tight jeans that hug her curves and a V-neck sweater that shows off her impressive cleavage. Her body is soft and tight in all the right places.

"Find the woman a seat," I say to Rurik, my eyes not leaving the girl. He nods and grabs a stool from the corner. He places it behind Courtney, but it isn't until I push on her shoulder that she sits down.

I pace the floor, drumming my fingers together. "This is an interesting turn of events."

"Please," Lawrence whispers.

I spin towards him, nostrils flared. "I told you not to speak."

He closes his eyes.

I begin my pacing again. "Lawrence owes me money. Did you hear that part, Courtney?" I ask, turning towards her. "I assume you've been eavesdropping for a while. You know what this is about?"

"I know what it's about," she says through gritted teeth. "It's about you compensating for your small penis."

I should slap her across the face, but instead I bark out a laugh.

My response surprises me more than anyone, but Courtney's eyebrow arches upwards.

"Your father and I had just reached an understanding," I continue.

"Twenty-four hours for him to come up with the five thousand dollars he owes me this month."

"This month?" Courtney asks, turning her attention to her father. "Dad, why didn't you tell me?"

Lawrence inhales to say something, but I spin around and shake my head. He closes his mouth and stares down at the floor.

"That's too much," Courtney says. "It isn't fair."

"Fair doesn't exist in the real world."

She rolls her eyes. "God, you are a cliché."

I find Courtney intriguing in the best way, but I also can't go on letting her think she can say whatever she wants without consequence. I take a deep breath and then spin around, pummeling my fist into Lawrence's stomach. For a second time, I pull the punch, but the force is enough to surprise him.

Courtney yelps. "Jesus, stop! I'm sorry. I'm sorry."

When I turn around, her eyes are wide and glassy, and she looks like a doll. Her skin is smooth and perfect and her hair is shiny and falling around her shoulders in messy waves. She is a picture, and I want to study her further.

"Are you, though?" I ask, balling my hand into a fist.

She nods frantically. "I'm. I'm sorry."

I turn towards Lawrence, but he isn't looking at me. He's looking over my shoulder at his daughter, shaking his head.

She is what Lawrence cares about. She's the reason he always paid on time and treated me with respect. Not because he actually respects me, but because he loves her.

And he'll do anything to keep her safe.

"This stop has taken longer than I planned, and now I'm not so sure I want to come back here tomorrow night to do it all over again." I frown. "And since we never got a chance to shake on it, our deal wasn't finalized."

"You rat," Courtney says behind me.

I ignore her. "I believe we should resolve this now. In my experience, once someone gets behind on one payment, they continually come up short on the next, and the next. It is a slippery slope."

"I can get the money—" Lawrence starts.

"Still not okay for you to talk," I growl.

He closes his mouth and breathes heavily through his nose. Sweat is beading up on his forehead and his cheeks are red with emotion.

"I'm not as interested in money anymore," I explain. "Do you have something else to offer me?"

Lawrence stares up at me silently and after a few seconds, I tell him he can answer my question.

"I don't have anything of value," he murmurs. "Just my shop, but even that isn't worth much. Really, I have nothing."

I spin away from him, pacing towards Courtney. I stand next to her stool and lay a hand on her shoulder. She tries to escape my touch, but I grip her harder. "Don't you, though?"

When Lawrence understands my meaning, his face goes pale. He shakes his head. "No, no."

I shrug. "Fine."

Then, I gesture for my men to move forward. Ready for blood, they advance all at once. Before they reach him, though, Courtney jumps to her feet.

"Take me," she says. "I'll do it. I'll go with you. Just don't touch him."

"No!" Lawrence yells.

For the first time in my relationship with him, Lawrence lunges forward and grabs the back of my shirt. He pulls me towards him.

"Don't touch her. Please. I'll do anything. Kill me. It's fine."

I shrug Lawrence off and turn back to Courtney.

Lawrence would die for his daughter rather than have anything happen to her. Which means this is the perfect punishment. Worse than a monetary fine.

"Six months," I say to her. "You'll come live with me for six months."

"No," Lawrence moans. "No. Courtney, run."

Courtney looks at her dad, and her lower lip trembles. Then, she looks back at me, and she turns to granite. She is fierce and fiery and tough, and I want to explore every facet of her.

"Will you hurt me?" she asks. "Will you kill me?"

I shake my head. "You will be of no use to me gravely injured or dead. Though, if you make any attempt to escape our deal, I will hunt you down and kill you. And your father."

She swallows, and I smirk, lifting an eyebrow.

"Do you agree to these terms?"

Lawrence falls into sobs behind me, but Courtney doesn't spare him a glance. She stares me in my eyes and nods. "Agreed."

I clap my hands together. "See? I knew we could all reach a compromise. Six months with me and this will all go away. Plus," I say, turning back to Lawrence. "This will give you a chance to save up for the seventh month when I come back to collect."

Lawrence has his head in his hands, his shoulders shaking. He is still weeping when I order my men to take Courtney out to my car.

4

COURTNEY

His car is dark and leather-detailed and smells like warm spice. The seat is warm underneath me, and in any other circumstance, I'd be thrilled to be in a vehicle as nice as this one.

Unfortunately, since the owner of the car is a monster, my excitement is tempered with fear.

Raw fear.

I didn't think before I lunged at him. He hit my father and something inside of me snapped. I hurled myself at him, but the moment our bodies made contact, I knew my attack was useless.

He was pure muscle under his clothes. Slamming my fists against him felt like hitting a brick wall. As useful as standing in the middle of a hurricane and screaming at the rain.

Now, I'm his.

For six months.

The thought makes my stomach turn, and I wrap my arms around myself and look out the window. At first, I try to pay attention to where we're going, but then I remember his threat. If I leave, he'll kill me and my father. And all of this will have been for nothing.

If I want my dad to be safe, I can't run. I have to do what he says.

"I don't usually listen to the radio, but you can turn it on if you want," he says.

The suggestion is so mundane that I can't help but look over at him.

His jaw is strong and square, and his golden blond hair is coiffed on top of his head, the sides buzzed short. The slope of his nose is flat and smooth. If I saw him painted in profile, I'd comment that the artist made him too perfect. *No one really looks like that.*

Except for crime bosses, apparently.

Tattoos cover his muscled arms, but I can't see enough to know what they are—just swirls of black peeking out from the collar of his shirt and the cuff at his wrist.

I reach out and turn the radio on, jamming the volume up as loud as it will go.

The man takes a deep breath and reaches out to turn it down to a normal volume. I expected a larger reaction.

"That was childish," he says. "Please tell me I do not need to repeat the conditions of your stay with me."

"You said I couldn't escape, and I'm not."

He looks over at me, and I meet his blue eyes with a hard glare.

"Your father's life is on the line." He turns back to the road and grips the wheel harder, his knuckles flexing against tan skin. "Do you really want to piss me off?"

I sink lower in my seat and as my adrenaline fades, the weight of what has happened begins to sink in.

Six months.

I'll miss school. Will I have to drop out? Will I lose the money I've already paid towards the semester? I can't afford to pay it again.

Panic builds up inside of me like a Jenga tower, and all it will take is one false move to make it all come tumbling down.

I poke at the tower gently, testing for an easy brick. Just a simple question to make this whole situation less uncomfortable.

"Who are you?"

The man looks over at me, one eyebrow raised. "Your father never mentioned me?"

He mentioned *someone*, but never in detail. He certainly never explained he was paying five thousand dollars per month for protection. There were times he would get frustrated and say he wished he had more money to buy me the things I needed—clothes, a car, tuition. But our house ran on a single income, and I understood that. I didn't ask for anything unnecessary, and still this 'lender' hung over my father's head for years, starting back when I was in middle school.

"I thought he took out a loan for the shop or something and was having a hard time paying it off," I admit. "He never corrected me."

"He probably didn't want to scare you," the man says, looking over at me again.

I feel his eyes on me like the lick of a flame against my skin, burning and uncomfortable. "How is that working out?"

"I'm not scared," I say quickly. "I just want to know who I'm not scared of."

He smirks, and I want to slap the expression off his full lips. "Dmitry Tsezar, boss of the Tsezar Bratva."

I don't know who he is or what a "bratva" is, but it sounds worse than a simple loan shark.

We drive in silence for a long while, and I steal glances at him when he isn't looking.

He sits up tall and proud in the seat, chin lifted, eyes focused on the road ahead of him. But I get a sense there is something more to him. A story behind the strong face.

I hate him for what he did to my father, but I also can't ignore that fact that Dmitry could have killed him. Instead, he threatened him, he bargained with him, and in the end, he traded my father's debt for me. It doesn't make him a good guy, but it precludes him from being a soulless monster.

A monster with a heart of gold, then. Or something like that.

That doesn't matter, though. Not when he's holding me captive. I can't feel pity for the man who is going to ... well, I'm not sure what he's going to do, but I'm certain he isn't sending me on an all-expenses paid vacation.

"So," I say, breaking the silence. "What are you going to do with me? Lock me up? Throw away the key?"

"If that's the kind of thing you like."

I turn to him with a frown. "It matters what I like?"

The corner of his mouth turns up in amusement. "I always try to make sure the women I'm with have a good time."

A prickle crawls down my spine as I realize what he means.

Sex. With him. The two of us. Together.

Heat floods my entire body at the same time like a kind of explosion, and I shiver.

"I can lock you up if you like," he purrs, reaching across the seat to drag a finger up my thigh. I shift out of his reach, but he isn't dismayed. He winks at me. "Or tie you up. My favorite option, if you want to know, is to pin you to the wall with my own body. I like the idea of your legs wrapped around my waist. It would give me a chance to show you exactly how *not small* my penis is."

My face has to be as red as a stop sign, and I'm grateful to the early autumn sunset for giving me some kind of cover.

I was too busy all semester to date much. School was my priority—passing my classes and keeping my GPA up. That mattered more than anything.

Perhaps my lackluster sex life is why Dmitry's words are like an arrow aimed directly between my thighs. I shift in my seat slightly, hoping it's a small enough movement he won't pick up on it.

Suddenly, the car stops, and I go on high alert. Are we pulling over to get a head start on what Dmitry was talking about? Has he changed his mind about taking me to his house? Maybe he'll just kill me and be done with it. My father won't be any wiser until six months from now when I don't come home. By then, there will be no trace of me for the police to find.

My heart is lodged in my throat.

Dmitry turns to me and drags his thumb across my lips with a mischievous smile on his lips. His blue eyes sparkle. "I'll be back."

Then, he's gone.

I watch him walk around the car and up to a small house set back from the road. The lawn is overgrown and the porch light is out, covering everything in shadow. I can see enough to know that the woman who answers the door is middle-aged and wearing a robe. Dmitry talks to her for a minute and then hands her an envelope. She grabs his hand with both of hers, whispering something to him, and then waves as he walks back to the car.

He slides into the driver's seat and pulls away without a word.

"What was that about?" I ask finally.

The woman seemed happy to see him. And it didn't look like she gave him any money in return, though it was too dark to really tell.

Is it possible Dmitry could have friends?

"Drugs," he says simply. "Or money. Or guns. Whatever you'd like to imagine it was."

"In a white envelope?" I ask.

He hums a dismissive assent and doesn't mention it again as he stops at another house and another, having a similar exchange with each middle-aged woman who answers the door.

After the fourth house, I push.

"Why won't you tell me what you're doing?"

"What makes you think you deserve answers from me?" he snaps back.

"Because you fucking kidnapped me," I spit.

"Ah ah," he says, wagging a finger. "Kidnapping implies you were taken against your will. I specifically remember you offering yourself up. Did you or did you not agree to this deal?"

I don't say anything, which he must take as a response.

"Since you did agree, I'm sure you remember the stipulations. I'm in charge."

I bite my tongue and sink down in my seat. I could argue, but he'll make more threats. Against me. Against my father. Or he'll continue telling me what he plans to do to me later, and I can't handle that kind of confusion right now.

∼

Twenty minutes later, Dmitry stops outside a large wrought iron gate.

It looks like a horror movie scene. The kind of entryway people walk through moments before stumbling into the abandoned house and being murdered by a ghost.

He hits a button on his visor and the gates swing open slowly. We pull through them, winding along a long drive with trees on either side, and I sit up.

"Is this where you live?" I ask.

He nods. "This is home. Yours, too, for the next six months."

The thought is a dark one. Six entire months.

However, my dread is interrupted when he rounds the last curve of the long driveway and the house comes into view.

Luxury.

That's the only word I can think of.

The house has a low, modern profile, all wood accents, stone, and glass. The lawn is immaculate, with obvious professional landscaping. It's magnificent.

Dmitry parks in front of the house in the middle of the semicircular driveway and turns the car off. I get out on shaky legs, suddenly much more nervous than I was in the car.

I'm going to live here. *Here.*

The reality of it isn't sinking in, and I'm not sure when it will. If ever.

How did I get myself into this mess?

Dmitry walks ahead of me, then pauses in the middle of a step and turns around. "Are you coming?"

I hesitate for only a second before I follow. Then, just as I reach him, he grabs my shoulder. His touch isn't rough, but firm. And I don't try to escape.

"There is only one rule," he says.

"Somehow I doubt that," I snort.

His eyes narrow. "I'm serious. There is only one *house rule* that you must obey: never go to the east wing."

"I'm bad with directions so you'll have to point out the wing I have to avoid."

He indicates to my left. "I'm serious, Courtney. Never go over there. I swear that you will regret it."

I'm curious. More than curious. But there is no way Dmitry will tell me anything, and I have too many warring thoughts in my head to devote to the mysterious wing of his house. First and foremost, I'm distracted by the fact that his house has wings in the first place.

Growing up, my dad and I lived in small rented bungalows and trailer parks. Nothing flashy or showy. We lived on the essentials.

This house is ... definitely more than the essentials.

Dmitry opens the door and waves me in ahead of him. Clearly, he at least knows how to be a gentleman, even if he's chosen to fall short of that standard for ninety-nine point nine percent of the brief time we've known each other.

The entryway is high-ceilinged and clean and shiny. Everything is marble and polished hardwood. Decorations are sparse; mostly mirrors and plants that might be real or fake. I can't tell.

A staircase leads up to a second floor and steps to my right lead down to a sunken living room. I've never lived in a two-story house before and now this one seems to be infinite levels. That's when you know a house is nice—it changes elevation for every room.

"Do you want a drink?" Dmitry calls over his shoulder as he walks through a door under the stairs and into a massive kitchen.

I nod without saying anything, but he must have seen it because he pours me a glass of whatever he is having.

I move to follow him into the kitchen, but I can't. It's too white and bright and right now, I need to sit down. My head feels fuzzy.

I walk back down the hallway and turn into the sunken living room. There's a gray stone fireplace and deep sofas with matching footrests. I drop down into the nearest one and take a deep breath.

It's comfortable, and I hate that.

This place should be a miserable dungeon. I should be chained to a wall and starved.

Instead, I'm sitting on the most comfortable sofa I've ever sat on while Dmitry makes me a drink in the other room.

Part of me wonders whether he isn't drugging it, but at this point, being unconscious might be a solace. My nerves are fried.

Dmitry walks into the room, saying nothing about the fact that I've made myself at home in his house, and hands me a drink with an amber liquid inside, one large ice cube in the middle. I take a sip and wince. But the burning helps me focus.

He sits on the sofa across from me, takes a sip, and then lowers his chin, staring up at me from beneath blond brows. "Your father said you're a dancer."

It isn't a question, so I don't answer it.

If memory serves, my father has been in "business" with Dmitry and his little gang for at least years eight. I wonder how much my father has told him about me during that time. Certainly, more than he told me about Dmitry.

"What does your bratwurst do?" I ask, clutching my hand around the glass.

Dmitry shakes his head. "Bratva," he corrects. "And I ask the questions."

"You didn't ask a question," I say. "It was a statement."

"Fine, then here's another one." He puts his glass on the end table next to the sofa and leans forward, blue eyes smoldering. "Dance for me."

My stomach drops, and I instinctively shake my head. "That's a command."

"I also give commands," he says, sitting back on the couch and letting his legs fall open. "So, dance for me."

Everything inside of me wants to run. I want to flee out the front door and disappear into the trees that surround this mansion.

But I can't.

Not unless I want my father to suffer the consequences. Not unless I want Dmitry's muscled meatheads to hunt me down and kill me.

Dancing is a better alternative to dying, so I set my drink down and stand on trembling legs.

Usually, I stretch before I perform. I limber up and listen to music.

Now, there is no sound but the thunder of my heart in my chest, and my muscles are cold and stiff with dread.

Dmitry raises his eyebrows, encouraging me, and then curls a finger to usher me forward.

I walk over to him stiffly, and he sits up and grabs my hand, holding it out to the side before dropping it, letting it slap against my leg. "Loosen up."

I scowl at him and begin to sway my hips, moving like a nervous teenager at a middle school dance.

He tsks softly. "You can do better than that. Don't make me return you to your father. Believe me, neither of you will like that option."

The threat is like a shot of adrenaline, and I turn around and roll my body in front of him. I stretch my arms above my head and shimmy down in a serpentine motion before pressing my backside out and standing up.

"Closer," Dmitry says, his voice lower and rougher than it was only a moment before. It's clear what he wants.

My limbs feel like they don't belong to me as I step between his legs and press my hands into his thighs for balance. I circle my body into him and ignore the jolt of electricity that shoots through me when he places his hand on my hip. His skin is warm on me, even through my clothes, and I grind down onto him, hoping to get this over with as soon as possible.

Dmitry begins breathing more heavily, his grip on my hip growing tighter. And rather than relaxing, I grow stiffer. More unnatural.

Suddenly, Dmitry wraps his arm around my waist and drags me down onto his lap. I can feel him pushing against my lower back through his jeans.

"You are so stiff," he whispers, his lips pressed against the shell of my ear. "Either you are not much of a dancer after all …"

I don't say anything. I can't deny it, and I'm not in the mood for a snarky remark. My tongue feels too big for my mouth, and there might be a hummingbird flapping in my chest.

"Or you just need to relax," he says, easing his grip and sliding his hand down my stomach until his fingers are wedged between my legs.

He uses his other hand to press my thighs apart, and I'm a mannequin in his lap. I watch what he's doing with a disconnected kind of curiosity, as though it's happening to someone else.

"Let me help you," he says, dragging his fingers up to flick open the button of my jeans and push the zipper down. When his hand slides inside of my pants, I'm amazed at the warmth, and I shiver from the pressure.

Dmitry massages his other hand up my body, sliding underneath the bottom of my sweater to lay his large hand across my stomach. He pins me against him and then slides his finger across my opening.

I can't help it. I gasp.

I try to shift away from his touch, but he presses his hand harder into my stomach, making it impossible to move, and circles his finger around the apex of my thighs, massaging my most sensitive area.

Immediately, I begin to squirm.

Sensation builds in my abdomen despite my attempts to stop it. I would love nothing more than for Dmitry to feel like a failure; than for him to think he can't please a woman.

However, that isn't possible.

As soon as he slides a finger inside of me, he knows my dirty little secret:

I'm wet for him. Wet and ready.

He presses one finger in and then two, using his thumb to continue the slow circles that are driving me wild.

I hold my breath until my vision goes black around the edges, and I have to gasp so I don't pass out. I lay my head on his shoulder, my body feeling heavy and drunk.

No one has touched me like this in so long. For the last several months, it has just been me under the covers of my twin bed in the precious few moments when Dandan left the dorm room and gave me a second of privacy.

Now, there is a beautiful, horrible man rubbing away every ounce of restraint and self-respect I have.

He's flipping my moral compass on its head.

He's turning my world inside out, and when he adds a third finger inside of me, pulsing to the rapid rhythm of my heart, he sets it on fire.

I moan and grab for something, anything to help me keep my grip on the world. I bring my arms up, and I don't realize I'm wrapping an arm around Dmitry's neck, my fingers finding his silky blond hair, until I've already done it.

As the climax comes, it's too powerful to move. Like a raging storm, it's better to shelter in place.

So, I curl my fingers in his hair and moan, squeezing my eyes shut as heat washes through me in pulsating waves.

Slowly, the waves begin to ebb, taking with them my power to move or walk or speak.

I just lie there on top of Dmitry, staring up at the ceiling, his arms still around me, his fingers still inside of me, completely spent.

"See?" he says, his breath warm against my neck. "I told you I wanted you to have a good time."

Then, he slides me off his lap, stands up, and walks out of the room.

5

DMITRY

The lights in the parking lot burned out years ago and trash lines the bottom of the chain-link fence and the grimy stone walls. The abandoned warehouse is annoyingly far out of town, which makes it the perfect place for a covert meeting.

Rurik lights a cigarette and leans back against the car, his feet crossed at the ankles. "Where is this guy?"

"We're early," I remind him.

I like being the first at a location. It gives me the upper hand and helps ensure I won't be surprised.

"But he'll be here. He's always on time."

My family has been working with Nico since I was a kid. Nico was one of the few people in this world my father truly trusted, which means I trust him as well.

"I just don't want to stand in this lot all night," Rurik complains. "There shouldn't be this many bugs this close to winter."

He swats at a small gnat flying around his face, but I can't think of anything to say.

I've been distracted.

Courtney has been living at my house for a week, and I haven't touched her except for the first night I brought her home.

When she sat in my lap and ground her tight body against me.

When I slipped my fingers between her legs and felt her fall apart.

I have to shift my position so Rurik won't see the small tent I've pitched.

And that's exactly why I can't focus. I've never thought about a woman like this. She has a fire that I admire. Usually, it's directed at me, which I could do without, but I still respect her drive. Her ability to speak her mind, no matter how the deck is stacked against her.

Also, her flawless fucking body.

I shift against the car again, hoping to disguise the growing hardness between my legs.

I need to fuck her. That's the problem.

Right now, she's this elusive woman. Beautiful and fiery and, aside from my fingers, unexplored. As soon as I get between her legs, the mystery will be gone, and I'll be able to focus on work. On what is really important.

I thought it would be nice to let her settle into the house before jumping into sex. Courtney put on a brave front, but I could tell she was freaked. I didn't want to traumatize her from the onset and then spend six miserable months together.

So, I've tried to make her feel comfortable at my house. We've eaten meals together and even had short but polite conversations. Every interaction has dripped with tension, though. Our first night together sits between us like an elephant in the room, and we won't be able to avoid it forever.

I wondered whether she's been thinking about it as much as I have.

I roll my neck on my shoulders and take a deep breath.

Tonight.

Tonight will be the night. We'll fuck and whatever spell she has over me will be broken.

My phone rings. I dig into my pocket and pull it out to see who's calling.

"Nico?" Rurik asks.

I shake my head. "I don't know the number."

Rurik stands up, arms crossed over his chest like he's going to guard me against whoever is on the other end of the phone. I answer.

"New location," an unfamiliar voice says. "I work with Nico, and he can't make it out there tonight. You have to come to him."

"This isn't a negotiation," I say. "We agreed on here and here is where we'll meet."

The man makes a disinterested noise. "Then I guess you'll be waiting all night. I just sent the address where we'll be for the next hour. Show up if you want your weapons."

Before I can say anything, the man hangs up.

I growl and shove the phone in my pocket. "Nico is fucking dead."

"Dead?" Rurik asks, eyes narrowed.

"He will be, once I kill him," I clarify. "One of his guys called to tell me they're changing the location."

"Oh." Rurik sighs and then turns to me, one eyebrow raised. "And you're going to let him do that?"

It's a show of disrespect to change the location last minute, especially through an intermediary rather than calling me himself. While I want to ignore the demand, I can't. Nico is a major key in our weapons shipments. Though, if I get my way, he won't be for long.

"I'll make sure Nico gets what's coming to him," I say. "But we need to go."

~

Rurik calls in more men to back us up. If the location is being changed, we don't want to take any chances.

"Not with the Italians on our asses like they have been the last few months," Rurik says. "You and I make a good team, but we won't win in a firefight that's just the two of us."

I nod in agreement and then pause. "Do you think this could be the Italians?"

He thinks on it for a minute and then shakes his head. "They're showmen. If they wanted to attack us, they would have done it at the first location. Probably with a pyrotechnics show to announce their arrival."

I laugh. "You're probably right. Subtlety isn't their strong suit."

Still, something about the situation rubs me the wrong way. Nico has always been up front with me. He's used middlemen to communicate a few times, but he's one of the few business relationships I have that I talk to directly. I mean, he came as a guest to my father's third wedding. The man is as close to family as one can have in this line of work.

The new location is closer to the city. It's on a frontage road just off the highway and cars trickle down the road despite the late hour. It's much more public than I care for.

Streetlights illuminate the sidewalk and part of the road, but the middle of the lot is dark. And in the dark center sits one car.

"That him?" Rurik asks, turning off the headlights and squinting.

"I can't tell." There's no signal to let us know the person in the car sees us or knows we're here. "Send a few men over to check it out."

Rurik nods and pulls out his phone. After a few seconds of sending out texts, I hear a car door open and close behind us and then two of my men walk towards the lone car, guns drawn.

I watch carefully as they approach the vehicle from both sides, surrounding the driver to ensure he can't get out. When they reach the front windows, they pivot and aim at the front side. Then, they drop their guns.

"What is going on?" I say, mostly to myself.

"Not good," Rurik says. "It's not good."

As proof of Rurik's guess, the two men turn and jog back towards our car. I get out.

"Who is it? What's wrong?"

I shouldn't have come here. I don't know what's going on yet, but clearly this was some kind of trap. I look around, expecting to see Italians approaching us from all sides.

"It's Nico," Pasha says. His face is so white, it's practically glowing.

"In the car?" I lean around to look over his shoulder.

Pasha nods. "He's dead."

I hide my shock. I already relented to a change in the location and now my supplier is dead. We are being played, and I don't want to look any more confused than I feel.

"Are you sure?"

They nod solemnly. "He's definitely dead."

I wave for Rurik to follow me, and we walk towards the car slowly, keeping an eye on the edges of the lot. There doesn't seem to be anyone else nearby, unless they're hiding in the trees. Still, there is no such thing as being too careful in a situation like this.

I inch around the back of the car, keeping my distance, and already I can see the blood splatter.

On the driver's side window and the rear window. There's a puddle leaking from the driver's side door.

No one could lose that much blood and survive.

Still, I want to make sure it really is Nico, so I walk up to the car and reach for the handle.

"Wait," Rurik says, grabbing my shoulder. "It could be a bomb."

He drops down onto his stomach and looks under the car, studying it. "I don't see anything, but stand back while I open it."

I wouldn't ask Rurik to risk his life for me like this, but I won't refuse his offer.

With a safe distance between me and the car, Rurik slowly pulls open the door. When nothing happens for several seconds, I approach again.

The smell of iron hits me like a wall, and I cover my nose with my forearm.

"Shit," I mutter, shaking my head. "This is bad."

There are blood smears all over the console and the steering wheel, and tears in the upholstery. Nico struggled. Hard.

Rurik turns away and wrinkles his nose. "It's rare to see a takedown this brutal. He must have pissed off the wrong men."

I shake my head. "I don't think this had anything to do with Nico. I think this has to do with me."

Rurik leans into the car and pulls out something smeared with blood. "I guess we'll find out. The killers left a note."

This will happen to every single one of your men and every single one of your contacts unless you back off. We will dismantle your tower brick by brick. Don't test us.

The note is signed with three slashes of color in the bottom corner: green, white, and red.

The Italians.

6

DMITRY

I throw the note on the ground and move quickly back towards the car. "We need to get out of here, now. And call Vadik. He's waiting at the docks for a shipment."

"You think this has something to do with that?" Rurik asks.

"I'm not sure," I admit. "But I want to know if it does."

Rurik calls Vadik while I call the number that brought me to this damn warehouse in the first place.

Predictably, there is no answer.

I open up a browser and search the number online, but no names pop up. Nothing to give me any clue where it could have come from.

Though, I don't really need additional proof.

The three-colored stamp on the bottom of the letter is enough.

For months, the Italians have been encroaching on our territory and questioning our hold on the city, and finally, they've taken action.

My father would berate me for not acting sooner if he were still alive to do so. My grandfather, too, for that matter.

I was always too soft for their taste. Too measured.

You have to act fast. Strike now. While the iron is hot.

I like to know every option. For instance, if I'd walked into Lawrence's shop and killed him outright for missing a payment, I wouldn't have Courtney back at my house waiting for me.

Though, when it comes to Courtney, I can't help but think I should have struck that iron while it was hot.

Because, oh damn, is it hot.

I squeeze my eyes closed and pinch the bridge of my nose, trying to focus. One of my most reliable suppliers is dead—murdered in a gruesome way as a message to me—and all I can think about is fucking Courtney. For fuck's sake, I need to break her and end this stupid mind game I'm playing with myself.

Rurik walks over, pulling me from my thoughts.

He shakes his head. "There was no answer. I called a few other guys, but no one has seen or heard from Vadik all night."

"Shit." I pull out my phone and make a few more calls. Rurik is right. No one has seen or heard from Vadik since he left to pick up the shipment.

Which probably means he's dead.

I'm just about to suggest a Bratva-wide meeting—something I do very rarely—when Pasha walks up, chewing nervously on his lower lip.

"What is it?" I bark when he doesn't say anything immediately.

"Vadik is in the hospital." He shakes his head. "He was ambushed. Luckily, he's alive and someone found him. But he's in rough shape."

"The Italians?" I ask, clenching my fist.

Pasha shrugs. "We don't know."

"But we can assume. Where is the shipment?"

"Gone," Pasha says, shrinking back like he's afraid I'll lash out at him for the mistake.

Unfortunately, even if I wanted to, there's no one to blame but myself. I should have dealt with the Italians when they first started overstepping the boundaries we'd established.

"What do you want to do now?" Rurik asks. "Should we call a meeting?"

I was considering it, but now it seems too reactionary. I've allowed the Italians to take ground and our weapons, which looks bad enough. If I overreact and call a Bratva-wide meeting, my authority will be called into question. I have to play it cool.

I shake my head. "It can wait until tomorrow."

Rurik frowns. "Are you sure?"

I snap my attention to him, eyes narrowed. He backs down without a word, lowering his head and nodding.

"Everyone should go home for tonight," I say. "Keep your guard up, but the Italians won't strike again just yet. They have what they want, so now we need to take time to formulate our plan as well."

Doing nothing after our supplier has been killed and one of our best runners has been beaten feels like defeat, but I need time to formulate the best way to strike back. As much as my father would push me to fight and charge and take no prisoners, maintaining my calm and not changing my behavior is the best thing to do. For now.

Rurik rides back with Pasha, leaving me alone in my car for the drive back.

I turn on the radio, but hate every song playing and flick it off. Sitting alone with my thoughts isn't any better.

I hear my father's voice in my head, giving life to all of the doubts I've ever had about my role as leader of the Bratva. I spy a half-full bottle of whiskey in the console. I brought it to share a drink with Nico, as was our tradition. Now, I decide to have some without him.

With no one to share with, I put the bottle to my lips and tip it back, taking a big swig. Then, I immediately take another.

The alcohol burns going down and then warms my chest and my stomach. I like the burn. I need it, so that this all doesn't feel like some fucked-up nightmare. I take another drink.

By the time I open the gate at the end of my drive and then pull up in front of the house, my head feels hazy. Usually, it takes more than a few shots to tilt me off my axis, but I haven't eaten anything most of the day, and the liquor is wreaking blissful havoc in my empty stomach.

I stumble on the first stair walking into the house and accidentally slam the front door closed. It's loud enough that everyone in the house must have heard it, but Courtney doesn't come to see who it is.

I walk down the hall, looking in rooms as I pass. She isn't in the sitting room or the kitchen or the dining room. So, I take the stairs to the second floor, gripping the railing to keep from tipping backwards, and go to check her room.

She's staying in one of the larger guest rooms in the house. Usually, it's the one I reserve for very important business associates, because it has a full bathroom with a vanity and a balcony.

I lift my hand to knock on her door, but then I hear the music.

It's the kind of music I heard on the radio on my drive home—bass-filled pop music that usually sets my teeth on edge. Apparently, it's what Courtney likes.

I turn the knob slowly and push open the door.

Courtney is facing away from me in the middle of the room—the desk chair and trunk at the foot of the bed pushed out of the way for additional space—dancing. She moves with the music, fluid and loose but also structured, like it's a routine she has worked on before. Watching her feels like a physical kind of poetry. Foreign, yet tangible.

She's almost near enough to touch. To tease. To taste.

Almost.

I lean against the doorframe and cross my arms, watching her move.

She's wearing a tiny pair of shorts that cuts off high on her thigh and a white tank top that is thin enough I can see the lacy white bra she has on underneath. Her tan skin pops in comparison with the white, looking deep and rich, and her dark hair is piled in an artful bun on top of her head.

I'm shamelessly admiring the curve of her body when she turns around, arms thrown over her head, hip jutting out, eyes closed so she can feel the music. Then, she opens them and yelps when she sees me.

She pulls her arms in to cover her midsection as though she's naked and then darts over to the radio to turn it off, plunging the room into a thick silence.

"I didn't know you were here," she says, breathing heavily. She wipes her forehead with the back of her arm and looks nervously at the floor.

"I didn't know you could dance like that," I say, making no move to hide my own arousal.

"I didn't know I was being watched," she says again.

I move into the room, closing the door behind me, and sit down on the office chair she has pushed into the corner. She follows me with her eyes like a nervous cat.

"Don't stop on my account," I say. "Please. Continue."

"I was done anyway," she says, crossing her arms.

Tonight is the night, I think, remembering my promise to myself earlier. I didn't act with the Italians when I should have, and if I don't act soon with Courtney, she's going to think she has more control than she does. She will think she can defy me.

It's my duty to show her that I make the rules. At least for the next six months.

"Continue." Any warmth is gone from my voice. It's an obvious command.

Courtney hesitates, staring at me for a moment, her eyes wide and glassy. When she realizes my decision is made, she walks slowly to the radio and turns it on.

The song has changed, this one a slower R&B kind of song, but I'm not paying any attention to the lyrics.

Even walking, Courtney is graceful. Each movement is thoughtful and measured, and she pauses for only a second in the middle of the room before she begins.

Her full hips taper into a tiny waist, and she circles her body, sending ripples of movement up her arms where her hands are swirling above her head. Then, she bends at the waist, popping her backside out towards me, and it's all I can do not to reach out and grab her.

Pull her into me.

Push into her.

She curls her body out and up, arching her back, and then turns to look at me over her shoulder.

I curl a finger for her to come to me, but she has only taken one step when I stand up and meet her in the middle of the room.

I grab her hips with greedy hands and press myself against her back. Courtney arches her lower back and grinds into me, letting out a moan.

The noise is small, but it rocks through me like she screamed out my name. In my drunken, horny state, it's all the encouragement I need.

I grab her arm and spin her around, threading my arm around her lower back; then, I walk her back towards the bed.

Her lips are full and pouty, mouth opened in surprise, and I lean down and capture them with mine. Her breath is sweet, like a cinnamon mint, and it smells like flowers when I run my hands through her hair.

Every inch of her is as soft as it looks. Her skin is smooth and warm, and I can't stop myself from sliding my hands under her shirt and feeling the flat plane of her stomach.

I'm about to pull her tank top over her head when suddenly, she grabs the hem of my shirt and yanks it up. I'm surprised she's taking any initiative at all, so I don't hesitate to lift my arms and let her pull my shirt free.

As soon as she does, she stands back as far as my grip will allow and studies my body, one eyebrow raised.

"Like what you see?" I whisper, circling my hips into hers.

Courtney doesn't answer, but based on the points of her nipples peeking through her lacy bra and tank top, I can guess how she feels.

I tug at the tank top again and Courtney brushes my hand away and grabs her own shirt, peeling it up her body.

She's golden brown everywhere, and I can see the muscles of her abs and obliques working as she twists and tosses the shirt on the floor behind her. Then, she turns back and immediately drops her hands to my waist, unbuttoning my jeans and shoving the material down to my knees.

I kick my pants off in two quick movements and then stumble forward—both drunk and hungry for her—grab her narrow waist, and lift her up. She curls her legs around me like she has done it a thousand times before, and I all but cannonball into the bed.

My fingers find the clasp of her bra while she licks a line across my collarbone. I moan and then grit back a groan of pain as she bites down on my shoulder. It feels hard enough to draw blood, but I can't help but notice how much blood the aggression is pumping elsewhere.

In jumbled, frantic movements, I peel her bra off and pull her panties down to her ankles. Whether she kicks them off or not, I don't know, because I crawl over her and position myself between her legs before I can see.

Then, not a moment too soon, I push inside.

She gasps as I fill her, digging her claws into my back, but then she goes loose. She spreads her legs wider, allowing me more space to fill her, and lays her arms out straight above her head, wrists crossed as though they're bound there.

I reach up to cover her wrists with my hand.

As soon as I pin her arms down, she comes alive. She arches her back and rolls herself onto me, and I realize this woman—full of fire and spunk—wants to be dominated.

So, I do just that.

I slide into her again and again, hard enough that our bodies slap together and she lets out a small yelp with every thrust.

Then, she begins to meet me in the middle until our bodies are ebbing and flowing in unison, making the sensation that much better.

I pull all the way out, teasing her, and then slide myself up and down her slit until she fights my hold on her arms, trying to break free.

I tighten my grip and then plunge back into her all at once. She gasps and just as she gets accustomed to my size again, I slide my hand between us and circle my thumb over the apex of her thighs. Over her most sensitive bundle.

It's like electric shocks moving through her with every stroke. Her back arches, muscles tighten, and it takes all of my strength to keep her down on the bed.

"Yes," she whispers softly, as though she's ashamed of wanting this. Of letting me know how good this feels.

I work my thumb faster over her, matching it with quick thrusts, and Courtney unravels.

Her breathing reaches a fever pitch and then her entire body goes rigid and still. She holds her position for one second, two, three, and then lets out a shuddering sob and collapses into the bed.

Tremors move through her arms and legs, and I let go of her hands. She curls her arms around me and smooths lines down my back as I continue to drill into her, riding out the last of her orgasm.

When she's done, I continue moving in her, searching for my own release, but Courtney shoves on my chest hard enough to knock me off balance.

Then, before I can complain, she presses me down into the bed and crawls over me.

I look up at her and am shocked at the woman I see.

She looks nothing like the rage-filled woman I met at her father's shop or the nervous girl who danced for me. Her pupils are dilated, the blackness driving out the caramel brown of her eyes, and her expression is focused; driven. She's a woman on a mission, and, at the moment, that mission is me.

She straddles my waist, then wraps a hand around my base and positions me at her opening. Then, all at once, she plunges herself onto me.

I tip my head back, mouth open, and breathe, doing my best not to lose it.

Thank God I don't, because Courtney rewards my restraint with sensual rolls of her body. She plants her hands on my chest and puts her dancer's body to use, bouncing against me before transitioning into a long, slow thrust, and then shifting back to staccato pulses.

The change of pace and the perfect view of her breasts bouncing in my face make it impossible to hold on for long, and I find myself gripping her waist and straining into her as pleasure warms through my body.

Not quite done yet, Courtney grabs my hand and slides it between us again. For a moment, I'm too lost in my own release to understand what she wants, but then she grinds herself against my finger, and I know.

She wants it again.

I flick at her nub, massaging and drawing circles against her while she rocks her hips over me, milking me of the last of my orgasm while I lead her to her second.

And just as I'm spent, Courtney stiffens and shudders.

Her face contorts into a brief flash of pain before easing. Her lips part, and she closes her eyes and lets her head loll to the side. Her body moves over me in soft, lazy pulses until she's done.

She slides off me and lies down on the bed next to me, eyes still closed, and I watch her, amazed at the interaction we just had.

It was nothing like what I expected. Yet, it was everything.

Incredible sex with a beautiful, fierce, submissive woman who isn't afraid to ask what she wants.

The thought of it is enough to have me ready for round two.

7

COURTNEY

The vinyl booth sticks to the back of my legs, and my neck is damp with sweat. The restaurant is sweltering—especially sitting this close to the kitchen—and Dmitry's guards are making me nervous.

Two large men, clad in black and clearly out of place in the mom-and-pop hamburger joint, take up a six-person table in the corner. They stare at me as though they're afraid I'll run.

The thought crossed my mind more than once, but Dmitry was pretty clear what would happen if I ran, and I can't risk my dad's life like that. Or mine.

Plus, as much as I hate to admit it, living with Dmitry hasn't been as terrible as I imagined. No dungeon, no rations of stale bread and water, no routine beatings. In fact, he has done his best to make me comfortable. Including letting me meet up with Sadie for lunch.

She's texted me every day for a week, asking to meet up, and I finally ran out of excuses and had to ask Dmitry if I could go. He said it would be fine as long as I took guards with me. I thought that seemed like a fair compromise, but now that they're sitting in the corner glaring at me, I can't help but think Sadie will notice their presence.

My phone rings and it's Sadie. The guards both perk up, brows furrowed, at the sound of me answering my phone.

"Hey, where are you?"

Sadie groans. "Stuck on the highway. There was some kind of wreck up ahead. Lights, sirens, a tow truck—the whole deal. I may be even later than I was already going to be."

I'm not surprised; Sadie is always late.

"That's fine, but don't get mad when you get here and I've already eaten," I say. "I'm starving."

"Please order something for me too! I skipped breakfast, so I'll need sustenance the moment I arrive. Ya girl is *famished*."

I take her order and then tuck my phone in my purse. When I look up, the guards are standing next to the table.

"God!" I yelp, hand pressed to my chest. "You scared me."

"Where is your friend?" one of the guards asks, his Russian accent thick.

I explain she's just running late, but the guards both look at each other, nervous.

"She'll be here soon," I say.

"Will you be staying later than planned?" the other guard asks. "We need a plan to report back to Mr. Tsezar."

I roll my eyes. "Do you have to report everything back to Dmitry?"

The question was an attempt to gauge the level of control Dmitry has over his men, but also a subtle jab at the fact these men act more like his loyal pets than his employees.

They both narrow their eyes at me, and the first guard nods his head. "Of course we do. Any attempt by you to convince us otherwise will also be reported. So don't try anything funny today. When your friend gets here, stick to the plan."

The plan: sit at booth, eat food, do not attempt to leave or tell anyone where or by whom I'm being held, and then leave with my armed escort to be taken back to my cell at Dmitry's house.

My cell that has an incredible bed, a closet full of luxurious—though revealing—clothes, and a housekeeper who cleans up all of my messes before I'm even done making them.

Yanka told me she has worked for Dmitry's family since he was just a little boy. However, unlike the guards, Yanka seems to love Dmitry rather than fear him. I even caught her teasing him about the state of his laundry one day, telling him if he kept staining all of his clothes, he'd have to do his own laundry.

I smiled at the exchange until she held up the shirt, and I saw what looked like blood splattered across the front.

Each interaction is just another puzzle piece I can add to the picture of the man who is acting as my de facto jailor.

Except, in this jail, I get to come and go as I please. As long as I take a couple guards with me.

The two guards stomp back to the corner, and the man behind the counter watches them with a furrowed brow. He keeps smiling at me, and I can tell he's trying to make sure I'm okay, so I just smile back.

When the waitress comes around—a red-haired woman with a half sleeve of tattoos on one arm and a large flower tattooed on her calf—I order a cheeseburger meal for me with a milkshake and a hamburger meal with a piece of apple pie for Sadie, who is lactose intolerant.

While I wait, my mind wanders. I think about where I'd be now if I hadn't made this deal with Dmitry. Where my father would be.

I can't help but think six months was overkill. Surely I'm worth more than what my father owed. High-end sex workers make high-end money, and with my age and experience in dance, I have to be considered high-end.

I mean, Dmitry sure seemed to enjoy what I had to offer.

My face warms with the memory of what we did last night. And the night before. And the night before.

The first time he came into my room and put his hands on me, I wanted to hate it. I wanted to lie like a lifeless doll on the bed and let him do what he wanted, hating him all the while, but I couldn't. Every brush of his hands over my skin and his hips against mine felt like an electric current. Each shock made me wilder with desire and want and need.

And the orgasm.

God, I've never felt anything like that before.

Being touched by Dmitry is so much different than touching myself. It's better than with anyone else I've ever been with.

I'm in the midst of remembering Dmitry on his knees behind me, drilling his considerable length—I was wrong when I teased him about being small—into me again and again, when Sadie slides into the booth across from me with a groan.

"Worst traffic ever."

I cross my legs, assuming she'll be able to smell the lingering scent of sex on me after my vivid replay of last night's events. "Sorry you got stuck in traffic. Was everyone in the accident okay?"

She shrugs and pulls her apple pie towards her, taking a bite out of the crust first. "I don't know. As soon as I got free of the standstill traffic, I blew out of there."

I roll my eyes. A real bleeding heart empath, this one.

"I just knew I needed to get here," she says around a gooey cinnamon slice of apple. "It took five days for me to get you to agree to lunch. I wasn't sure I'd get so lucky again."

"Sorry," I say with a wince. "I've been busy."

"With what?" she asks. "Your dad? Because I went by the shop the other day. I needed my oil changed, but you weren't there, and he didn't seem to think you'd be around anytime soon."

Okay, Sadie would smell a lie, but I couldn't tell her the entire truth. So, I settled on a half-truth.

"I'm staying with a guy," I say quietly, hoping this isn't against the rules. "I just met him, but—"

"But he brainwashed you?" Sadie finished, mouthing hanging open in shock. "Since when do you do anything spontaneous? Ever?"

"Hey!" I say, wrinkling my nose. "I'm not that boring."

"Yeah, but, no offense, you aren't this interesting usually, either," she says with a shrug. "So, who is he?"

"His name is Dmitry," I say quietly, feeling the guards' eyes on me the entire time. "He's a ... small business owner."

"What business?"

"You wouldn't know it," I say quickly. "It's online. I don't know much about it. It's pretty boring."

Sadie frowns and chews on her lower lip. "Courtney, this all sounds pretty fishy. Why are you staying with this guy? Did you and your dad have a fight or something? Because you can stay with me if you want. Devon has been over a lot lately, but I can kick him out."

"Are you and Devon—" I start to ask.

"No," she says, shaking her head. "We're just friends ... with occasional benefits."

I try not to, but I wrinkle my nose.

"Don't judge," she says with a smile. "He's good."

If Sadie knew the truth about my situation, she'd know I have no right judging anyone's sex life. Mine is currently so fucked up, I'm not sure it will ever be made right again.

"But anyway, what is up with you and this guy? Dmitry?"

I'm spared answering the question when a car pulls up in the lot right in front of our window and Devon climbs out of his tiny, rusted car. He sees us through the window and winks.

"You invited Devon?"

"Well, I told him we'd be here," Sadie says, a grin spreading across her face. "I guess he wanted to surprise me."

"That sure sounds like you two are—"

She shushes me and then slides over to make room for Devon. Except, when he gets to our table, he slides in on my side, scooting me over with his hip until our legs are pressed together.

"Hey, ladies," he says, draping an arm over the back of the bench and stretching out. "I hope you don't mind me crashing. Sadie told me you'd be here and it sounded like a good time."

I'm so relieved I don't have to talk about Dmitry anymore that I almost don't mind Devon's sudden appearance. Though, that quickly changes when he drops his arm around my shoulders.

I try to shrug away from his touch, but he squeezes me into his side. "I've been telling Sadie to bring you around more often. I'd like to get to know you more."

"I've been busy," I say with a grimace.

"Busy with a *new man*," Sadie emphasizes.

"A man?" Devon raises his eyebrows in surprise but then squeezes me even tighter, adding his other hand to my upper thigh. "Is this man taking care of you?"

I can feel Sadie's eyes boring into me, and I hope she doesn't think I want this. Because even though she said Devon was just a friend, I know her well enough to know when she likes someone. And despite Devon being a lumbering, handsy idiot, she likes him, and I refuse to get between them.

"Yep," I say, shrinking away from his arm. "I have a new man."

Devon leans down until his nose is almost against my cheek and whispers, "Is he the jealous type? Because Sadie and I, we like to share."

My eyes go wide, and I look up at my friend, but she's staring daggers at Devon.

"We like to get a little wild," he continues, oblivious to the swirl of emotions around him. "If your new friend isn't insecure, maybe we could go for a little swing, if you know what I mean."

Sadie's face flares red, and my stomach flips.

I'm already a sex slave to a Mafia boss, which is bad enough. The last thing I need is to start swinging with my best friend and her "just a friend" boyfriend.

Devon drags a hand down my neck towards my collarbone, inching dangerously close to my breasts. "You seem like the kind of girl who could do with a little unwinding."

Just before his finger can hit the curve of my chest, I turn and shove him away from me with both hands.

Devon is bigger than me, but he also was not expecting me to fight back, so he tips sideways and falls flat on the diner floor, yelping in surprise. Sadie scrambles up to help him, and I open my mouth to give him a piece of my mind and tell him what a creep he is.

Before I can, however, two large shadows descend on our table.

"Time to go," the guard with the thick accent rumbles.

"Who the hell are you?" Sadie asks, looking from the guards to me and back again.

I try to explain, but before I can, one guard grabs my arm and pulls me from the booth. They each pick me up by an elbow, lift me over Devon, and rush me towards the exit.

I wave over my shoulder at Sadie, but she just stares after me, slack-jawed.

8

DMITRY

Dried blood covers my hands and there are splatters of it across my shirt. Yanka is not going to be pleased about having to stain-treat more clothes, so when I peel the shirt off, I drop it in the trash. I may be the boss of a Bratva, but in a fight, my money would be on Yanka.

Luckily, none of the blood is mine.

Our Bratva-wide meeting this morning—yes, I decided we needed one after all—ended when Pasha showed up with news of the Italians trying to interrupt another shipment. Vadik finally regained consciousness and told him he overheard the Italians talking about where they would strike next. So, we grabbed our guns and ran.

It wasn't organized or well-planned like I usually like, but my men needed to be let loose. After the losses we suffered the night before, they wanted their pound of flesh, and I wasn't about to hold them back.

We got to the docks just as some Italian goons were arriving and a shootout ensued.

We killed the men easily with just a few shots, but I searched through their pockets for identification and got myself covered in blood in the process.

My phone rings, and I quickly wipe my hands on my jeans, though it proves useless. Giving up, I fish my phone out of my pocket with two fingers. I know who it is without bothering to look at the Caller ID.

"Any change?" I ask, pinching the phone between my ear and my shoulder as I slip out of my jeans.

"No, sorry," Amanda says. "I'm calling to make sure it's fine with you if we change a few of her dosages."

"Oh yeah," I say, trying to hide my disappointment. "Whatever you both think is best will be fine."

Amanda starts saying something else, but my phone beeps to alert me to another call. It's Fyodr.

"Do whatever you need to do," I say, cutting her off. "I have another call, but call back later if you need me for anything."

"What's going on?" I ask, switching lines. I let Courtney go out for lunch with her friend, and she should still be there. I told the guards to call only if there was trouble.

"We're coming back," Fyodr says, his voice deep and obviously annoyed. "There was an unexpected visitor to the table. He appeared to be very ... close to her."

"To Courtney?" I ask.

"I think he was a boyfriend."

I hear Courtney saying something in the background, but I can't make it out.

Fyodr starts relaying the events, talking over her increasingly loud commentary, and tells me the man had his hands all over her and they looked very cozy in the booth.

Suddenly, I hear a small struggle and then Courtney's voice comes through the phone loud and clear.

"That man was a scumbag. I didn't want to have a threesome or a foursome or whatever with him. I hate him."

Clearly, I've given Courtney too much free rein. One day out of the house, and she's testing my rules. She isn't supposed to be with another man for the entirety of the six months. Plus, she's disrespecting my soldiers.

There is a struggle for the phone, but I've heard more than enough. I hang up and grab a fresh pair of pants. I wanted to shower, but there's no time now. They'll be back soon, and I want to deal with Courtney right away.

They must have been closer to the house than I thought because I've just slipped into my pants when I hear the front door open and close, followed by the sound of Courtney's voice echoing through the house.

"Get your hands off me!" she snaps.

With every second, her voice gets louder, and I know the guards are hauling her up the stairs.

I pad into the hallway, shirtless, and meet them.

Fyodr and Alexi each have her by one arm, and her legs are bicycling as she tries to reach the ground.

"Get your hands off me," she shouts.

I nod for the men to put her down, and they let go. Courtney is surprised by this and drops to her knees, scrambling back up and brushing off her shirt.

She flips her hair over her shoulder and huffs. When she sees me, her brown eyes harden. "This is wholly unnecessary. I didn't do anything wrong."

I move towards her fast, stopping only a few inches away. "Because my guards stopped you."

"What they didn't tell you is that I pushed that creep out of the booth and—"

Her cheeks are flushed from exertion, and her lips are glossed and shiny. Being so close to her makes me feel off-center. To ground myself, I wrap a hand around her neck and pull her to my lips.

She hesitates for a moment before her mouth goes soft and she kisses me back. My tongue pushes her lips apart and slides inside, twirling with hers. Courtney drags her hands down my bare chest until her fingers are at my waistband, teasing what she wants—what we both want.

I break away and grab her shoulder, holding her back.

I see my men sneaking quietly down the stairs, not wanting to interrupt our moment, and I'm grateful to be alone with her.

"You are mine," I growl, grabbing her hip and pulling her against me. "Only mine."

Courtney lays her hands on my chest like she's going to push me away, but she doesn't. She looks up at me with hooded eyes, her gaze unfocused from our kiss. "For twenty-two more weeks."

The reminder of how little time we really have makes me kiss her again.

Her mouth is sweet and warm, and I walk her backwards until we hit the hallway wall. Courtney throws her arm up over her head, her hand knocking a picture frame askew, and I quickly grab her wrist, pinning her arm down as I claim her mouth as my own.

For twenty-two more weeks.

When I nip at her jaw and her neck, she takes a shuddering breath.

"That guy is a creep. He's my friend's friend. I don't even know him."

I follow the curve of her waist down to her waistband and around to unbutton and unzip her jeans. With her free hand, she helps me push them down her hips.

"Then why were you letting him touch you?" I ask. "If you remember, I'm the only man who can lay a hand on you. Otherwise, the deal is over."

She gasps when I cup my hand over the warmth between her legs and arches her back to give me better access. "He cornered me in the booth and touched me, and I didn't want him to. I tried to get him off."

Courtney tilts her head back, letting me lick and suck on her neck and earlobe, while her hand is massaging circles in the tight muscles of my back and shoulders.

"I should kill him," I mutter against her skin, driving my excitement against the front of her lace panties. "I'm the only man who can touch you, whether you like it or not."

Suddenly, Courtney pulls her hand out of my grip and unbuttons my pants, sliding them down just far enough that she can slip me out of my boxers and wrap her hand around my length.

I hiss as she slides slowly to my tip, and then her mouth is at my ear.

"I'm not exactly resisting, am I?" she whispers, stroking me again.

I pull back, surprised. I knew our sex felt good to her. There's no way she couldn't feel the sexual tension between us. Still, I never expected her to admit she wanted this. I never imagined she would admit this is more than a business deal.

And it's so fucking sexy.

I slide my hand down her smooth stomach and inside her panties. She widens her legs, letting me flick my finger against her and massage until she's moaning, her hips bucking against my hand.

"You want this?" I growl. "You like this?"

She bites her lower lip and nods.

"Tell me," I demand.

"Yes," she breathes. "I want this. Yes, please."

I slide a finger inside of her, curling it up and towards myself, massaging her inside until she's panting.

"More," she says, throwing her head back against the wall.

I add a second finger.

Courtney lifts herself onto her toes and then lowers down on my finger, riding my hand, and it's too hot to handle.

I pull my fingers out of her and capture her mouth again.

"Please," she mumbles against my lips. I'm in no mood to deny her.

I know we should go into my room, but it's ten feet away and too far. I can't wait. I need her now. *Here.*

Not caring how much the skimpy lace panties she's wearing cost, I tug at the sides, tearing the delicate material, and position myself at her opening. She inhales, ready for me to impale her, and I do just that. All the way to the hilt because the fire of need inside of me is raging. I have to put it out before I explode.

"Dmitry?" a voice from the stairs asks.

Courtney gasps and throws her arms over her chest, and I lean forward to pin her against the wall, covering her body with mine.

"I'm obviously busy," I bark, looking over my shoulder to see Fyodr staring straight ahead, trying not to look at us.

"I know," he says with a wince. "But the police are here. I don't think they're willing to wait."

9

COURTNEY

Dmitry waits until the guard is gone and then he pulls me into his room and shuts the door. Without a word, he rifles through his closet for a shirt, tugs it on, and buttons up his pants. Then, on his way out the door, he stops and looks back over his shoulder.

"Get dressed."

I roll my eyes, but I'm not sure he notices.

Obviously, I'm not going to hang out half naked in his room while the police are downstairs.

My panties are ruined, but I pull up my jeans anyway and try to get used to the feeling of denim against my rather sensitive skin. Then, I move to his walk-in closet to check my appearance in the full-length mirror.

My dark hair is tousled from his hands and my shirt is rumpled. I try to smooth it out, but there's no use. So, I do what I can with my hair, and clean up the edges of my eyeliner with my finger.

As I'm leaving the closet, I notice something hanging halfway out of a small trash can. I almost walk right past it, but then I see what looks like blood splatter.

I bend down and pull the fabric out of the trash can, pinching it between two fingers, and realize it's a shirt. There are drops of blood around the collar and a smear of it on the hem where it looks like someone tried to wipe their hands.

I drop the shirt on the floor.

What kind of man am I living with?

I just begged him to fuck me in a hallway, and there was a bloody shirt a few feet away in his bedroom. He mentioned murdering Devon, but I thought it was mostly an act. Now, I'm not so sure.

Dmitry is dangerous. I knew it from the moment I saw him punch my dad in the shop, then when he kidnapped me, but I somehow managed to push aside for a little while, caught up in the red-hot sex and chemistry between us.

Now I know the truth and it scares me.

More than anything, it scares me that I still want him despite it all.

Suddenly, there is a knock on the door and it cracks open. "Courtney? May we come in?"

It's Dmitry, his eyes wide in warning.

I quickly kick the bloody shirt to the back of the closet and pull the upholstered bench in from the middle of the room to hide it.

Just as I finish and walk out of the closet, Dmitry opens the door wide and lets in two police officers.

They're both portly men, their hands resting on their belts, eyes narrowed and searching. They scan me up and down.

"Can I help you?" I ask as sweetly as I can.

"I was just about to ask you the same thing," the bald officer says, puffing out his chest. "We heard a report that you might be being held here against your will."

Dmitry's eyes flare and then crinkle at the corners in a friendly smile when the officers look in his direction.

I could tell the officers I'm here against my will. I could tell them everything Dmitry has done—to me, my father, and probably scores of others. The bloody shirt is sitting in the other room as proof.

Except, what if it isn't enough? What if they can't arrest him and then he kills me and my father just as he said he would?

Or, what if it *is* enough? What if they cart him away in handcuffs and arrest him?

I hate that both options seem equally unthinkable.

I laugh, the sound so genuine I almost fool myself. "Who on earth told you that?"

"Your friend, Sadie," the other officer says. "She called and said you were dragged out of a diner by two large men."

"There has been a misunderstanding," I say. "Those were my bodyguards."

The bald officer raises a pale eyebrow. "Bodyguards?"

"I hired them to watch over her," Dmitry jumps in, walking over to curl his arm around my waist. "And lucky I did, because a man at the diner was groping her."

"I managed to push him away, but my guards got me out of there before he could make a scene," I finish.

Both officers narrow their eyes and look at one another. I can't tell whether they're buying my story or not, but I lay my head on Dmitry's shoulder just in case.

"Would you like to file a report?" the bald officer asks. "If a man was assaulting you, then—"

"No, no," I say, waving them away. "I don't plan to ever be near that man again, so there's no need for that. I'm just glad we could resolve this misunderstanding. I'm sorry you had to take the time to come all the way out here."

They both shake their heads like they're having the same thought.

"Please tell your friend she was mistaken. She seemed very worried about you."

"I will, right now," I say earnestly.

The bald officer nods and then turns to Dmitry. "Sir, do you think we could speak with Ms. Palillo alone for a moment?"

Dmitry squeezes my waist and then presses a kiss to my cheek. His breath is warm, and I feel a rush of cold when he moves away from my side and walks into the hallway.

The officers move closer to me and lower their voices. "If you are being held against your will, you can tell us. We will escort you out of here right now."

I smile, but it's more strained now. "I'm being honest with you. I'm in total agreement with everything that's happening here."

Technically, it's true. I agreed to this deal.

"If I didn't like it, I'd tell you."

Also true. Part of me feels like Dmitry may have hypnotized me with his touch. *Why* does it feel so good? And why can't I get enough of him? Maybe if the sex was worse, I'd risk my life and tell the police the truth.

"Okay," the bald officer says, raising his hands. "We just had to do our due diligence."

"Of course." I smile and lead them towards the bedroom door. "I appreciate your concern, but it's wholly unnecessary."

They step into the hallway where Dmitry is leaning against the wall, arms crossed over his chest. I didn't notice before but his hair is disheveled, his lips are swollen, and there is a bite mark on his neck.

The officers nod to him to let him know things are fine, and then I see the other officer glance down at his feet.

Where my ripped panties are lying.

He turns back to me, his cheeks red, and then makes a beeline for the stairs.

One of Dmitry's men shows them out, and Dmitry stays in his position against the wall until the front door is firmly shut and locked behind them. Then, he bends down and picks up my panties.

"Do you think they bought your lies?" he asks, twirling the torn fabric on his finger.

I reach out to grab them, but he yanks away and then tucks them in his front pocket. "I'll keep these, thanks."

I roll my eyes and take a deep breath. "I hope so. I'm a terrible liar, so I did my best to tell the truth as much as possible."

"Clearly, since your friend sent the police here on a welfare check," he grumbles. Then, he seems to register what I said, and his eyebrows quirk up. "You're telling me you actually believe you are here of your own accord? And you … like it?"

He bites his lip on the last words, and I ignore the flutter of nerves in my stomach.

"You weren't supposed to be eavesdropping."

He shrugs. "I had to make sure you weren't betraying me. Now, back to you liking it here. What exactly do you like?"

I swat at him, but he catches my hand and presses it against his chest, stepping forward until there is no space between us. Until we're breathing the same air. Until I don't need to breathe at all.

"What do you like?" he whispers.

I try to keep my composure. Dmitry doesn't need to know exactly how much he affects me. Because I'm certain he's the kind of man who would abuse that power.

"I'll tell you what I *don't* like," I say, prying his large hand off my waist. "I don't like being questioned by the police. How often can I expect that to happen?"

"Ask your friend," he snaps. "She's the one who brought them to my house, after all. I should end our deal for that reason alone. You're already a risk to my operation."

"Your operation must be pretty flimsy if I'm a risk," I retort.

Suddenly, Dmitry's arm is around my waist, and he's bending over me, his mouth moving an inch from my face. I can't see or smell or feel anything but him. Everywhere.

"I control more than one law enforcement agency in this city," he whispers. "You say the word, and I could have those two cops who were in here murdered within the hour. My operation is bigger than you can even imagine."

He's trying to scare me, and it's working. Though, I'll never let him know that.

I roll my eyes. "You don't strike me as a cop killer. You seem to be more honorable than that."

Dmitry lets go of me all at once, so suddenly that I nearly fall over and have to catch myself on the wall. "There you go again, talking about things you don't understand. I'm not honorable."

Most people would take that as a compliment, but I'm learning quickly that Dmitry doesn't like being called on his soft spots.

"You're right," I admit with a shrug. "After all, how many honorable men have bloodstained shirts lying in their closet?"

He doesn't say anything, so I walk back into the bedroom with Dmitry following slowly behind and grab the shirt from behind the small bench. I hold it up between two fingers like a piece of evidence.

"That's trash," he says, grabbing it out of my hand and throwing it in the trash can. "And it's nothing."

I cross my arms, one hip pushed out to the side. "You seem to want to convince me how bad you are. So, convince me. Whose blood is that?"

He stares at me silently, his face blank and unreadable.

I wonder why he isn't telling me, but then a horrible thought crosses my mind.

The words are stuck in my throat, and I have to lick my lips to even get them out. "It isn't … it isn't my dad's blood, right?"

Dmitry runs his hand through his hair, looking over my shoulder, and I feel my heart drop into my stomach.

It's my dad's blood.

I wish I could call the police back and change my answer.

"I guess I did convince you I'm not honorable," he says bitterly. When he finally looks at me, his jaw is tight. "No, the blood doesn't belong to your father. We have a deal and if you don't break it, then I won't either."

My heart once again begins to beat, and I can feel the blood flow returning to my limbs, but I'm still frozen in a state of panicked relief when Dmitry turns on his heel and stomps out of the room.

10

DMITRY

I toss another ruined shirt in the trash. I'm less worried about Yanka's wrath now. Really, I don't want Courtney to see it.

When she looks at me like she sees something good inside of me, I try to squash her hope. But when she looks at me like I'm a monster, I lose all of mine.

Something about her gets to me.

Even this morning when the setup Rurik and I orchestrated together was successful, and we caught several of the Italian members responsible for stealing our weapons, I couldn't find any sense of joy or satisfaction in it.

Even when I pressed my gun to the back of their heads and executed swift and merciless justice, I wondered what Courtney would think about all of it. Whether she would understand or be horrified.

That's why I throw the shirt with the stains on the cuffs away—so I don't have to find out.

When Courtney thought I killed her father, the reality that she had so little trust in me nearly sent me over the edge. A kind of anger I haven't felt in a long time—the kind my father was prone to—rose up in me, and I had to get out.

Now, I have even less control over my emotions.

I had little patience to begin with and now even my precious reserves are depleted thanks to the growing Italian problem. They're attacking on all sides, and this is the absolute worst time to have my head in knots over some damned woman.

Shirtless, I drop down into my desk chair and tip back as far as it will allow, my hands dragging down my face.

Then, my phone rings.

I growl and answer it without looking, prepared to tell whoever is on the other line to fuck off and never call back. Whatever problem has arisen, people need to learn to take care of shit by themselves. Because I'm done.

"What?" I bark.

"Dmitry?"

It takes me a moment to place the soft male voice, but then I can see him perfectly—his short round frame, and his eyes that look a little too much like his daughter's.

"Lawrence." I sigh and sit up, elbows resting on my desk. "To what do I owe the pleasure?"

If he's calling me to renegotiate, I will extend her time with me. Courtney didn't agree to that, but her father is breaking his side of the arrangement by trying to talk me out of it.

I'll add another month. Maybe two.

Perhaps Courtney will realize what a monster I really am if I do that.

I can't decide if that would be a good or a bad thing.

"Courtney," he says, his voice shaking. "Is she ... is she okay?"

The man sounds terrified and on the verge of tears, and despite my frustration with the day's events—not to mention the fact I haven't touched Courtney in three days—I soften towards him slightly.

"She's fine. Perfectly healthy."

There's a sigh of relief on the other end of the phone. "I want you to know I'm working on getting you your money. I will have it to you by the time our contract is up."

"Courtney is the payment," I say. "There is no need."

"There is a need," he says. "I don't want my daughter to feel like my bartering chip. I want her to know I paid my dues on my own. I'm not sure that will be worth much to her when this is all said and done, but ... it's the least I can do."

In a way, I admire his dedication—to his daughter, to paying his debts.

In another, I find his emotional vulnerability sickening.

"Courtney's mother left when she was a little girl," he continues. "It was my fault. A lack of ambition, according to her. So, when she left me to raise Courtney on my own, I started my business and built us a life that we could both be proud of. Though, sometime during all of that, Courtney realized why her mother left me and picked up the idea that you have to work for love. That you have to do something to earn it. And well ... I don't want her to think she has to do something like this to earn my love. I just ... I couldn't stand it if she thought she owed me this."

I hear soft, muffled sobs coming through the phone and groan. "This has all been very touching, but I'm busy."

"Wait," Lawrence calls out. "Please don't hurt her. Please be gentle. She's my only daughter. I love her and—"

I hang up before he can finish. There is only so much sentimentality I can take in one day, and I've had my fill.

None of this shit has any bearing on me.

Except, hard as I try, I can't get the conversation out of my mind for the rest of the day.

∼

I'm halfway home when I get the call.

Just before, I was mentally preparing what I would say to Courtney when I got home.

We haven't had a real conversation or physical interaction since the day the police arrived, and I can't remember whether I'm avoiding her or whether she's avoiding me. Perhaps we are both avoiding each other.

The lines in our relationship have gotten blurry and when that happens, there are bound to be uncomfortable moments. Maybe sitting down and explaining that she's nothing more than a bargaining chip will clear things up. Her father would hate to hear me say that, but it seems the most apt description of what she is.

Right?

Then, the call changes everything.

Rurik is screaming into the phone before I even answer.

"Get there *now!*" he shouts. "The bar on 43rd !"

"What are you talking about?"

"The building is on fire, and they're trapped!" he shouts. "I'm on my way now, but you need to get there!"

The bar on 43rd is ten minutes from my office, which luckily, I've already driven eight of. So, as soon as Rurik hangs up, I slam on the gas and take the next exit off the highway.

I'm driving down the frontage road when I see the telltale swirl of smoke above the tree lines. To anyone passing by, it looks like exhaust or a chimney, but I know my men are at risk.

From the street, the bar looks much as it always has—windows covered in posters advertising open mic nights and ladies' night and happy hour, parking lot littered with trash, and a slew of shiny black cars parked in no discernible order. The fire must be in the back, I presume. That's where the smoke seems to be coming from, anyway.

I sprint out of my car, leaving the door open, and run for the front of the bar.

I bought the place a few years back as another source of income, but also to let the men have a place they could gather and drink and hang out. It has been a huge hit and at any given time several of my lieutenants can be found half drunk inside.

The Italians must have known that.

Because surely this could only have been perpetrated by them. There is no way this is a coincidence. Not with the murder of Nico, Vadik's beating, and attacks on two of my weapons shipments.

No, this is part of their plan. They want to decimate my organization.

I reach the front door and notice a thick metal chain wrapped through the handles. I tug on it uselessly, opening the door little more than a couple inches before it falls shut. Though, in those few inches, a stream of heavy smoke pours out of the bar.

I pull my gun and blast my way through the chain. It takes almost all my bullets, but it finally snaps. Almost immediately, men start flooding out of the door, falling over one another in an effort to get out. Once out, they collapse on the sidewalk, soot-covered and coughing.

We do a head count and then another, and amazingly, it seems everyone made it out okay. The fire trucks finally arrive and douse the flames, though not before considerable damage is done to the building.

I managed to save my men, but looking around, the message is obvious:

The Italians aren't standing down.

~

By the time I get back to the house, it's way later than normal, and I'm exhausted.

I have no desire to talk to anyone about anything, least of all to Courtney about our arrangement. That can wait until tomorrow. Or, if I sleep through tomorrow, then sometime next week.

Whenever, just not tonight.

I unlock the door and slip inside, pressing my back against the cool wood for a few breaths before continuing on into the house.

I told myself I would walk inside and head straight to my room without looking for Courtney, but I can't help but glance in rooms as I pass, seeing if she's inside.

She isn't in her usual spot on the sofa in the sitting room or cooking in the kitchen, and based on the lack of noise coming from upstairs, she isn't dancing in her room. Then, I peek in the dining room and see her sitting at the table.

Her hair is down around her face in a shiny black curtain, and she's stooped forward over what looks like a textbook.

Since she came to stay with me, I've seen her with her nose in various books on cognitive neuroscience and neuroanatomy, but I've never really asked her about it. It never exactly comes up.

Usually when I come home, she's doing something active—cooking or dancing or working out. So, seeing her hyper-focused and oblivious to my presence is a new side of her. It's another facet of her personality I don't know anything about.

Part of me wants to step around the corner and clear my throat, let her know I see her.

I could clear the air about our arrangement the way I'd planned to do before the fire or I could ask her what she's studying in school; whether she plans to go back during our arrangement.

It would hardly feel like imprisonment if she was able to continue her education. Though, I'm not sure I want this to feel like imprisonment anymore.

That idea bothers me.

I shouldn't care about Courtney.

She's a bartering chip.

Payment for a debt I'm owed.

I should take what I want from her and forget the rest.

Except, she tucks a strand of hair behind her ear so I can see her lips, pink and pursed in thought, and something flares in my chest hotter than the flames back at the bar.

She's becoming more important to me than she should be, and I would be wise to keep myself in check.

I watch her for another moment, relishing the way she presses the end of her highlighter to her lips, and then slip away and pad quietly upstairs without her noticing.

11

COURTNEY

The days are starting to run together.

When the sun is up, I spend my time preparing for my next semester of school. Dmitry hasn't said anything to lead me to believe I won't be able to attend, so until I hear otherwise, I'm going to try and get ahead.

If I'm not studying, then I'm dancing, trying to burn off the energy that gets pent-up being inside Dmitry's house all day.

There really isn't anywhere for me to go, and with the Italians attacking Dmitry's Bratva regularly, he's told me the safest place for me is his house. So, I listen.

I stay inside and wait for him to come home.

I wait for him to mount the stairs and find me in my room. I don't turn around until his hands are on my waist and his breath is on my neck.

Then, I let him lead me to the bed and strip my sweaty clothes away.

Dmitry's hands are warm and all-encompassing as he touches me.

His palms brush across my pointed nipples and grip my hips. I can't help but arch into him, leaning into the warmth and stability of his presence.

Because when he comes home and touches me, I know it will be thirty minutes or an hour or two where my thoughts aren't swirling. Where I can breathe and feel and forget.

For a while.

Dmitry nips at my collarbone with his teeth, and I whimper and draw him up over my body, wrapping my legs around his hips. I find his mouth and pinch his lower lip between my teeth. I kiss a line across the stubble on his chin and lick his earlobe.

More than anyone I've ever met, I want to devour Dmitry. Kissing isn't enough. Touching isn't enough. I need to taste him and dig into him.

Dmitry doesn't seem to mind as he moans with every stroke of my tongue and matches my movements with his finger between my legs.

"You taste good," he says between my legs.

I ignore the flutter of excitement in my stomach.

Dmitry is a distraction. A beautiful, strong distraction with unreal stamina.

And more importantly, he's my captor. A criminal who threatened my father, threatened me.

So, I can't have butterflies for him. Any response I have towards him is nothing more than a chemical response, an instinctual response left over from before humans evolved. My body recognizes that Dmitry would make strong babies.

That is all it is: my human instinct to survive.

Though, as much as I want to view Dmitry as a monster, the more I learn about him, the harder it becomes.

During the day while he's gone, I run into his household staff. Yanka has been with Dmitry for years. One day, I helped her sort through the laundry, and she told me that Dmitry paid for her son to have his tonsils removed when he got really sick. He also paid for a nurse to stay with her husband at their house so they wouldn't have to live out of a hospital room while he received cancer treatments.

The landscaper got in a car accident and was late to work, and by that afternoon, Dmitry had bought him a new truck.

Everyone in Dmitry's house seems to worship the ground he walks on, which is not at all what I expect from the staff of a mob boss.

While their stories do soften my heart towards Dmitry, it hardens again whenever I remember the fact that he's holding me ransom and threatening my father.

I can't allow his hands or his mouth or his deeds to erase that one truth.

"You taste sweet." Dmitry's voice is muffled by my thighs.

I buck my hips up, pressing myself against his lips and his tongue. I wrap my hand around his head, curling my fingers in his hair, and hold him against my trembling center.

When his tongue pushes inside of me, I gasp and arch my back. I go stiff as the ball of heat in my belly explodes and sends waves of pleasure to my furthest extremities.

The orgasm is still tearing through me when Dmitry slides his length inside.

I claw at his back as he pumps away, feeling every inch of him while also reminding myself to remember who he is.

To remember what he has done.

∼

Dmitry comes into my room early one morning while I'm still in bed. He crawls beneath the blankets with me and whispers that he will be home late tonight, if at all. I wonder why he's telling me this, but then I feel his body warm against my back. I feel his length hard against my spine.

He wraps his hand around to my front and pulls me firmly against him.

Eyes still closed and sleepy, my body responds to his touch. I circle my hips against him and reach around to curl my fingers in his hair.

Soon enough, he has my pajama shorts tugged down, and he's pressed against me from behind. When he slides in, I forget that it's morning and I haven't brushed my teeth yet. I forget that my hair is oily without a shower and my face is creased from the pillowcase.

I become a raw bundle of nerves, desperate for release, and I work myself back onto him, rolling my body against his front.

We both come at the same time, grasping and breathing heavily. Then, he places a kiss to the top of my spine, slides out of me, and pulls away.

When I wake up a few hours later, I almost convince myself it was a dream except I can still feel him inside of me, between my legs. There is a delicious ache there, and I circle my hand between my thighs, finding my second release of the morning as I relive the earlier encounter.

After I finally get up, shower, and get dressed, I'm ravenous, and I head down to the kitchen for my usual breakfast of toast and half a grapefruit. Then, I move into the dining room and pour over my books.

I don't bother changing into proper clothes or getting ready. My hair air-dries in loose waves and my makeup is buried somewhere in the bottom of my duffel bag. I don't see anyone aside from the staff during the day, anyway. And when Dmitry gets home in the evenings, I'm usually all sweaty from dancing, so I know he doesn't mind.

After a quick lunch of an apple, walnut, and spinach salad, I go upstairs to dance.

Except, today, I don't want to dance.

I have over five months left in Dmitry's house, and if every day is spent in this same routine, I'll lose my mind.

I pause at the top of the stairs and look towards the door that leads to the east wing of the house.

The forbidden east wing.

For weeks, I've ignored the door and the burning questions I have about that portion of the house because Dmitry warned me, but boredom, and the knowledge that he will be gone all day propel me to take one step. And then another.

Soon enough, I'm standing in front of the door, my hand on the knob.

If the door is locked then I'll walk away. I'll ignore it, just like I have for the last few weeks. If the door is locked, then I won't search for a key or attempt to pick the lock in anyway. I'll respect Dmitry's wishes.

I twist the handle slowly, waiting for the lock to catch and keep me from opening it.

But it never happens.

I twist the knob all the way to the right, and the door pushes open.

Looking around to be sure I haven't been seen by anyone, I quickly rush through and close it behind me.

The east wing looks remarkably similar to the west. Just another hallway. More doors.

This part of the house is darker, with the windows drawn and fewer lights turned on, which is why I notice the bright strip of light coming from beneath the door at the end of the hallway.

I gravitate towards it like a moth to a flame and press my ear to the door. There is no movement inside. No muffled conversation or rattle of chains.

Again, I try the knob. And again, the door is unlocked.

I push it open and immediately blink against the brightness.

A window is open, allowing the afternoon sun to stream inside, and it takes me several seconds to be able to see anything at all.

Then, I begin to make out the shape of a bed and a chair and a desk. There is a trunk for clothes and a closet, just like in my room.

Unlike my room, however, there are electrical cords running across the carpet and wires dangling from the ceiling and across the bed. Surprise pushes me back through the doorway and into the dim hallway. Curiosity pulls me forward again.

I step inside, eyes narrowed against the brightness, and see a small, pale, blonde-haired girl lying in the center of a bed that is much too large for her.

Then, I see a man walk through a narrow door to the right. I start, but don't retreat. There is nowhere to go. He has already seen me, and I can't leave the house.

"I'm sorry," I say quickly, hoping I can claim directional dyslexia as an excuse. "I didn't mean to—"

"Amanda?" the man calls over his shoulder. He has on a slim-fit button-down with a skinny tie tucked into straight-legged jeans. He looks like an accountant.

A red-headed woman in bright green scrubs walks through, looking like a medical elf. "Doctor?"

He nods towards me. "What is she doing here?"

The woman—Amanda, apparently—goes mute at the sight of me and simply shakes her head.

"You didn't ask her to come here?" he asks.

"No one asked me," I interject. "I'm sorry. I didn't mean to interrupt ... this. What is this?"

"You need to go," Amanda finally says, rushing towards me. She moves between me and the little girl as though hiding her from me will keep me from remembering I ever saw her in the first place. "You shouldn't be here."

"Where is *here*?" I ask. "What is going on?"

"You need to go," Amanda repeats.

"Get her out," the doctor says from behind her, as though she wasn't already trying.

Amanda grabs my arm, but I pull away from her weak grip and charge fully into the room until I'm standing next to the bed.

The little girl is hooked up to machines that monitor all of her vitals. There is an IV pumping fluids into her bruised and battered arm. She doesn't stir at all from the commotion.

"What happened to her?" I asked. Then, a horrible thought washes over me. "Did Dmitry do this?"

"Get her out," the doctor orders, more forcefully this time. "Before we both lose our jobs."

"What is your job?" I ask, voice high and frantic.

Amanda moves towards me again, but I dodge her and bump the side of the bed, shaking the frame and the little girl.

"Why are you here? Why does she need to be hooked up to all of this stuff? What did Dmitry do to her?"

Was this little girl taken from her family in the same way I was? Was she payment for a debt?

The thought turns my stomach, and I try to push it aside until I know the facts.

"What happened to her?"

"Courtney," Amanda says gently. I assume Dmitry or one of the other members of staff in the house told her my name, but it's still unnerving to hear her use it. "Dmitry doesn't want you here. I have to ask you to leave."

I raise a hand like I'll hit her, and she backs off. "I'm not leaving until I know what happened."

The doctor comes for me this time, his eyes narrowed. "I'm not going to let you cost me my job. You have to go. *Now*."

I sit on the edge of the bed, careful not to touch the girl, though I see her roll slightly from the addition of my weight on the mattress.

"Don't touch her!" Amanda warns. "Don't bother her."

"I'm not. I don't want to hurt her. I just want to know what happened."

I look back and the girl is shifted on her side, and I scoot away, trying to bother her as little as possible. As I do, I realize she didn't roll onto her side because of me. The girl rolled onto her side because she ... rolled onto her side.

"Is she awake?" I ask.

As soon as the words are out of my mouth, the room goes silent. The doctor and nurse freeze next to the bed and study the small girl.

When the girl blinks, Amanda gasps and makes me jump.

"Is that unusual?" I ask.

The doctor runs around to the other side of the bed and presses a stethoscope to the girl's chest. The nurse follows behind him.

"What is going on?" I repeat for what feels like the hundredth time.

The two of them whisper amongst themselves, though their words dry up when the little girl lifts a hand to her face and rubs at her eyes as though waking up from a dream.

"Call him," the doctor says suddenly. "*Now.*"

Amanda runs for a phone across the room as the little girl becomes more and more aware.

"Tati?" the doctor asks, laying a hand on her cheek. "Can you hear me, Tati?"

Finally, the little girl opens her eyes, wincing against the light, but rather than look at the doctor, she turns and looks directly at me.

I'm frozen, stunned by the little girl's beautiful brown eyes.

So stunned that I don't hear Amanda call him or hear the doctor say anything. I just stare at the little girl and watch as she's looked over and inspected and checked.

It feels like only a second has passed when the door bursts open and Dmitry rushes inside. He glares at me for one second, but then turns his attention to the little girl. He drops to his knees next to the bed, his eyes creased with worry and awe.

"Tati?" he asks. "Can you hear me?"

The girl turns to him, and her dry lips lift into a weak smile.

Dmitry smiles back, and I think what a beautiful sight it is—his smile.

"Out." I look up and realize Dmitry is looking at me. "Get out. Now."

I'm too confused to argue, so I stumble through the door and into the hallway. Seconds later, the nurse follows me.

When the door closes between us and the small child, Amanda turns on me. "If I get fired because of you—" Her voice cuts off, too angry to finish, and she shakes her head. "This is bullshit. Not my fault at all. I didn't do anything wrong."

"What happened to that little girl?" I ask. "What is going on? Was she unconscious? Who did that to her?"

"She was in a coma," Amanda says as though it was obvious. "She just woke up for the first time."

I gasp. "Did Dmitry hurt her? If he did, you have to go to the police. If he's keeping you here, then we can both try to get out together. That little girl doesn't deserve this kind of life. She doesn't deserve—"

Tears well in my eyes. I'm overwhelmed and confused and heartbroken, and Amanda must sense that because her nursing instincts take over. She lays a hand on my arm.

"The girl is Dmitry's niece," she says. "She was in a bad car accident with her family a few months ago. Her parents died, and Dmitry took her in. He hired me and the doctor and swore us to secrecy. He didn't want anyone to know in case his enemies decided to use her against him. Tati was helpless and vulnerable."

I absorb the information as well as I can, but I feel like a sponge already full of water. "Dmitry didn't hurt her?"

Amanda shakes her head. "He saved her."

I sigh, unsure what to feel. Then, I reluctantly add another checkmark for Dmitry in the "good guy" column.

After a few minutes, the doctor steps into the hallway and hitches his thumb over his shoulder towards the door. "Dmitry wants to see you."

"Me?" Amanda asks.

He shakes his head and nods to me. "Her."

I hesitate for only a second before Amanda pushes on my back, and I walk back into the bright room where the little girl is now sitting up in bed.

Dmitry turns to look as the door clicks shut behind me.

12

DMITRY

Amanda doesn't explain anything on the phone. Just: *It's Tati. Come quick.*

In the middle of a meeting with Rurik about the Italian problem and without explanation, I jump up and run from the room. I drive like a madman through town, grateful I don't pass a police officer, and sprint through the house and into the east wing with no thought for anything or anyone aside from Tati.

I see Courtney.

Sitting on the edge of Tati's bed.

Then, I see Tati.

Eyes open, blinking.

There's too much going on. Too much happening at once, and I need to get everyone out of the room and figure out what's going on.

After sending Courtney away, I interrogate the doctor, trying to figure out why she was in Tati's room, why she was in the east wing at all.

"She just walked in the door," he says, shaking his head. "There are no guards here, so there was no one to stop her. I tried to get her out, but she wouldn't leave. She was worried about the girl and sat on the bed, and the next thing I knew, Tati was waking up."

"Is she really awake?" I ask, looking down at her.

Tati's brown eyes look up at me; they study me, but she doesn't try to sign anything. Doesn't try to communicate at all. She just stares.

"It isn't some kind of reflex?"

"No," the doctor assures me. "She's truly awake."

He removes a few of the wires and the tube. Tati coughs, and it's the first time I actually believe any of it is real. It's the first time I've allowed myself to believe she could be okay.

Then, Tati lifts her hand. *Hello.*

Tears spring to my eyes, and I have to force them back down as I lift my hand and stroke my niece's blonde hair.

Still, questions nag. So, I send for Courtney.

When she walks in, her finger is twisted in a strand of her black hair, and compared to the bright light in the room and Tati's pale face, Courtney's skin looks like an even richer shade of tan than normal. She's beautiful, and I have to push those thoughts away to focus on what matters.

"What were you doing in here?" I demand.

Courtney looks down at the floor. "I just ... I wanted to know what was back here. I didn't know it would be a person. Your family."

I narrow my eyes. "Amanda told you?"

She nods. "I'm not sure why you didn't."

"Because Tati was vulnerable. *Is* vulnerable. If my enemies knew she was here, they could have attacked the house the way they did the bar. I didn't want to risk it."

"I'm not your enemy."

We look at each other for a long moment, and Courtney shrugs. "I don't want to be your enemy. I don't think of myself that way. Not anymore."

I don't think of her that way either, but I don't say so.

Then, I feel a small hand on mine. Tati frowns at me and then begins to sign, her fingers stiff and slow, as though it takes her a while to remember the right movements.

Where are my mommy and daddy?

My heart seizes in my chest, and I'm glad I don't need to speak to respond to her because I wouldn't be able to get through it without breaking down.

Not here right now, I sign, and then smooth down her hair.

"What did she say about her parents?"

I look up and Courtney is watching us.

"How do you know sign language?"

"I worked at a coffee shop," she says with a shrug. "We had a few deaf customers, and I learned the basics."

I turn back to Tati and smile. *Give me a second.*

Then, I move towards Courtney, grab her just above her elbow, and pull her towards the corner. "How much do you know?"

"Enough," she says. "I took a class in school about trauma at an early age. The way you handle this is so important. I just want to help."

"Don't." I shake my head and look back towards the bed. Tati is watching us, so I turn so she won't be able to read my lips. "She's my family. I will handle this."

Courtney opens her mouth to argue, but I raise a brow and she stops.

"I should end our deal since you broke the rules and came to this side of the house."

"Dmitry, no!" Courtney pleads, laying a hand on my chest. "Please."

I step away from her touch. "The only reason I'm not going to is because, for whatever reason, you're good for my niece's health. Your presence brought her back."

"I didn't do anything," Courtney says. "I didn't even touch her."

I'm not usually a superstitious man, but after months of visiting Tati with no change, no movement, no improvement, I have to take it as a sign that she woke up the first time Courtney walked into her room.

It has to mean something.

"I don't know what happened," I admit. "But you brought Tati back, and I will not punish you for that."

Courtney relaxes, but I step forward and press a finger under her chin, lifting her face to mine. Her brown eyes gaze into mine, wide and searching, and I find myself drawn to her lips, to her warmth. I have to bite the inside of my cheek to keep from kissing her.

"But if you disobey my orders again, I will not be so forgiving."

I hold Courtney's chin up, forcing her to look into my eyes and see the truth of my words.

She blinks, and I finally let her go. She takes a deep breath, releasing a shaky sigh. "You know, sometimes it feels like you might be two entirely different people. It doesn't make sense that the same man who would care for his niece like this could also threaten me and my family."

Courtney has seen enough for one day, so without responding, I grab her arm and drag her towards the door. She doesn't resist, and I've just opened the door to allow the doctor and Amanda back into the room when Tati lets out a raspy kind of cry.

Before the accident, she rarely vocalized at all, so the sound surprises me. When I turn around and see tears pouring down her face, I freeze.

I don't know how to handle this.

I love her because she's family, but she's still a six-year-old girl. I know nothing about children. Especially when they're upset.

I let go of Courtney's arm and stand in the doorway, frozen and uncertain.

Then, Courtney moves to stand next to me and whispers in my ear, "She's overwhelmed."

I can relate. I've just barely figured out, on some level, how to deal with Courtney, and now Tati is awake and needing me, and I don't know where to give my attention first: to the woman threatening my power in my own house or my orphaned niece.

"She doesn't recognize the doctor or the nurse," Courtney says, laying a hand on my shoulder and urging me forward gently. "She needs someone to explain to her what is going on. She needs her uncle."

I move blindly towards the bed and reach for Tati's hand. With my other, I gesture for the doctor and nurse to step back. Eventually, I tell them to leave altogether.

Then, I sit with her and hold her hand and try to make sense of things for her.

Am I sick? she asks.

You were sleeping. That man and woman were helping you. Making sure you ate and had enough water.

Where are my mom and dad? she asks again, looking around the room for them.

I tell her in as few words as possible that they aren't here. When she asks if they will be soon, I distract myself with adjusting her blankets around her waist.

Then, suddenly, Tati stiffens and shakes her head. I follow her gaze and realize Courtney is slipping through the door, trying to sneak away without being noticed.

"Wait," I call.

When Courtney turns around, Tati grabs my hand and claims my attention. *Stay. Tell her to stay. I want her here.*

"Sorry," Courtney says, tucking her hair behind her ear. "I didn't mean to disturb you two. I'm just going to go—"

"Nowhere," I finish for her. "Tati doesn't want you to go. She asked you to stay."

"Me?" Courtney asks, looking from me to Tati.

Tati smiles at her, tears still making her eyes glassy, and waves for Courtney to sit on the bed.

Seeing her smiling, making requests of people she doesn't know—acting like a child—makes me happier than anything has in months.

When I lost my brother and sister-in-law, and I thought I was going to lose Tati, too, everything felt dark. My father is gone, as well as my grandfather. I have no family. No other blood relative in the world left.

But now, Tati is awake and healthy, and I have Courtney to thank … for some reason.

Courtney watches me as she crosses the room, gauging whether I'm okay with her getting so close. Finally, she feels comfortable enough to sit on the edge of the bed, and Tati reaches out for her hand.

As soon as their fingers are intertwined, Tati lies back on the pillow. There is still sadness in her face, but for the moment, she's content, and that is all I can hope for. For now.

Her eyes start to droop closed and panic grips my chest.

"Tati?" I call, even though she can't hear me. "Is she okay?"

Could the coma come and go like that? Could she slip back into it if I'm not vigilant? I look to the door, wondering if I should call the doctor back in, but Courtney reaches across the bed and lays a hand on my cheek.

"These kinds of injuries require rest," she says. "She's going to be very tired for a while. She's just resting."

I ease back onto the bed, studying Tati and the slow, deep movement of her chest. The panic in my chest slips away, and I take a deep breath.

"Thank you."

Courtney's attention snaps up to me, clearly surprised, and then nods. "Of course."

We both sit there for a long time, watching Tati sleep, neither of us saying anything.

13

COURTNEY

I'm in my room with one of the three new sign language books I ordered in my lap when the door opens and then quickly closes. Before I can even look up, the book is off my lap and Dmitry is between my legs.

He pushes me back on the bed and unzips my jeans, slipping the denim from my hips.

"Hello to you, too," I say as he drags his palms down my now-bare thighs.

He responds by kissing his way up my inner leg, and I don't mind at all.

The sex has been frequent and mind-blowing. Dmitry seeks me out most days of the week and, without any discussion or conversation, we tear into one another.

It has become an incredible release. Whenever we skip a day, I miss and crave it.

Still, he hasn't opened up to me. Actually, he has barely spoken to me since the day Tati woke up. All of his time is split between dealing with his men and the Italians, and Tati's rehabilitation, though I've taken on a large role in the latter aspect, as well.

For some reason, Tatiana likes my presence. She requests to see me in the evenings and wants me to read books with her. I've been learning more sign language so we can stop reading the same children's nursery rhyme books over and over again, and she has been teaching me little things like the sign she made up for Dmitry's name—the letter 'D' with her right hand while both arms move towards the front in the 'strong' sign.

Dmitry puts his strength to use when he wraps a hand around my lower back and slides me further up on the bed so he can rest on the edge of the mattress while his mouth goes to work on my center.

I spread my thighs for him and curl my fingers in his silky hair.

Yesterday, he came home bloodied again. I tried not to stare, but it's hard not to. I'm not accustomed to the violence of his life.

"Things aren't usually this bad," he said when he caught me looking at him. He threw his stained shirt in the hamper and turned to me, bare-chested and beautiful. "The Italians are still after us."

Then, we transitioned into precisely what we are doing now.

"You seem clean today," I say. "No trouble at work?"

Dmitry looks up at me, eyebrows raised. "Do you really want to talk right now?"

No, of course not. I want to scream his name and beg him to never stop, but if we don't talk now, we never will.

"There doesn't seem to be another time to talk," I admit as he swirls his tongue inside of me. My entire body goes to jelly.

Dmitry sighs and crawls over me, kissing his way under my tank top, eventually lifting it up until I help him pull it over my head and toss it on the floor. He unsnaps my bra with a quick flick of his fingers and has my nipple in his mouth in an instant.

He's efficient.

At this rate, he'll get good enough there won't even be time to talk during the act.

"Tatiana's physical therapy is going well," I say through a moan when he nips at my breast.

"I do not want to talk right now," he says, grinding his hips against mine like he wants to pound me to dust. I can feel his excitement against my thigh.

Dmitry and I haven't had a lot of time for anything other than carnal conversation, but he has thanked me a few times for looking after Tati. I tell him it's my pleasure, and I mean it. Tatiana gives me a purpose in the house. Something to do aside from study and dance.

She's an easy little girl to love.

I'm sad that one day, she won't be in my life.

One hundred and twenty-seven days left in our deal.

Dmitry grabs my arms and pins them above my head. Then, with his eyes locked on mine, he drives himself into me, thrusting to the hilt.

I tip my head back and cry out, and Dmitry muffles the sound with his mouth, kissing me until I feel drunk.

He pounds into me, our bodies slapping together, and I curl my legs around him and hook my ankles behind his back. I pull him into me even as the orgasm becomes too much to contain. Even as I fall apart, I keep ahold of him. Because I know when this is done, he'll leave.

And for reasons I don't understand, I don't want him to go.

"Courtney," Dmitry groans in my ear, his breath hot on my neck as he comes.

When he's done, he kisses me, slides out, and leaves.

One hundred and twenty-six more opportunities for that to happen.

The next day, I'm walking down the stairs after a physical therapy session with Tatiana and pulling my hair up into a ponytail when the door slams open.

My hands are occupied, so I don't have any way to brace myself as I slip down the remaining three stairs and land on my butt on the marble floor.

I scramble to standing as fast as I can. "What is going on?"

The guards are grunting and hauling something through the door, and I step back and press myself against the wall, not wanting to interfere. Dmitry usually tries not to bring his work home with him but things have been crazy lately. Apparently, he has to interrogate someone here.

I gesture towards the basement door, thinking I'll at least try to be helpful even if I don't agree with what is happening, but then I see who the guards are holding.

"Sadie!" Her name is a question and a plea, and I rush forward and try to pull the guards' hands off her. "What is going on? What is happening?"

"She was trespassing," a guard barks. "She climbed the fence."

"She's my friend." I pull on their hands again, but they keep a tight hold on her. Sadie lets out a frustrated scream as she thrashes back and forth, but her fighting does little. The guards are much stronger than her.

"I'm calling Dmitry," I shout over the commotion.

"Not necessary."

Dmitry appears behind the guards and nods at the guards. Immediately, they drop Sadie, and she falls to the floor in a heap. I kneel down and lay a hand on her back. "Oh my God, Sadie, are you okay?"

"Fine," she says sarcastically. "Great."

"Courtney," Dmitry says, eyes serious and searching. "You should have your friends call next time. We'd be happy to open the gate for them."

I glare up at him, but his expression doesn't change. I wonder if he's going to kick Sadie out. She did call the police on him, after all. He has good reason to not want her around. However, he crosses his arms over his chest and turns for the stairs.

"I'll be upstairs. Make yourself at home, Sadie."

The guards clear out, though I know they'll stay close, and I wait until Dmitry is upstairs and the door slams behind him before I stand up, hauling Sadie with me.

"What in the hell were you doing climbing over the fence?" I ask. "You could have been shot."

"Shot?" Her eyes go wide. "Who keeps armed guards at their house?"

"Important people. People with a lot of enemies." I'm not going to lie to Sadie, but I'm not going to tell her the whole truth. She doesn't need to know. I made a deal with Dmitry—for my father—and I intend to see it through. "Come into the kitchen."

"No." Sadie stumbles back against the door and shakes her head. "Not until you tell me what you are doing here. Are you safe?"

"What did the police tell you?" I ask. "They talked to you, right?

Because they came here to talk to me, and I told them I'm fine. I told them I wasn't kidnapped. Did they relay that to you?"

Sadie bites her lip and nods. "Yes, but I didn't know if I could trust them. You hear stories about dirty cops. What if they were working with the guys who took you? I wanted to see you for myself."

I hold my arms out to the side and spin in a circle. "I'm fine."

True.

"I'm here of my own free will."

Mostly true.

I feel Sadie studying me, but she isn't as frantic as when she first arrived. On some level, I can tell I've calmed her worries, and this is confirmed when she follows me deeper into the house.

"Do you want tea?" I ask, grabbing the electric kettle from the counter and filling it with water before she can answer. Then, I grab two mugs from the cabinet and drop a spiced tea bag in each one.

When I turn around, Sadie's dark brows are raised. "You really are here of your own free will, aren't you?"

I nod. "I wasn't lying to you. I'm fine."

She sighs and drops down onto the nearest barstool. "Then you need to tell your family that. I went to talk to your dad, and he said you were okay, but you should see him, Courtney. He's pale, and thinner by the day. He's worried sick about you. Even your mom is worried."

My stomach twists at the news of my dad, but at the mention of my mom, I stop my movements and spin around. "What about my mom?"

"She couldn't get ahold of you, and your dad kept making excuses, so she finally came into town. She went to the police station to demand they come here and haul you out of this house."

"What?" I lean back against the counter, mouth hanging open. "My mom?"

My mom, who wouldn't show up in my life in any kind of meaningful way for years, is suddenly in town. With my dad.

Looking for me.

It's all too bizarre to be real, and also too dangerous.

"Tell her I'm fine." I move to Sadie and grab her hands. "Tell her to go home. I don't want to leave."

"But why?" Sadie looks around at the sparkling kitchen and shrugs. "Okay, I mean, I guess I get it. This is a freaking mansion. But this is also not like you at all. You're all about school and your dad and your future. Why are you suddenly with this guy?"

"Dmitry," I correct, though I don't know why it's important to me that she call him by his name. "And because I want to be. Please just let it go."

Sadie stands up and takes a deep breath. Then, she smiles at me. "No, I'm sorry. I won't. Something weird is going on here, and I'm not going to stop until I'm positive you are safe."

We go back and forth on it for a few minutes, but there is no use. Sadie has always been stubborn, and she won't budge. She doesn't believe all of my half truths and deceptive storytelling, and she isn't going to stop.

I could tell her the truth, but that isn't an option.

Number one, it probably wouldn't do anything to end her crusade to free me.

Number two, it would put her at risk. Dmitry didn't make it explicitly clear, but it was implied that no one can know who he is or what he does or why I'm actually here.

So, I hug Sadie goodbye and beg her one last time to let it go.

"I'll let it go when you're home," she says, poking me in the side. Then, she looks past me into the house, eyes narrowed. "Take care of yourself, please. Be safe."

I promise her I will, and I hope I can keep that promise.

One hundred and twenty-five more days until this will be over.

I head upstairs to find Dmitry, but when I'm halfway up, I hear the sound of Tati's bell. Dmitry and I run into each other in the hallway, both headed towards Tati. He doesn't say anything as he follows me down the hall to her room.

I poke my head in her room and wave to catch her attention. When she looks at me, I sign. *What is it, kid?*

There are crayon masterpieces hanging from the walls, dolls in various stages of undress with tiny princess dresses strewn about the bed, and juice boxes all over the nightstand. It looks much more like a six-year-old girl's room now than a hospital unit.

I'm bored. She slumps down in the bed.

Dmitry smiles and walks into the room. *Then get out of bed. The doctor wants you to walk around more. You have to work on your endurance.*

Me and Courtney already did that today, she signs. *We walked the halls forever. It was boring.*

I know enough sign language now to guess at what is being said, but I still miss things from time to time. When I do, Dmitry translates for me.

Dmitry smooths down her blonde hair with a surprisingly gentle touch. *Is everything boring?*

Yes, she pouts. Then, suddenly, she sits up. *I want to go to the movies. You won't let me go to school yet. So I want to see a movie.*

They've had this discussion about school more than once. The doctors don't think Tati is ready. Neither does Dmitry. Based on my college psych classes, I'm torn because I know she desperately needs the normalcy of a classroom but also likely needs more time to recover. For now though, Dmitry has put his foot down, so it's a moot point.

Dmitry frowns. *The movies? Like, the theater?*

She nods, mouth open in a gap-toothed smile. *Can we get popcorn? And candy? I want a soda!*

Whoa, hold on. Dmitry bites his lip. *I'm not sure if that's such a good idea.*

Tatiana's face falls at once, and then she turns to me. *Courtney? Please?*

I hold up my hands. *That isn't my decision, kiddo. I'm sorry.*

You never let me do anything fun, Uncle Dmitry. She lowers her chin to her chest, bottom lip pouted out. *It isn't fair.*

Dmitry looks up at me and then double-checks to make sure Tati is reading his lips. "Thanks for backing me up. Now I'm the bad guy."

I almost remind him that he is, definitionally, a bad guy. Instead, I just shrug. "I like the movies. It would be fun."

It would be nice to forget about the drama of my life for a few hours. Plus, the house is pretty boring. Tati isn't wrong there.

"It isn't safe," he says.

Tati looks up at him and waves a hand in front of his face. *Don't talk about me. I'm right here.*

He lays a hand on her forehead and winks down at her. While she's distracted, I argue her cause. "We have guards. It would be easy to keep the movie theater safe. And it isn't exactly a common haunt of yours. No one will suspect it."

Dmitry sighs, narrows his eyes at me, and then looks down at Tati. As soon as she sees the smile on his face, she jumps up. *Are we going?*

He nods, and she throws her arms around his neck. Then, she points to me. *Courtney, too?*

Dmitry wraps an arm around the girl's middle and lifts her up on his hip. Then, he nods and looks at me, a small smile on his lips. "Yes, Courtney, too."

14

COURTNEY

The movie is captioned, but Tatiana is having a hard time reading. So, Dmitry spends a few minutes every so often signing what is going on to her in the dim lights. I would think that would be a terrible way to enjoy a movie, but Tati doesn't seem to mind. She just eats her candy and popcorn and takes long drinks from the soda she's supposed to be "sharing" with Dmitry.

When he isn't signing the events of the movie to his niece, Dmitry is scouring the theater.

It's a mid-afternoon showing of a cartoon, so the theater is filled with parents corralling kids to and from the bathroom, splitting snacks between arguing siblings, and perpetually telling them to shush.

Still, Dmitry can't seem to relax. He glances back at the doors every few minutes and jumps whenever the dad in the row behind us slides past to keep his toddler from crawling under the seats.

For the first time, I consider how difficult it must be to be Dmitry. How exhausting it must be to constantly be wary of threats to your life or the lives of your loved ones.

He can't take a day off. He can't forget his worries for a few hours in a movie theater. If he did, there is a possibility he'd be caught unaware. Attacked. Killed.

"This movie is terrible," I whisper in his ear.

He starts and then looks at me, eyes narrowed. "I don't think it's meant for us."

I shrug. "Still terrible."

He turns away, but I see a small smile pull at the corners of his mouth.

Truthfully, I haven't watched the film much. Dmitry has been busy monitoring the theater for danger, and I've been busy monitoring him.

When we got to the show, Tatiana led the way into the row, Dmitry trailing behind. So, I somehow ended up sitting next to Dmitry, and his knee keeps brushing my thigh. At first, I pulled it away, but now I'm letting our bodies touch, and it's almost more exciting than when we have sex.

The sex is good—obviously. But being close to him, near him when I know nothing more is going to happen, stokes a fire in my belly. It makes me want it even more than I usually do.

I bump my knee gently against his, readjusting in my seat so it looks like an accident. Then, I lay my arm on the armrest, the back of my hand brushing lightly against his arm.

"Stop that."

I look over, and Dmitry is staring straight ahead, but his jaw is tense.

"What?"

His hand reaches out and catches mine before I even know it's happening. Then, he pulls my arm over the armrest and settles it along the length of his thigh. He presses his lips to my ear and whispers, "Stop touching me when I'm at a kids' movie and can't do anything about it."

A shiver works down my neck, and I turn away, hiding my smile. I see a couple a few rows ahead of us. I nudge Dmitry and point to them. "They obviously don't care we are in a kids' movie."

He follows my finger and then blanches. "Are they making out in a theater full of kids?"

"Let's hope that's all they're doing."

He laughs into his arm and it feels good to see him be something other than serious all the time.

He smiles with Tatiana and is gentle with her, but otherwise, Dmitry is stoic. I know he has to be to survive in the world he inhabits, but I'm glad I can help him relax every so often. I'm worried that the man might implode if he doesn't blow some steam off every once in a while. Even if a kids' movie about an animated rabbit isn't exactly his first or second choice for relaxation.

"Not everyone here is deaf. We should stop talking before we get in trouble," I say.

Dmitry nods to the dark, muscular figures on either side of us. I hadn't really noticed them, but now I see they're obviously Dmitry's guards.

"No one is going to walk past my men. They're intimidating enough to keep any grouchy fathers away."

He's right; his men are scary. But so is Dmitry. In a moment of honesty, I say so.

Dmitry turns to me and studies my face. I can feel my skin heat under his gaze, and I hope it's too dark to notice. Then, he shakes his head. "*You* are intimidating."

"Me?" My eyebrows shoot up. "No, I'm not."

"You are," he insists. "You're intimidating because it's difficult to intimidate you. You aren't afraid of anything."

That isn't true in the slightest.

I'm scared of everything.

I'm especially scared of Dmitry ... and the way I feel for him. But I decide not to say any of that.

Instead, I brush my knee against his leg again and stare up at the movie screen as though I'm giving it all of my attention. He releases a frustrated growl next to me.

When the movie is over, none of us are ready to go home, so I suggest we walk around the adjoining mall. Dmitry is hesitant, but Tatiana yanks on his arm and all but drags him through the front doors and straight to the toy store.

Once we are inside, the guards keep a safe distance behind us to the point I can almost forget they're there at all.

I want a pretzel, Tati says, pointing to the food court.

After popcorn and candy? Dmitry asks. *Aren't you full?*

Tati insists she isn't and then grabs my arm and drags me into the argument. *Courtney wants one, too.*

Dmitry raises a brow at me, and I shrug. "I wouldn't mind a pretzel."

He rolls his eyes, but I can tell he's having a good time. He enjoys seeing Tati be a normal kid just as much as I do. Her days are busy with resting and physical therapy and lessons from a tutor Dmitry hired, so it feels good to let her get out of the house and enjoy the simple offerings of the local mall.

Tatiana is only halfway through her pretzel when she looks over and sees princess-style dresses in a store window. Her eyes go wide and glassy, and she doesn't sign anything; she just points.

Those? I ask.

She nods, mouth hanging open, and I turn to Dmitry. "Can we try one on?"

He groans. "Only if I don't have to go in. I'm tired."

"Maybe you're the one who needs physical therapy," I tease.

He smiles and then hands me his credit card. "Don't let her go too crazy."

Tatiana grabs my hand and pulls me inside. I follow her around the store, grabbing dress after dress and throwing them over my arm. The saleswoman, excited about the possibility of a large sale—and a large commission—gets us a dressing room and gives Tati a bottle of water to drink as she goes through the arduous task of dressing up like a princess.

She's excited and signs things too quickly for me to keep up, but I don't need an interpreter to understand the smile on her face. She's having the absolute best time.

The dress she's most excited about—a purple one with glittery lace around the middle and shimmery beads stitched into the skirt—is too tight around her arms and a bit too short, so like the princess she is, Tati sends me out to the store to get her a larger size.

The sales associate who had been helping us, an eager blonde woman with bright red lipstick, is nowhere to be seen. Instead, there is a middle-aged woman standing near the cash register.

"Excuse me," I say, waving a hand. "Do you work here?"

The woman doesn't answer but presses her lips together in a smile and nods in a way that makes me believe she's happy to help me.

"I need this dress in a larger size, but I don't see one on the racks."

She squints and scans the store floor. "Let me see, let me see."

I follow her in circles around the racks, thinking that if I wanted to scour the entire store, I would have found the dress myself.

"Let me look in the back," she says, waving for me to follow her towards the back of the store.

The dressing rooms are just to my left, and I peek in to see that Tati's door is still closed, frilly dresses scattered over benches and hanging over the top of the door.

The woman tries every key on her ring for the back door, but none of them fit.

"I know I have the key somewhere," she says, sounding as exasperated as I feel. "Wait here."

I stand next to the door, the too-small dress still in my hands, and wait for the woman to rifle through the desk and her pockets. Finally, she walks over to me with the key ring held in the air, a silly smile on her face.

"It was on the key ring the whole time. Silly me."

I laugh, but I'm no longer feeling very forgiving. It only takes her a few seconds to walk inside and come back with the next size up in the purple dress, and I walk it back into the dressing room.

I throw the dress over the top of the door and shake it around to catch Tati's attention. When she doesn't grab it, I shake it again. Then, I stick my foot under the door and wave it around.

Still, nothing.

Finally, I push on the door and realize it isn't even locked.

I also realize Tatiana isn't inside.

My heart jumps immediately to my throat, and I run to every other door to make sure she isn't hiding in another dressing room. When I can't find her anywhere, I jog back onto the main sales floor. The woman who helped me find the dress isn't there anymore, and I don't have time to wait for her, anyway.

I run out of the shop and find the guards standing near a cell-phone stand. "Did you see Tati?"

Both men straighten at my arrival and shake their heads. "She was with you."

Panic crushes my chest, and I feel breathless. "She isn't here."

Immediately, one of the men breaks away to find Dmitry.

To tell him I lost his niece.

~

Dmitry walks too fast for me to keep up without jogging. His strides are long and furious.

"I can't believe you lost her."

"She needed another dress size," I say, as though that's any kind of excuse. I let a six-year-old out of my sight. A six-year-old who was recently in a coma. Whose parents are dead. Whose uncle is a Mafia boss.

Please be alive. Please be nearby. Please don't be gone.

I send the silent prayers up to the sky and hope she hasn't gone far. She needed Dmitry to give her a piggyback ride through a lot of the mall because she was tired. How can she suddenly be gone?

Dmitry isn't saying anything, but I know it's only because he's too angry to speak. His jaw is clenching and unclenching, his teeth grinding together as we walk. He has already called for more backup to get to the mall, and his guards are spread out in every direction, sweeping through the place with ruthless military-like efficiency.

"I'll go check the food court again," I say, hitching a thumb over my shoulder and backing up in the opposite direction.

Dmitry doesn't even turn around. He waves a hand in the air to tell me to go, and I do.

I don't know a ton about kids, but I know they're creatures of habit. If Tatiana got lost, she would go to a place she'd been before. She'd follow the same paths we walked. So, I do that.

I walk back to the dress store to make sure she didn't go back there looking for us and then I make my way over to the pretzel stand. From there, I dodge the crowds coming out of the movie theater and head for the claw machine where Dmitry failed to win Tati a stuffed unicorn after three attempts.

Nothing.

A panicked sob works its way out of me, and I swallow it back as fast as I can. If I let myself fall apart now, I won't gather myself up again.

This was my idea. Coming to the mall after the movie. It was my idea.

Dmitry would have taken us home where it was safe, so if Tati is gone, it will be my fault.

Thoughts spin in my head too horrible and fast for me to keep up with, and I feel dizzy when I suddenly see a flash of purple moving through the crowd.

I stand on my tiptoes and arch around a group of emo teenagers in baggy black pants and chains, and I see her.

Tatiana.

She's in the too-small purple dress, the back of it unzipped, holding the hand of a large man.

For a second, I think it's one of Dmitry's guards, but then I realize that can't be true. If it was one of the guards, they would be heading back towards Dmitry. They would be on the phone with him, trying to return the little girl to her uncle.

This man is taking Tatiana to the exit doors.

Purpose and adrenaline pump through my veins as I run through the crowd, knocking people to the side in an attempt to get to the little girl.

When the man takes her through the exit doors and into the bright sunshine beyond, I lower my head and run even harder.

I can't let her get away.

The light outside temporarily blinds me, and I hold up a hand to shield my eyes from the afternoon sun. As soon as my vision begins to return, I see the flash of purple again to my right.

The man is kneeling down next to a large black truck and it takes me a second to realize he's signing something. To Tati. He's talking to her.

"Hey!" I scream as I run towards them.

The man doesn't hear me at first, and I'm not sure if he's deaf too, so I scream again. If nothing else, I want to try and attract as many eyes as possible to our situation.

"Hey, asshole!" Usually, cursing in front of a child would not be my go-to, but Tati can't hear me, anyway. "What in the fuck are you doing with my kid?"

Screaming the truth—*what are you doing with the recently orphaned niece of the man holding me captive as collateral for my father's illicit Mafia debts*—seemed a little long-winded.

The man turns around and Tati follows his gaze. She steps forward when she sees me, but the man extends a hand out to hold her back.

I'm getting closer to them now, only ten feet away, but I don't slow down.

I don't have a weapon. Not even a purse to hit him with. So, I have to use my body.

When I'm only a few steps away, I leap into the air and slam my body into the man's front as hard as I can.

He grunts with the force of the impact and stumbles back a few steps but doesn't fall.

I, on the other hand, have the wind knocked out of my chest. The man is built like a brick wall.

"Get away from her," I wheeze, falling away from him and reaching blindly for Tati.

When her little hand slips into mine, an ounce of my panic disappears.

She's alive and safe. *For now.*

"I was just talking to her," the man grumbles.

"Well, don't!" I yell. "Ever again. Never come near her. You creep."

The man has dark olive-toned skin and dark hair cut into a flat-top. His nostrils flare as he moves towards me, but before he can do anything, I hear yelling behind me. I turn and see Dmitry and his guards rushing towards us.

Again, another bit of panic floats away.

We aren't alone. Dmitry is here.

"What in the hell is going on?" Dmitry yells.

The man backs away further but doesn't leave. I expect him to make a run for it, but he holds his ground.

"I knew you wouldn't tell her the truth!" he yells as Dmitry gets closer. "She deserves to know the truth about her parents."

The situation gets more and more bizarre at every turn. I thought the man wanted to kidnap Tati, but now it seems as though he's more determined to tell her the truth about her dead parents?

What is happening? And why?

Dmitry arrives and throws his arms around me. For a second, I lean into his touch before I realize he's grabbing Tati from my arms. He pulls her away from me and runs a hand across her cheek, checking that she's safe.

Once he's satisfied, he sets her on the ground and turns his flat gaze on me. "Take her inside. With the guards. *Don't* let her out of your sight."

"Who is she?" the strange man asks.

I realize he's talking about me. When I look at him, he studies me with hungry eyes, an eyebrow arching. "I don't recognize her."

Dmitry steps forward, his eyes murderous. "Well, I recognize you, asshole. If you care about breathing, I'd suggest you leave."

The two men stare at each other, and I watch, frozen, until Dmitry shouts at me.

"Leave. Now."

I jump and then grab Tati's hand and pull her back inside the mall. Luckily, one of the guards steps forward to grab Tati because I feel lost. He takes Tati to another claw machine and has her point to a toy she might want. I watch the exchange without really seeing it, my mind focused on Dmitry in the parking lot.

Is he okay?

Are they fighting?

Does he need help?

Before panic can bloom in my chest, a shadow appears over my shoulder. It's Dmitry.

He stands next to me without saying a word or looking at me. His eyes are trained on Tati.

But I'm watching him.

He has blood on his shirt.

15

DMITRY

This is why I can't have nice things.

Normal things, really.

We went to the mall for one afternoon and everything went to shit.

Tati is having nightmares, Courtney and I aren't speaking, and I'm not sure how I feel about any of it.

At the time, I was mad. Beyond mad.

I thought it was because Courtney lost sight of Tati, but it wasn't. I was afraid. That fear turned into rage, and I took it out on Courtney.

Usually, I don't feel bad about these kinds of things. I just forget it and move on, but I can't do that with Courtney. Every time her brown eyes land on me—which has been less and less frequent now that she's studying for her first exams of the semester—I remember every shitty thing I've ever done to her. To her father.

Even though Courtney is at my house as part of our deal, I know that she cares about me. On some level, at least. And she adores Tati.

Courtney would never do anything to hurt Tati, and I know she's bothered by the fact that I don't trust her. The thing is, I do. I trust her more than I probably should.

I don't trust the Italians, however.

When they were messing with my business, that was one thing. But talking to my niece? That is another situation entirely.

As soon as I know more, we can strike. We can fight back. Things will certainly spiral out of control, and I know I'll be condemning us to war, but there is no other way. The Italians want to play dirty? Fine, so will I.

I have Rurik monitoring things for me, trying to figure out how the Italians know enough to follow my movements and how they know about Tatiana, but he doesn't have any useful information for me yet. So, I wait.

While I wait, my mind wanders to Courtney more than I would like, and after days of mulling things over, I decide to make a call.

Lawrence is breathless when he answers the phone. "Is everything okay? Is she safe?"

"She's safe," I assure him, surprised that my annoyance is only mild at best. "She's going to school and staying busy, and I just wanted you to know."

Courtney's father sighs with relief. "Thank God."

After Tati was taken, even for just a few minutes, I had a small glimpse into what daily life is like for Lawrence right now. I couldn't continue ignoring his calls and shutting him out.

Still, I also don't have time to call him every day.

"That's all I wanted to say. I have to go."

"Please take care of her," Lawrence says before I hang up. "She's a good girl. She deserves it."

I don't say anything on the phone, but Lawrence's words stick with me. Courtney does deserve ... something. Though, I'm not sure what.

It isn't until a few days later that I finally figure it out and make the call.

∼

Courtney gave me a printout of her class schedule and my guards text me when she leaves campus for the day, so when I get home after work, I know she and Tati will be upstairs together.

If Courtney isn't at school or studying, she's with Tati. Always.

When I walk in the room we decorated for Tati in the west wing, my niece is teaching Courtney how to sign one of her favorite songs. The music is deafeningly loud so Tati can feel the bass, but Courtney doesn't act like she minds. She's smiling, her dark hair pulled back in a messy ponytail that swishes over her shoulders as she bobs her head with the beat.

When Tati notices me, she opens her mouth wide and hurls herself at me, hands swirling in the air in celebration.

Courtney turns down the music and grins. "You're home early."

It's the first genuine smile she has given me in days, and I soak in the warmth of it.

Then, I stop.

I can't count on this. If the experience at the mall taught me anything, it's that I can't have a normal family life. I can't have a beautiful woman waiting for me at home with my kids. I can't be greeted with hugs and cuddles and smiles.

My enemies will pounce on that weakness.

If I let myself depend on seeing Courtney's face at the end of every day, she'll be taken from me.

So, I rub my hand over Tati's head and give them both a pinched smile before stepping away. "I had to come home and show you a surprise."

Surprise? Tati asks, having read my lips.

I nod. *In your old room.*

Before I can even finish signing the sentence, Tati is running out the door and down the hall towards the east wing. Her physical therapy is going well. She only has a slight limp in her right leg from the car crash and her weakened muscles post-coma.

"What is this about?" Courtney asks. Her voice is closer than I expected and a shiver runs down my spine at the feeling of her breath on my neck.

"Go see," I say, gesturing for her to follow Tati.

She does, walking ahead of me, and though I'm trying to have more self-control, I can't help but watch her hips move as she walks.

Courtney moves around the house in tiny shorts that reveal every inch of her tanned, toned legs. Her shirts are loose but the material sticks to the curves of her body in suggestive ways that make it hard not to imagine what lies underneath.

Though, I don't have to do much imagining.

I've seen Courtney in just about every position known to man—naked—and yet it still isn't enough. The usual feeling I have at this point in a relationship for something new, something different, is glaringly absent.

I don't want new or different.

I want Courtney.

I slide my hand into my pants to adjust myself before walking into Tati's old room.

Tati is standing in the middle of the room, eyes wide, mouth open in a smile, taking in the changes I've made.

"I thought you were redoing the bathroom?" Courtney says from just a foot away inside the door.

"I did that, too." I nod to the en-suite bathroom which now has a jacuzzi tub and a white-tiled shower with three shower heads. "But I also did this."

This being a new dance studio.

The floors are smooth and wooden and shiny. Floor-to-ceiling mirrors cover one wall with a bar running down the length of the opposite wall.

For me? Tati signs, her cheeks glowing pink with excitement.

Whatever the Italian man said to her the other day, Tati never told me. But I know it had something to do with her parents. Clearly, he didn't tell her they're dead, but he made her think more critically about it. So, seeing her excited and unburdened is like seeing a triple-fucking rainbow.

I nod. "For you."

As I say the words, I look to Courtney as well. Her eyes meet mine for just a second before she throws herself at me.

I grunt in surprise and then instinctively wrap an arm around her waist.

Her body is warm and soft, and she stretches up onto her toes to press herself more firmly against me. I'm very grateful I paused outside to adjust myself, otherwise she'd know exactly how excited I am.

"It's perfect," Courtney says, spinning away from me to help Tati practice at one of the barres.

Soon, Tati wants Courtney to show her moves, and I stand in the doorway, content to watch them swirl around the room. Tati worships Courtney. They've only known one another a few weeks, but my niece is smitten, and I worry what it will be like when Courtney is gone. When it's just me and Tati alone in the house.

Right now, I'm Uncle Dmitry, but will that change if I get busy with work? If I can't be here every day to dance with her and listen to music?

I try to push the worries away, but the more I look at how happy Tati is next to Courtney, the more I can't imagine how she'd ever be happy with just me.

The thoughts eat away at the bright moment until the doctor arrives to take her for more physical therapy. To me, it looks like she doesn't need it, but the doctors insist Tatiana still has a lot of recovery ahead of her.

Tati grabs the doctor's hand and runs down the hall. When I move to follow, Courtney reaches for my arm.

"She does okay on her own," she says. "Actually, the doctor asked to see her alone today. They don't want any distractions."

I look down at where her fingers are wrapped around my forearm and swallow. "She won't be upset we aren't there?"

Courtney pulls her hand away slowly, and I miss the warmth immediately. "She'll be okay. It's good for her to be a bit more independent. As long as she knows someone she loves is close by, she does okay."

Love.

That's what I feel for Tatiana. I have no trouble saying that.

But what do I feel for Courtney?

For this brave, bold woman who stormed into my life and invaded every corner of it? A few weeks ago, I would have said that I was the one holding Courtney captive, but now the roles feel reversed. I can't imagine walking away from her.

"You're probably right about the independence," I admit. "After what happened at the mall, I can't let Tati out of the house for a while. If she doesn't learn to be alone more often, I'm worried she'll get sick of us."

"Maybe sick of you," Courtney teases, nudging me with her elbow. "She likes me. I'm *cool*." She does the sign for 'cool,' showing off her newly acquired sign language skills. "Though, with this dance studio, you're pretty cool yourself."

I shrug. "It was kind of for you, too."

She looks up at me, a smile pulling on the corners of her mouth, and I know she knows. Tati has only taken a few dance classes in her life. She would have been just as happy with a dog or a trampoline.

The dance studio was for Courtney.

"Thank you," she says softly, stepping towards me.

Her toes hit the floor first, moving like a dancer. I move to hold onto her, but she walks past me. For a second, I think she's going to leave, but then she closes the door and twists the lock. When she turns around, her back pressed to the door, her lips are pouty, eyes lidded, and I understand perfectly what is happening.

I've shown enough self-restraint for a lifetime, so I finally give in to my baser instincts.

The moment she's within reach, I drag Courtney's body against mine and capture her mouth with my own. I kiss her like I need her lips on mine to be able to breathe. I run my hands over her body, groaning whenever my fingers meet skin.

When she jumps up and wraps her legs around my waist, I immediately walk us further into the room and find the nearest wall.

I press her against the mirror, pinning her in place with my lower body, and lean back to allow her to unbutton my shirt.

She sighs as she runs her hands over my chest, and I bite back a growl when she leans forward and nips at my bare skin.

I want to enjoy this. Her.

But my mind is still torn. So, I decide to let it all out.

"I'm sorry about what happened at the mall."

Courtney freezes and looks up at me, brows knit together. "Are we talking about this now?"

I roll my hips against her, making her lips part in a sigh and nod. "Yes. I should have prepared you for what to look out for, what to do. I shouldn't have left you two alone. It was my fault."

Courtney kisses her way up my neck, nibbling on my earlobe. "I'm sorry for not staying with her. I shouldn't have let her out of my sight."

"Don't apologize." I grab her hands away from my body, mostly because I can't focus while she's touching me, and pin them against the glass above her head.

Suddenly, the expression on her face changes. Her eyes narrow, one eyebrow raised, and I think I've made her angry.

Her legs drop from around my waist and land on the floor. Keeping eye contact, she slips her fingers into the waistband of her shorts and slides them down her legs until they're a useless puddle on the floor.

My pulse quickens when I realize she's taken her panties off with them.

Courtney grabs my hand and lays it on her bare hip. Then, she turns around so her perfect ass is in front of me and her palms are flat on the glass.

When she looks over her shoulder at me, it's a miracle I don't lose control right there.

In a second, my pants are unbuttoned.

I feel more unwound than I've ever felt before. Less in control than I've felt in a long time. My fingers are jittery and my legs shake as I position myself at her opening. She arches her back, pushing into me, and I groan with every centimeter of contact between us.

Courtney moans, and I look up to see her watching me in the mirror.

This position has always appealed to me for the lack of eye contact, the lack of intimacy. It was about relief and physicality and that was it.

However, I'm not so certain anymore.

Courtney licks her lips and bats her eyes. She slides up and down my length while nibbling her lower lip between her teeth, while watching me to see exactly what every roll of her body is doing to me.

There is a whole other level of connection happening that I've never felt before, and I want to look away, to break it off, because who the fuck knows what happens if I let this continue? But I can't.

So, I grab her hips to ground me and slam into her.

Her mouth opens in an 'o' of surprise, and then she smiles.

The smile undoes me.

I thrust into her again and again until the sound of our bodies fills the room and echoes off the new floors.

Courtney reaches back to grab my thigh, and her eyes stay on me the entire time.

And my eyes stay on her.

I watch as her breathing gets more ragged, as her fingers flex on the mirrored surface. I watch as her brows pull together and her lips part in a moan.

When she comes, I see it and feel it, and the force of it brings me down with her.

I collapse forward onto her back, throwing out a hand to catch myself on the wall so we both don't fall down.

Still inside of her, I wrap my other arm around her stomach and pull her to standing, pressing her body against the wall. Bodies flat together, I hug her from behind and pulse into her with the last remnants of my energy.

When we finish, our handprints are smeared all across the glass, along with the perfect outlines of Courtney's breasts.

I'm tempted to ask the maid to never clean it off.

16

COURTNEY

Another day, another fight.

Dmitry stares at me, his gaze hard and immovable, and I want to grab him and scream.

Up and down, up and down.

Usually, I'm good at reading people, but I never know what Dmitry is thinking.

All I know is that sometimes he seems to like me—like at the mall before the kidnapping stuff and in the dance studio—and other times, he looks at me like I'm a piece of gum stuck to the bottom of his very expensive shoes.

"It's just a suggestion," I say, rolling my eyes.

"A suggestion you've made loudly and repeatedly," he says. "I hear you, and I disagree. Drop it."

So, I do.

I leave the kitchen and go back to studying and try to focus on my schoolwork, but it's difficult with my six-year-old shadow.

I love Tati. More than I ever expected to. Before her, I was never great with kids. But she likes me. Most of the time when I leave for class, which started up again not too long ago, she wants to come with me. It's only thanks to the superhuman strength of her nanny that she doesn't rush out the door every morning and cling to the bumper of the car.

She's trapped inside without even an hour of yard time a day offered to most prisoners. I understand Dmitry is worried about the Italians waging another attack or trying to hurt her, but she's just a little girl. A little girl without her parents or any friends or any sense of normalcy.

I wish I could help, but the decision isn't mine to make.

A week after Dmitry put in the new dance studio, which Tati and I have been enjoying thoroughly, I wake up to her screaming.

I've only been asleep thirty minutes since Dmitry climbed into bed with me and distracted me for over an hour, but I bolt upright at once. The covers are on the floor and I'm in the hallway before I've even fully grasped what is happening.

I've never heard her scream before.

Usually, if she wakes up in the night, she rings the bell until one of us comes to her. But now, she's shrieking.

I sprint down the hallway and suddenly run into a wall of half-naked man. It's Dmitry, and once he ascertains that I'm not an intruder, he takes off for Tati's room.

The guards are already there when we arrive, bleary and confused.

Tati is sitting up in bed, eyes closed, and screaming at the top of her lungs in a panic.

Dmitry and I rush for her and envelop her in hugs until she calms down and begins breathing normally.

She refuses to let us leave her alone, and we end up staying with her until the wee hours of the morning, stroking her hair and reminding her we're with her.

Dmitry barely looks at me the entire time, and I know it's because he knows I'm right.

Something needs to change.

Dmitry comes home the next night and goes straight to his office. I try to catch him before he shuts the door, but I'm too late, and when I go to knock, I can hear him on the phone.

"They can't get to another shipment. We have to cut them off or risk looking like fucking screw-ups." He pauses, waiting for the other person to respond. "I don't care. Take care of it. If you have any questions, call Rurik."

I wait a few minutes after he has hung up before I knock on the door.

"What?"

Not exactly a warm welcome, but I take what I can get and go inside.

Dmitry is in a pair of jeans that hang low on his hips, his shirt is in a ball in the corner, and his hand is running through his hair.

All of it is enough to distract me from my true purpose, but I swallow the ball of lust in my throat and focus on my task.

"We need to talk."

He looks up, one eyebrow raised. "About?"

"Tatiana," I say, sitting down in the chair across from him. "You need to tell her, Dmitry."

He sighs. "If that is what you're here to say, then go. I've heard it."

"No you haven't," I argue. "Well, you've heard it, but you aren't listening. I know what I'm talking about."

"Your parents aren't dead," he says. "I talked to your dad about you just this morning."

His eyes widen like he didn't mean to say that, and I make a mental note to circle back to that surprising revelation.

"My mother might as well have been dead." I take a deep breath and blow it out through pursed lips. "My mother left me and my father, which was bad enough. But worse, my father refused to acknowledge it. He swore to me over and over again that she would come back. Then, she'd come back for a weekend, and I'd think he was right. I'd believe him. And then she'd be gone again."

"You had a shit mom," he says, his voice wavering between a question and a statement.

"I did," I agree. "It would have been nice if someone had told me that at the time. If my father had been honest with me, it might not have hurt so bad when she left. I might not have been as hopeful when she'd come back for a visit. If he'd been honest with me, it might have kept me from resenting him so much."

I've never said that out loud before, but it's true.

I resented my father. Resent him still; present tense.

I love him so much, but part of me doesn't trust him. Part of me always feels like he's hiding something from me.

That feeling was only made worse the night I walked into his shop and overheard him talking with Dmitry. My father had been paying Dmitry off for years and never told me. He never explained why we were in financial trouble or why he couldn't buy me the nice things all of my friends had.

If he'd told me, it wouldn't have bothered me so much. I could have found a job and helped him out. He could have come to me when he got behind on payments, and we could have figured it out together.

"Honesty is always the best policy," I say, hating how cliché it sounds. However, it's true.

Dmitry stares at me for a long while, not saying anything. But I can tell he's thinking.

His fingers are drumming against his denim-clad thigh, and his jaw is working in the way it only does when he's deep in thought.

Finally, he sits down at his desk and lowers his chin, looking up at me beneath thick brows. "How do you suggest I approach this subject?"

I'm momentarily stunned because I didn't expect to get this far in the conversation.

I wanted to make my opinion known, but I had no reason to believe Dmitry would ever take my advice. Or ask for.

So, I stammer for a moment before finding my footing. "Oh. Well, I mean … I think the best thing to do is tell her the truth. About all of it. Tell her what happened and then explain that it's normal to be sad. Explain that you're sad, too. Let her know that grief is a normal process and that you will be there for her through it all."

Dmitry lets me finish, but I can almost see another few feet of wall going up around his heart.

Showing any emotion isn't exactly Dmitry's strong suit, let alone grief.

"Thanks for the suggestion," he says coolly. Then, before I can say anything else, he grabs his phone and slides it across the table to me. "Speaking of your father, he called me this morning wanting proof you're still alive. Apparently, he doesn't trust me."

I reach for the phone but hesitate at the last second, my hand hovering over it. "You want me to call him?"

He nods and then shrugs. "Or video chat. Whatever."

My heart leaps, and I grab the phone and find my father's name in his contacts. I stand up, but Dmitry clears his throat and points to the chair.

"Stay here. I want to know what is being said."

I call my dad, and he answers on the first ring. "Hello?"

The screen is black. "Dad? Where are you?"

"Courtney!" He screams my name and then lets out a sob. "You're alive."

The screen is still dark, but I see a shift in it, and I realize my dad has the phone pressed to his ear.

"Pull the screen away from your face." Two months away and nothing has changed. It almost makes me cry.

He pulls it back and then stares down at me, confused for a second before he understands. When he finally gets a good look at me, he sobs again.

Sadie was right. He looks thinner than I've ever seen him. There are dark circles under his eyes and a gray color to his skin I've never noticed before. He looks older, if that's possible in two months' time.

"I'm alive," I say. "I'm fine. Better than fine. Things are great."

Dmitry shifts in his seat at that, and I hope he knows I'm exaggerating for my father's sake.

Then again, am I exaggerating?

This arrangement began as a bargain, but more and more, I find myself excited when I hear Dmitry come home. Nervous when he knocks on my door. Thrilled when he crawls into my bed.

His presence is electrifying in a way I've never experienced before, and while I'm still counting down the days until our arrangement is over, I'm no longer certain whether I'm happy to see the number of days remaining shrink smaller and smaller.

My father asks details about what I'm eating, where I'm sleeping, and how school is going. I try to do the same with him, but he insists he's fine. That he's eating well and sleeping, though I have visual proof that he isn't.

Dmitry doesn't interrupt once. He doesn't sigh with boredom or urge me to hurry the conversation. He lets me sit and talk with my dad for half an hour before I cut the call short. If I don't, I know Dad never will.

"Please take care of yourself," my dad says, his eyes getting teary.

"You too," I say. "I mean it. Don't worry about me. I'm fine."

When I hang up and slide the phone across Dmitry's desk, he doesn't say anything, so I stand up to leave. As I turn, however, he clears his throat.

"How is school going?" he asks. "You told your dad it was going well. Is that true?"

His hands are folded in front of him on his desk, and he still doesn't have a shirt on. It's disconcerting to be so close to him half clothed and not be trying to get him the rest of the way naked.

"It's true. I'm doing well. I have plenty of time to study."

He nods. "Are you happy here?"

The question bewilders me. Dmitry has time in his life for Tati and work and sex with me, but I didn't imagine he concerned himself with much else.

He gave me the dance studio—though he disguised it as a gift for Tati—but even that felt more like an apology than a show of affection.

This, however. This simple question feels like care. Concern.

For me.

I'm happier than I was living with my dad in our trailer, waiting for my mom to come home. Happier than I was studying my brains out in school and living in my tiny dorm.

Here, I have Tati. I dance and eat delicious food and play hide-and-go-seek in the many nooks and crannies of Dmitry's mansion.

I have Dmitry.

Admitting that feels big and too much. So, I opt for a quick nod. "I'm happy."

Dmitry seems relieved. "Good."

I know he needs to get back to work, so I stand up and move towards the door. But I'm not ready to leave yet, so I divert towards his bar cart.

"Do you want a drink?"

He raises his brows in surprise, his jaw clenching in consideration, and then nods.

I know his favorite drink from ones we've shared many nights after putting Tati to bed together. An old-fashioned.

Even the bar cart in his office is well-stocked, and I quickly portion out the bourbon, add the bitters, and drop a sugar cube in. When money got tight in school, I spent a few weekends working open bars for a catering company. It's like riding a bike.

When I slide it across his desk, he smiles up at me, the corners of his mouth hesitant, as if he's doing so against his better judgment.

He doesn't touch the drink until I'm at the door. He takes a sip and nods his head in appreciation as I'm closing it.

I'm halfway down the hallway when I realize that Dmitry's life is lonely. It's hard to see at first because there are so many people in his house and under his command. So many people calling him and needing his help. However, there are very few people taking care of him. Being concerned about whether or not he's happy.

Even I didn't ask him the question in return.

Dmitry takes care of Tati and me ...

But who takes care of Dmitry?

17

DMITRY

The call comes midmorning.

I have some men out collecting for me, making a few stops to clients who could become problems unless reminded of our presence. I expected them to call with progress reports.

I didn't expect an emergency.

Get here. Now.

The words are the same as the night of the fire at the bar, though the location is different.

I drive without seeing, sure I can't count how many traffic laws I'm ignoring. My men are in trouble, so nothing else matters.

As soon as I pull onto the road—warehouses and crumbling buildings dating back to the city's earliest days, rising up to block out the sun on either side—a shot pings off the roof of my car.

A firefight.

I slam on the brakes and dive down into the passenger seat, digging through the glove compartment for my gun. Two more shots ricochet off my car, though none of them hit the windows. Apparently, the Italians can't shoot for shit.

Taking a deep breath, I open the driver's side door, roll down the window, and duck down behind the door, peeking up through the window, gun at the ready.

My men are in similar positions, guns aimed at a building on the right side of the road. It used to be a shoe factory, recently converted into apartments, though the tenants haven't moved in yet. I know because the owner of the building pays my Bratva for protection. From the Italians … and us.

The territory has been in dispute, control constantly in flux, but we have controlled it for the better part of a year without any problems. Now, apparently, the Italians have taken issue.

"How many?" comes a voice from behind.

I drop down and spin around, aiming my gun at Rurik before I realize it's him. He holds up his hands and curses.

"Shit, Dmitry. It's me."

"Don't fucking sneak up on me in the middle of a gunfight," I growl. "And I don't know. I just got here."

"Me too."

I didn't hear his car pull up, but I also didn't hear him approach me, so I don't ask any questions. There is no need to look even more incompetent than I already feel.

"We can't hold this position," Rurik says. "We have to advance. They have the high ground."

I look where he's pointing and finally see the Italians in the third floor windows.

"You think we should storm the building?"

Rurik shrugs. "It's better than holding point in the street so the police can conveniently find us and arrest us. We need to end this now, before word gets out."

He's right, but I don't say so. Instead, I call for the men to move forward.

One by one, with everyone else keeping cover, the men run forward and into the lobby of the building. The door is locked but the glass panes have been shot out, so we all just step through the shell of the door.

The lobby is still uncarpeted and smells of fresh paint, though now there are bullet holes marring the new drywall.

We scour the first floor but don't find anyone.

"They didn't even protect themselves," I mutter to myself as we run up the two stairwells, converging on the men on the third floor from both sides.

The planning is shoddy, at best, and the attack seems like an idea thrown together last minute.

Still, when we reach the third floor and pull open the door, shots ring out.

Immediately, Maksim hits the ground with a limp thud, a bullet through his head.

I take out the man who shot him and the second Italian who comes out of the door trying to see where his friend went.

The floor is in a U-shape, so I lead a group of men down one hallway to a forced left, and when I turn, I see the rest of my men coming from the other side. I gesture for my men to stand back and wait for the other team, lest we end up on either side of an Italian, forced to shoot in the direction of our own people to defend ourselves.

No one else comes out, though.

Four men.

Four Italians sent to snatch a building in disputed territory? It's a poor showing, and I can't decide if it means the Italians are running low on numbers or if this is a small faction that broke away and tried to make a name for themselves.

I don't have much time to contemplate it, though. There's too much to be done.

I sent some of my men to speak with the owner of the building to discuss what happened and help him arrange repairs. Then, Maksim has to be dealt with.

"I can take him to the funeral home," Rurik says. "Are you going to speak with his wife and kid?"

As the leader, it's my duty to deliver the news to Maksim's next of kin. I nod to Rurik, then turn to leave.

I hate every fucking second of the task.

Maksim's house is on my way home, so I stop off there, blood still splattered across the front of my shirt.

His wife wails when I tell her, though she knew it was a possibility. Everyone in this lifestyle does. There are no guarantees of another day. That reality does little to soften the blow, however.

She hugs her child, still too young to fully understand what his mother's crying means, and I can only think of Tati.

Of what I would want someone to tell her if I died.

I don't know what time it is when I walk inside. Sometime in the afternoon.

I'm not thinking about Courtney or her class schedule or Tati's physical therapy. My only focus is getting to Tati and telling her the truth of what happened to her parents. While I still have the nerve.

My hand is on the door to her room when I feel a small yet firm hand on my shoulder, tugging me back.

"You can't go in there like that."

It's Courtney. Her long dark hair is pulled back in a ponytail, and she's wearing a tiny pair of athletic shorts with a white tank top.

I lay a hand on her waist without thinking, mostly as an instinct, and she leans against my chest, her brows knit together in concern.

"You have blood on your shirt," she says by way of explanation, pointing at my collar.

I left the house in a white undershirt and suit pants. I was too distracted to worry about a button-down.

When I still don't say anything, Courtney runs her hand down the length of my arm and then grabs my hand. She leads me to the nearest bathroom and helps me clean up.

I watch her as she wipes a cool towel across my face and neck. Her eyes are cool and assessing, even though there is a blush high on her cheekbones. Her lips are pursed and incredibly kissable, but I force myself to resist the urge.

"You're calm in a crisis," I say suddenly.

I know Courtney knows about my violent side. It's the entire reason she's at my house in the first place. But I'm not sure how I feel about the fact that she's so accustomed to seeing me covered in blood that it hardly fazes her anymore. Is she afraid of me?

When she looks up at me, her eyes are wide with surprise. She quickly recovers and gestures for me to lift my arms up so she can peel my shirt up and toss it on the floor. Then, she looks at my chest, and I can almost see her heart beating beneath her collarbone.

"Even at your father's shop," I continue, "you didn't panic."

She shrugs and looks down at the floor for a moment before looking up again, her eyes heavily lidded. "It's because I didn't really think you'd hurt me."

The words sit between us like a wild animal we're both too nervous to touch.

Finally, I take a breath. "I'm going to tell Tati. About her parents."

Courtney lets out an involuntary breath. "What changed your mind?"

I step away from her, the bathroom suddenly feeling too small, and turn on the shower. "I'd want her to know if I was dead. I wouldn't want Tati to be expecting me home at any minute. Or, even worse, to think I'd left her of my own choosing."

I stare at her for a minute before peeling down my pants. I want to grab her and pull her into me.

But not now.

Not yet.

I need to focus.

Courtney leaves, and I shower. When I get out, there are new clothes hanging from the bathroom door for me, and she's sitting in the hallway, one of her sign language books in her lap.

"I can go in with you if you want," she says. "As support."

"For me or Tati?" I tease, though it isn't much of a joke.

We go in together.

Tati is sitting cross-legged on the floor, a plastic doll in her lap. She's brushing the Barbie's long blonde hair, tiny clothes and shoes scattered around the floor. When we walk in, she grins and runs forward, hugging us both with one arm.

But her smile fades when she looks at me.

What's wrong?

I lead her to the bed, and the frown on her tiny face deepens.

I hate that this happened to her. That she has already had to face so much death and loss in her young life.

And I hate that I'm the only person left to take care of her. I'm not good enough. Not ready.

I can't be in charge of a child's well-being.

Except, I am.

I have to be.

I want to talk to you about your parents, I sign. *Where they are. What happened to them.*

The man at the mall told me about an accident, Tati signs. She takes a deep breath. *He told me people were hurt.*

I should have killed that man on the spot. I knocked him out and dropped him in the back of the truck, but I should have ended his life for talking to a six-year-old about something like this.

People were hurt. You were hurt. Do you remember it at all?

She shakes her head.

I unravel the story slowly, giving her as much time as I can to absorb the details and understand. I tell her about the mystery driver who hit her family's car, knocking it from the road and halfway down a cliffside. I tell her that she survived for hours before being found and then was asleep for several weeks.

Then, I tell her about her parents.

They didn't make it? she asks, confused about my phrasing. Part of her knows the truth, though because her lower lip is trembling.

Courtney lays a hand on Tati's leg, and she lays her hand over Courtney's, gripping her fingers until Courtney's hand turns white.

I explain it again and again until she doesn't have any more questions, until the only thing she can do is cry and be held by us.

When Tati is finally asleep, tears still on her cheeks, Courtney and I slip from the room and go straight into mine across the hall.

She stands nervously in the doorway as I pad inside.

I pull open the bedside drawer, remove a bottle of whiskey, and take a swig. Then, I hold it out to her, wondering what she'll say.

She reaches for it and then pulls back. I nod.

"You've been here two months," I say. Courtney doesn't look up, but she nods her head. "And I haven't heard you request any ... feminine products."

Her breath is shaky.

"Our first time was unprotected."

"I know," she says. "I didn't think it would happen after one time, but—"

"Maybe it hasn't." I shrug. "We don't know yet."

"No, we don't," she agrees. "But I should be careful."

The day has been a nonstop rollercoaster of emotions and adrenaline, and I feel more spent than I have in a long time. Even considering the idea that Courtney could be pregnant feels like too much, so I decide not to think about it until we know for sure. Courtney appears to want to do the same thing, as she leans back against the wall and takes a deep breath.

"We need to get our minds off—" I gesture indiscriminately around the room. "Everything."

"Agreed." She licks her lips. "How do we do that?"

"How do you usually clear your head?"

She thinks for a moment and then her eyes brighten. Suddenly, she steps forward, grabs my hand, and leads me out of the room and down the hall. We're halfway to the dance studio before I realize where we're going.

The windows along the back wall are open, letting in the moonlight, and neither of us moves to turn on the lights.

The room seems to be steeped in a gray fog, but I can see Courtney clearly as she turns on the music low and faces me.

"Do you want to dance with me?" she asks, her voice soft.

The first night we met, Courtney danced for me.

It seems only fitting after the evening we've had that she would now dance with me.

"I'm not a very good dancer," I say, taking her hand and pulling her body close to mine.

She arches her body against me, grabs my upper arms firmly, and then bends back, her head circling so low her hair brushes the ground. I can't hold back a groan as her hips grind against mine and her shirt slides up, revealing the smooth plane of her stomach.

The moment she circles back up and is in my arms, the dance is over.

I catch her mouth with mine, bending her back, a hand curled in her hair.

She must be feeling it too, because she grabs my face, holding me to her, and jumps, wrapping her legs around my hips.

Our movements are rushed and clumsy as we peel off our clothes and ending up on the floor, Courtney naked and splayed out in front of me.

I run my fingers over her smooth skin and crawl over her, kissing my way between her breasts and over her neck. She digs her fingers into my shoulder blades when I press myself against her opening, and when I slide in, she tips her head back and moans louder with every inch.

The sounds of our bodies coming together echo off the hardwood floor and the mirrors until it sounds like we're at an orgy rather than alone in the room.

Courtney hooks her legs around my lower back, drawing me in deeper, and almost immediately I feel her body tense and shake. Her mouth opens in a gasp, and she squeezes her eyes closed as the orgasm rips through her.

The moment she can relax her hold on me, Courtney pushes on my chest and rolls me over.

Watching her climb over me, straddling my hips, is the sexiest thing I've ever seen. And that's only compounded when she slides onto me slowly, grinding her hips in slow circles.

Our sex before this was hurried and fierce and desperate. This feels slower. Softer.

Courtney leans forward, her breasts brushing against my chest, her mouth a few inches from mine. But we don't kiss. I look up at her, watching expressions flit across her face as she rolls herself over me, using her dancer's body to its full potential.

I let my hands roam down her back and over her ass, massaging and exploring. But for maybe the first time in my life, I let a woman take control. Of our pace, our motions, our depth.

I lie back and let Courtney take care of my needs in a way I didn't know I needed them to be taken care of.

So, when I finally come, it's hard and long, and I could sleep right there on the wood floor.

When Courtney tries to pull away, I wrap my arms around her, holding her against my chest, staying inside of her as long as I can. I'm not ready for it to be over.

I don't realize I've spoken out loud until Courtney laughs and kisses my nose. "Well, sir, as soon as you're ready, we can do it again."

The suggestion sends a surge of renewed energy to the lower half of my body, and I immediately pick Courtney up and carry her, naked, across the house and into my bedroom where I hold her to her promise.

And we do it again.

18

DMITRY

I sit in my office, phone in front of me, and wait.

Several times, I've reached for my phone, certain it was about to ring, but nothing happened.

It's midmorning, just after 10:00, and they should be done by now. Everything should be in place, and I should be getting a call. Any moment now.

Just as panic begins to creep in, my phone rings.

"It's done."

I sigh, realizing it's the first full breath I've taken all morning. "Are you in position?"

"Yes," Pasha says. "At a hotel down the street. As soon as they come outside, we're ready to act."

The Italians are holding their council meeting at an abandoned funeral home. Apt, considering what is about to happen to them.

After the shootout at the apartment building, I sent several of my men on a reconnaissance mission. We needed to know more about the Italians' plans and their movements so we could stop reacting and start acting. While watching a bar where many of the Italians liked to hang out, Pasha and a couple other men grabbed a drunk Italian and brought him to me where he was sobered up and then tortured for information.

Finally, under threat of having both of his femurs broken, he relented and told us about the meeting time and location of many of the Italian lieutenants.

"Good," I say. "I'm leaving now."

I use the alley to get to the hotel so I don't draw any unnecessary eyes our direction. The men are set up in the lobby of the hotel. There is a closed sign in the front window and the manager has been threatened into loyalty.

Rurik and Pasha are both near the front window, staring towards the boarded-up building down the street.

"They'll be leaving any minute," Rurik says. "We planted a bug, too. The feedback is shit, but we'll hear when the meeting is over."

I've only been there ten minutes when Rurik tenses and gestures for everyone to pay attention. Slowly, men start to come out of the building. A few of them get in their cars towards the back of the lot and reverse, and Rurik looks at me with a question in his eyes, but I shake my head.

"Wait for more. There will be more."

He nods, and we watch as the trickle of people from the building turns to a flood. There are twenty men heading for their cars. We won't get that many again, so I nod.

And the plan begins. There are two parts to come: A set of explosives to scatter the Italians, then a massacre to take them out like rats escaping a sinking ship.

First, the ground seems to crack beneath our feet.

The sound comes next, a deep rumble like thunder that rattles the windows of the hotel. When I'm certain the glass won't shatter, I step forward and see the plume of smoke moving into the sky.

Then another. And another. And another. Bombs like fireworks, each one a dull boom followed by the screams of dying men.

And with each successive explosion, the rats begin to scurry.

"Nice job, Pasha," Rurik says, clapping him on the back.

Pasha grins, proud of his bomb work.

"Now we move," I order. "Rurik, you and your squad take the east approach. I will circle around from the west. And men..."

I look up. All eyes are on me.

"Leave no one alive."

I hear the cocking of guns, the murmur of assent, and then we depart in two waves to rid the city of the Italian stain that I have let linger for far, far too long.

The Italians have attacked us again and again, fucking with our supply lines and threatening my men, so it feels good to fight back. To retaliate.

To destroy.

We squint through the smoke, tripping over shrapnel and body parts, and we don't find each other again until we get inside the front door.

I can hear shouting.

Panic.

But it's coming from all over.

There's a door to the left, another to the right, a hallway that extends deeper into the building, and a set of stairs. I have three men with me, and I send them each in a different direction. Rurik goes upstairs, and I head towards the back of the building.

The sound of their shouting is too loud for the Italians to hear my footsteps, so the two men in the kitchenette don't even turn around as I lift my gun and take aim.

They hit the floor without ever knowing who shot them.

I search the rooms at the back of the house, but there is no one left, and when I get back to the lobby, my men are waiting there.

Everyone except Rurik.

I'm halfway up the stairs, shouting his name, when he appears from a side bedroom. There's blood running down his cheek from a cut, but otherwise, he's fine.

We load up and leave as sirens approach, feeling victorious for the first time in months.

Why don't you and Uncle Dmitry go to dinner by yourselves? Courtney asks Tati. I'm impressed with how good her signing has become in such a short amount of time.

Tati grabs her hand and shakes it, jumping up and down. *No.*

She's insistent that Courtney come to dinner with us. Tati is also insistent that Courtney wear a dress.

A princess dress, she corrects when either of us forgets that small detail. *It has to be beautiful. Like Courtney.*

The days since we've told Tati about her parents have been up and down, a constant fluctuation of good and bad moments. For now, this is a good moment.

Tati is excited about something, and when I look at Courtney, I know she doesn't want to disappoint her. So, we climb in the back of the SUV and head to a dress shop downtown. No one even considered the mall after the last trip we had there.

The shop is small, and I pay the owner to lock it from the public while we're inside. She hesitates at first, until she sees the wad of cash I'm holding out to her. Then, suddenly, she's more than willing to do that, as well as personally design and tailor a dress for Tati, who loves that idea more than anything. For the amount of money I just handed to her, I almost expect her to plant cotton seeds and harvest the fabric for the dress herself.

"She isn't as concerned about my dress anymore," Courtney comments wryly as we stand back and watch Tati pick out gowns in every color of the rainbow.

"No, but I am," I say, grabbing her shoulders and turning her towards the racks. "You deserve something nice. Pick whatever you want."

Courtney groans. "I don't need a dress."

"You can't wear jeans to dinner," I say. Though, truthfully, Courtney looks in jeans the way most women look in ten-thousand-dollar dresses. The woman knows how to wear denim.

She turns to me, her lower lip pinched between her teeth. "I don't want you to have to buy me anything else. It doesn't seem right. You're giving me more than I'm giving you."

Her father's words flash in my mind. *Courtney picked up the idea that you have to work for love. That you have to do something to earn it.*

I step around her and grab a long black dress with a deep slit in the front and hold it in front of her. Even imagining her in something like that sends blood rushing to places that it should not rush while in public. I drape the dress over my arm and keep looking.

"You've been so good with Tati. You take care of her more than I ever expected, and she clearly loves you. That has been an amazing gift," I say slowly, choosing my words carefully. "I've been busy. Knowing you're there to take care of her has been a huge help."

Her cheeks go pink, and she twists her lips to the side, still uncertain.

"Tati has a hard time trusting people. A lot of people look at her strangely because she doesn't talk and can't hear; they don't take time to get to know her. So, she's closed off."

"She loves you," Courtney says.

"Because I was close with her dad," I say, swallowing the lump that rises in my throat whenever I talk about him. "My brother and I were close ... mostly because my father was such a piece of shit. We only had each other. Tati looked at me like a second father, almost. Now, I guess, I'm her dad, in a matter of speaking."

Her hand on my shoulder settles the storm in my chest, and I give her a tight-lipped smile. "It wasn't all bad. My father raised my brother and me to be strong men. To be good leaders. My brother became the world's most amazing father to Tati, and I went on to do what I do. To be a leader of men."

I grab a red dress and lay it over the black one, and Courtney grabs them both from my arm, offering to hold them while I continue to browse the shop for her. Under normal circumstances, I'd never go dress shopping. But for Courtney ... well, it isn't so horrible.

"You and your brother may have turned out okay," she says, pausing for a long time. "But I guess now you need to decide who you would rather emulate as a father: your father or your brother?"

The question is one I've considered too many times and for too long, and I still don't have an answer. Not because I don't know who I would like to be, but because I'm not sure if it's possible.

Courtney tries on the dresses alone and doesn't show me which one she decided on, so my only job is to hand over my credit card when the cashier asks for it.

As we're leaving the store—Tati running ahead to see a display in the window of a toy store—Courtney bends forward slightly and grabs her stomach.

"Are you okay?" I ask, rubbing a circle across her lower back.

She takes a deep breath and nods. "Just a little nausea. I've been feeling sick all week."

I raise a brow, and she looks up at me, nodding her head. "I know, I know. I've also been really tired and the smell of eggs makes me want to hurl."

There's a small corner store at the end of the street, so I tell Courtney to watch Tati—ignoring her nervous expression at the thought of being alone with Tati again—and run ahead to purchase a pregnancy test.

The clerk, a teenage kid with acne on his chin, asks under his breath whether I've missed my period, but I'm nervous enough that I ignore him instead of putting the fear of God into his heart, like I ought to do.

The box feels like a weight in my pocket, slapping against my leg as we walk to the car. By the time we get to the house and Tati goes in for her physical therapy, I'm desperate to hand it off to Courtney.

Her hand shakes as she grabs it and walks into the bathroom.

I pace outside the door, trying to consider what this means.

For me. For us.

Tati just came into my custody. I'm still trying to figure out how to be a father to her, and now there's a possibility I will have a newborn.

I didn't plan for this. Didn't prepare for it.

When Courtney walks out, she nods her head immediately, dark hair tumbling forward over her shoulder. Her bare feet squish nervously in the carpet.

"Positive."

I can tell she's waiting for my reaction, but I don't know how to react. I don't know how to explain how I feel without it all coming out ... wrong.

"How do you feel?" I ask finally.

She sighs, her pink lips puckered around an exhale. When she looks at me, her brown eyes are soft and warm. "I'm terrified. Scared shitless," she admits. "But also ... "

"Also what?" I ask, encouraging her.

"It may sound crazy, but this also feels like what I've always wanted," she says. "I just never knew it until now."

I take a step towards her and wrap an arm around her lower back, pulling her against me. "Me too."

She snaps her attention up to my face. "You want this? Because you don't have to. I can do it on my own. I know this isn't something you planned, and—"

I quiet her with a kiss, my lips brushing softly against hers. Then, without meaning to, the kiss grows heated. I pin her to the wall, my hands sliding down to her hips.

Then, I realize Courtney is pushing on my chest. I step back and let her lead me to my room, where she shuts the door and pushes me towards the bed.

"I'll be here for you," I tell her as she lays me back and crawls over me. "I'll take care of whatever you need."

Courtney unbuttons my pants and slides them down my legs along with my boxers. I spring free, at full attention, and Courtney licks her lips as she straddles my thighs.

"I'll be the right kind of father," I say, though I'm not sure I know what that means.

She wraps her hand around my base and nods. "I know you will."

Then, her mouth is on me, warm and tight, and I can't think about anything. Not what we just learned or what is to come. I can only think about the sensation of her body on mine, her mouth around me.

I watch her bob up and down until I can't stand it anymore. I tangle my fingers in her hair and drag her up. Then, I roll us both over and, being careful not to crush her beneath my weight, I hook my arm behind her knee and lift one of her legs over my shoulder.

When I push into her, it goes on forever. Deeper than I've ever felt, and we both shudder from the connection.

It's deep in more ways than one. Intimate.

The position doesn't allow me to kiss her, so I study the way her chest heaves with every breath. I watch her lips part in sighs.

She's beautiful and honey-warm beneath me, and I don't want it to end.

But, like all things, it does.

I feel Courtney clench around me and that's it. I groan as I come, and she falls with me.

Our bodies pulse together until we're limp and sink into the bed, limbs tangled irreversibly.

I've almost dozed off, unconsciousness creeping at the edges of my mind, when I feel Courtney's warm hand slide down my chest, across my abs, and towards my still throbbing member.

"No way," I chuckle, shaking my head. "I'm spent, woman."

She giggles. "We'll see about that."

Her mouth closes around me for the second time and the impossible happens. I want her again.

I wonder if there is an end to this want for her? If there is a point at which I'll grow tired of the taste of her and the feel of her against me.

I've never wanted anyone the way I want Courtney, and I'm not sure what it means.

Perhaps it's because she's carrying my child. Though, I felt this way from the start. Before we'd ever been together.

Once again, I grab Courtney and drag her up my body, but this time she takes control. She grabs the sheet, pulling it over her shoulders, and falls forward until we're inside of a white globe. Sunlight streams through the sheets in bright white light, and I wish my eyes could take photographs. I wish I could remember the way Courtney looks, naked and backlit above me, her eyes closed in pleasure as she rolls her hips against me.

I grab her hips and direct her onto me again and again, harder and harder until we're both breathing heavily, losing control.

Then, I hear the rattle of the handle and the squeak of a hinge.

Courtney yelps and falls on top of me, the sheet deflating around us.

"Get out," I growl to the door, frustrated at the interruption.

When no one answers, my heart lodges in my throat.

I pull the sheet back just enough so my eyes peek out, and I see Tati staring at the bed, forehead wrinkled in confusion. When she sees me, she smiles.

What are you doing?

"Is it Tati?" Courtney whispers.

"Yes."

Wrestling, I sign back. It's the first thing I can think of. *We'll be in your room in a minute. Go wait for us.*

I want to play, she says, moving towards the bed.

"No!" I shout in a panic. Then, I shake my head. *No. Give us a minute. We'll come to your room and play.*

She frowns but obeys, closing the door behind her.

As soon as she's gone, Courtney collapses on top of me in laughter. "We just got caught. What did you tell her?"

"That we were wrestling."

Courtney sits up, the sheet falling around her waist, and laughs. The vibration moves through her body and into mine, and despite the interruption, I'm still ready.

I grab her hips and slide her across me all while she's still cracking up.

"Oh, are we still wrestling?" she whispers, leaning forward to press a kiss to my nose and then my lips.

I drive my hips into her, wiping the smile from her face. "Absolutely."

We finish quickly, panting and sweaty from our "wrestling," and as Courtney pulls on her clothes and slips out of the room to go into Tati's, I can't help but think that this could be our future.

Sneaking sex between play sessions with our kids.

The thought comes on unbidden, but I can't push the image from my mind. And when I go into Tati's room and find Courtney helping her dress her many dolls and arrange the furniture in her doll house, the image cements further.

It scares me a little less than it once did.

19

COURTNEY

Tati's seventh birthday party is a roaring success.

Since she only recently found out the news about her parents, Dmitry didn't know if she'd be up to a celebration. Especially since we can't exactly invite over a bunch of children and parents to his house. Not while the Italians are still looking for any way to attack Dmitry and his Bratva.

However, as soon as I mentioned the idea to Tatiana, she began signing so quickly I couldn't keep up, telling me she wanted unicorn cupcakes and streamers and music so loud it would rattle the walls.

So, we have all of that. And more.

Dmitry has a miniature horse brought in and fills the entire dance studio with balloons from floor to ceiling that Tati runs through for half an hour, the widest smile on her face.

At the end of the day, we're sitting around the table eating cake for dinner, and I can picture this long-term.

I'm still counting down the days until the end of our agreement, but I'm not counting down the days until I leave.

I don't want to leave.

I love Tati and Dmitry … Dmitry is complicated. He's the father of my child and a man I have electric chemistry with. He's violent and bloody, but I've seen him be gentle. I've seen him open his heart and be vulnerable, and I think I could bring out even more of that side of him.

I think, with time, we could become a family.

Can we watch a movie? Tati asks.

Dmitry looks to me, eyebrows raised. *What do you think?*

Only if it has a princess in it.

Dmitry laughs and Tati shakes her hands in celebration. She's still cheering when the doorbell rings.

Dmitry stiffens but doesn't move to answer it. The maid will get it and there are guards posted all over the property to ensure no one unauthorized gets inside. We're safe.

When one of his guards walks into the dining room, Dmitry is on his feet in an instant.

"It's the police."

"What do they want?" Dmitry asks.

The guard shakes his head. "They wouldn't say."

Tati turns to me. *What is going on?*

Let's go to your room to rest a bit before the movie, I urge her, standing up.

She tries to resist, but Dmitry repeats the order, and she follows me up to her room. I tuck her into her bed with a promise to be back soon, and the nanny assures me she'll keep Tati upstairs until we know what is going on.

By the time I get back downstairs, Dmitry is talking with the police in the sitting room.

"What does the bombing have to do with me?" Dmitry asks.

When I walk in the room, he gestures for me to sit next to him on the couch, and I do, tucking in close to his side.

"It was a bombing and a shooting," the officer says. He has a thick mustache that looks like it belongs in a porno, but his brow is furrowed and serious. "It was an attack, and one of the people shot was a young woman I believe you are both acquainted with."

My heart leaps into my throat. "Who?"

He looks down at a notepad in his lap. "Sadie Hatch."

I gasp and Dmitry immediately wraps his arm around me, though I have a feeling it's meant more to restrain me than comfort me.

"You do know her, then?" he asks, looking from me to Dmitry and back again.

"Yes. She's a good friend," I say, voice breaking. "Is she alive?"

The officer doesn't answer, instead continuing with his line of questioning, and a pit forms in my stomach. "Everyone else at the scene belonged to the Italian Mafia. Except for Sadie. We didn't understand her connection to the scene, so we searched her phone settings and found that she had come here within the last several weeks."

"She did," Dmitry admits. "She actually sent the police here as well. I'm sure you have a record of that."

"The kidnapping claim," the officer says, reading once again from his notepad. "She believed Miss Palillo was being held against her will, but we investigated and discovered that was not the case." He turned to me. "Unless things have changed since our officers were last here?"

I shook my head. "No, I'm here because I want to be. Now, is my friend dead or alive?"

The officer's lips press together in a thin line, his mustache hiding any sign of his mouth at all, and he sighs. "She's alive and being treated at a local hospital. She's expected to recover."

I nearly sob in relief, and Dmitry hugs me closer to his side. "Sadie's charge was found to have no merit, so why are you here again? What does any of this have to do with us?"

The officer turns his attention to Dmitry, eyes narrowed to slits. "Well, it's no secret you have … issues with the Italian Mafia."

Dmitry shakes his head. "I don't know what you mean."

The officer rolls his eyes and continues. "Sadie also had the address of a local pub owned by the Italian Mafia in her phone. Our suspicion is that her visits to this house were noted by the Italians, and she was approached to work as a spy. That would explain her presence at two known Mafia hangouts, and why she was present during the attack."

"That sounds like top-notch police work, officer. I commend you," Dmitry drawls. "I'm still not sure why you're here to see me, though."

His tone is casual, light, almost. At first, I thought it was just a façade to get through the interview, but now it seems genuine.

He doesn't care about Sadie at all.

He doesn't care that my best friend was shot.

And he doesn't seem to care that—as far as I can tell—he or one of his men is responsible for it.

I shift away from his touch, and he glances over at me for only a second before returning his attention to the officer.

"We're wondering if either of you knows anything about the attack," the officer says. "Considering your connections, both personal and business, with those attacked."

Dmitry hums in thought. "No, I'm afraid not. We've been celebrating our daughter's seventh birthday today, so if you have no further questions, we'd like to get back to it."

The officer stares at Dmitry long enough that even I become uncomfortable, though Dmitry just returns a disconnected smile.

Finally, the officer presses his palms to his knees and stands up. "No, that's all. I'm sure you won't mind if I stay in touch, though."

"Please do," I say quickly. "Whoever did this should be brought to justice."

Dmitry closes the door behind the officer and then lingers in the entryway, not looking at me or making any move to apologize or comfort me. He just stands there.

"Don't you have anything to say?" I finally ask. "My best friend was just shot."

"Some best friend," he says with a shrug. "She sent the police after you."

"Because she thought I'd been kidnapped," I spit. "Which I was."

Dmitry's eyes flare to life—the first sign of any emotion I've seen from him. "Hardly. You came here willingly."

"Under threat," I correct. "She sensed that and wanted to help me. I lied to her, and now she's recovering in a hospital. Some fucking thanks that is."

"At least she's alive," he says. "It's more than she deserves for feeding the Italians information about me and my Bratva. Men died because of her."

"Clearly you feel that way, since you had to have approved the shooting. Nothing happens without you know about it. Isn't that right, *boss?*"

Dmitry runs a hand through his hair and shakes his head. "I gave the go-ahead for my men to kill everyone inside that building because everyone inside was working for my enemies—your friend included. But if you're accusing me of knowingly having your friend shot, you're wrong. I did not do that. Though, if I had a good reason, I would have."

I let out a scream of frustration and spin away from him, pacing towards the fireplace. "I need to get out of here," I say, spinning in a circle, looking for shoes and keys and my purse, though I know they're all upstairs. I walk past Dmitry towards the stairs. "I need to see Sadie."

Dmitry grabs my arm and pulls me towards him. His hand is gentle, though his grip is firm. "No."

"No?" I glare at him. "You're forbidding me from leaving?"

He nods. "I am. I'm sorry, but you can't go."

I rip my arm out of his grip and stumble backwards. My foot catches the bottom step, and I fall back on the stairs. Dmitry moves like he wants to help me up, and I wave him away. "Are you going to have me shot if I leave? I shouldn't even ask. I know you would."

"Are you fucking kidding me?" Dmitry growls. He narrows his eyes on me, cold and dark, and a chill runs down my spine. "It doesn't matter what you think of me. Your friend was working for the Italians; how do I know you weren't helping her? How do I know you didn't come into my house with the purpose of betraying me to my enemies and getting me killed?"

I'm angry—beyond angry—but his words still hurt. To think he doesn't trust me, that everything we've been through in the last few months was for nothing ... something in my chest cracks.

"You don't care about me or Tati," he continues. "You're a liar. I've changed my mind. You need to go. Don't even think about going near the hospital to visit Sadie—I've got guards on her who'll report back to me and I'll make your father pay. But anywhere else you want to go, I don't care. Go. Now. I can't have you in my house anymore."

A second ago, I wanted nothing but to leave, but now his command hits me like a brick. I fall back, my spine hitting the steps hard, and stare up at him, mouth open.

"You want me to leave?"

"Now," he reiterates.

I don't have the words to ask what this means. For me. For us. For our deal.

Will he kill my father now that I'm no longer living in his house? Will he punish my family? Will I even be able to return home or will he track me down and have me killed? What about our child?

I don't want to think Dmitry could be capable of something like that, but I truly don't know him anymore. Not the way I thought I did.

Suddenly, Dmitry's attention snaps up to the top of the stairs, and his face goes pale with horror. I turn and see Tati standing there, tears rolling down her cheeks.

Don't make her leave, she signs. *Please.*

Clearly, she read his lips.

"Tati," Dmitry whispers. He rushes past me to grab Tati.

Please, she signs again, looking down at me, her big innocent eyes cutting me straight to my core.

Dmitry takes a deep breath and looks down at me. His expression is livid, lip pulled back. All of the emotion and concern he had for Tati only seconds before is gone.

"You can stay," he relents. "But stay away from me. Far away."

Before I can say anything or argue, he carries Tati upstairs and disappears, leaving me alone on the stairs.

20

DMITRY

I hear Courtney leave for class in the morning, but I don't leave my room to say anything to her.

I'm not sure what to say.

The day before was … a lot.

Information was coming at me quickly, and I didn't know what to think. Who to trust.

I'm still not sure.

Did Courtney manipulate me? It's possible. I knew from the moment I met her that she was a smart woman. This could have been her plan from the start—revenge for the years her father was forced to pay me for protection. Revenge for me hitting him.

I don't know whether she's the vengeful type or not.

Though, I do know she wouldn't knowingly put her friend in danger.

Courtney wouldn't send Sadie to the Italians if she thought there was any danger of her being hurt, and since she knows me and my men, she knows there is always a chance of being hurt.

No, Courtney would have found some way to work directly with the Italians. She wouldn't have brought her friend into it.

Which begs the question: why was Sadie there at all?

I told Courtney I would have shot Sadie if I had any reason to believe she was conspiring against me, and I'm not sure if that's true.

Knowing what would happen to my relationship with Courtney if I killed one of her best friends, I don't think I could have pulled the trigger. Especially since everyone else in the house—that I saw—was a known Mafia member. Seeing a cowering woman amongst the group would have given me pause.

I think I would have saved her. After all, I'm not in the habit of killing women. I don't even kill men unless there's a good reason.

So why didn't Rurik?

Why didn't he even mention that she was there?

There were four of us there shooting that day, but Rurik was the only one on the second floor, so that's certainly where Sadie had to have been found.

Another question that needs to be answered: who else survived? If Rurik failed to kill Sadie, how many other men did he leave alive? Anyone who will testify against us? Anyone who could put me or my men in prison?

I have to speak with him.

But before I do, I can't walk away without making things right. Or, at least, as right as they can be.

I call the hospital and cover Sadie's medical bills. I also increase her care to full-time private nursing.

None of it's for Sadie, though.

It's for Courtney.

She's been through enough pain in her life that she doesn't need to lose her best friend, too. Even if her best friend is too nosy for her own damn good.

When I'm done with my good deeds for the year, I grab my keys and arrange a meeting with Rurik. Just a simple text: *Meet at my office. Now.*

I'm down the stairs and halfway to the front door when I hear small footsteps behind me. When I turn around, I'm hit with forty pounds of sobbing seven-year-old.

"What is it?" I say, pulling away and signing the question to her. *What's wrong?*

Don't go. Tati wraps her arms around my legs and squeezes tightly again.

I pry her off me and kneel down so we're face-to-face. *I'm just going out to take care of some work.*

What if you don't come back? she asks.

Of course I'll come back. I'll always come back. I swallow, realizing that her parents didn't come back. *As long as I'm able to, I'll come home to you.*

Stay, she signs again. *Call Courtney and tell her to come home and then both of you stay here with me. Please don't kick her out.*

Her sobs overpower her, and she falls forward against my chest. I pat her back as the emotions work themselves out. When she's ready, she pulls back and lets me explain.

Courtney isn't going anywhere. Not yet, anyway. Not for a few more months. *She'll be home after her classes for the day, and I'll be back before dinner. I promise.*

Tati looks unconvinced, but she gives me a weak smile as her nanny takes her back upstairs. As soon as she's gone, I take a deep breath, pull my phone from my pocket, and read the newest message.

Rurik is already at the office waiting for me.

Rurik is reclined in the seat across from my desk, looking more relaxed than he has any right to be.

"I asked you here because we need to talk," I say coolly.

He raises a brow in understanding but says nothing. I swallow back my frustration, hoping to keep this conversation civil.

For anyone else under my command, this kind of mess-up would warrant immediate punishment, but Rurik has always been loyal. He's one of my most trusted lieutenants, and I want to give him the opportunity to explain himself.

"It's about the raid at the Italians' meeting the other day. The bombing."

He nods. "I remember."

"The police came to my house last night."

At least he has the good sense to look surprised. "Did they connect you to it?"

"They connected me to one of the victims. A young woman was there."

Rurik blinks, and I know immediately he knows who I'm talking about.

"She was shot but survived," I say, pausing to let the gravity of it sink in. "She's in the hospital right now."

"How did they connect her to you?" he asks. "Were you fucking her, too?"

He didn't say Courtney's name, but I know that's who he's thinking of. And the very idea that he would mention her name so flippantly, with so little respect, is enough to make me stand up and begin to pace.

I have to work off my energy. I can't sit still.

"She's Courtney's friend."

He shrugs. "So, you're telling me your slave's friend is working for the Italians?"

Is Courtney my slave? Is that how I should refer to her?

Technically, I suppose. Though things feel far beyond that now.

"I'm telling you that you shot a defenseless woman and let her live," I growl.

Rurik stands up as well, leaning across my desk in what can only be described as a hostile posture. "Are you angry that I shot your girlfriend's friend or that I let her live?"

I pull my arm back and swing, throwing my entire body behind the punch.

My fist connects with Rurik's jaw. He isn't expecting it. He spins back and trips over his chair, falling across the floor.

In the next second, my guards are in the room, lined up around the edges, eyes and weapons trained on Rurik.

They're loyal to me, not him. Even if he's their friend, they will do as I command.

"What in the fuck, Dmitry?" he shouts, grabbing his jaw while he works it back and forth.

"Talk to me with respect," I spit. "I'm angry because my top lieutenant shot a woman without mentioning it to me. And I'm angry because his shot is apparently shit. You let the girl live, and now I have no idea whether she will turn against me. She' already accused me of kidnapping Courtney. Now I have to consider what I'm going to do if she wants to implicate me in this attack, too."

"I was told to kill everyone in the building," he said. "That's why I didn't mention the girl was there. I'm sorry I missed, but it sounds like you wish I hadn't shot her in the first place."

"She was a defenseless woman. What was the point?"

Rurik stands up and takes a step away. He looks around at the guards along the edge of the room and then levels a glare at me, eyebrow raised.

"It sounds to me like you're allowing your emotions to cloud your judgment," he says. "You care about your slave more than you should, and now you care about her friends, too."

I stare daggers at Rurik, my jaw ticking, trying to decide how to respond.

I'm not entirely sure there isn't some truth to his words, but that doesn't mean he has the right to say any of it to me. In front of my men.

So, I have to act swiftly.

I circle a finger in the air, and my men surround Rurik. He fights them for a second but is quickly overpowered.

"Am I going to be killed?" he asks, looking properly cowed for the first time since he walked into my office.

I don't address him, instead talking to Pasha on his right. "Take him downstairs and have him beaten. Leave him alive."

The men drag Rurik from the room as I sit down and attempt to continue my work. As soon as the door is closed and I'm alone, I lean back in my seat and cover my face in my hands, wondering how things have gotten so completely out of control in such a short amount of time.

If I thought things were handled with Tati, I'm cured of that belief the moment I walk into her room.

Rather than her usual hugs and smiles, she's sullen. She looks up at me as I walk into her room, but she doesn't wave or ask me about my day or tell me anything about hers.

What is going on? I sign.

When Tati doesn't look at me, I'm forced to walk to her bed and lift her chin to force her to acknowledge me. Her eyes are hard.

What happened?

You ruined everything, she signs in an angry flurry. *Courtney and I used to have fun, but now she just cries all the time. Because of you.*

I shake my head, confused. *Have you talked to Courtney today?*

If there is any sign at all that Courtney has tried to turn Tati against me, I'll kill her. No one messes with my family.

She won't come out of her room, Tati pouts. *She went in there right when she got home from school and won't answer the door. She's crying in her bedroom. She hates me.*

Whoa, whoa. She doesn't hate you. She's angry with me, I say. *Not you.*

Tati's arms are still crossed over her chest, but she looks slightly relieved. *Why?*

It's complicated.

She sighs, and I know I have to fix this. Somehow.

Tati lost her parents already. I can't let her lose another adult she cares about.

I'll talk to her, I promise her. *Don't worry.*

Tati pushes me towards the door, insistent I fix things with Courtney now, and I leave without making any promises. I'm not sure I'm ready to talk to her yet.

However, when I run into Yanka in the hall, I stop her.

"Have you seen Courtney?"

"Seen?" she asks. "Yes. Talked to? No. She won't talk to anyone."

"Do you usually talk to her?" I wasn't under the impression Courtney spoke with anyone else in the house.

"You work an awful lot of hours," Yanka says cryptically. "That girl is lonely. And based on what I overheard yesterday, she wants to see her friend."

I frown at her for eavesdropping, but Yanka shrugs her shoulders, unbothered. She knows I trust her, and she knows I couldn't keep my house running without her.

Courtney already asked to see Sadie, and my answer was no. And it still is.

I can't relent on that point because I don't know if Sadie and Courtney are working together to bring me down. If they are, I have to limit contact until I know what I'm going to do about it.

"I need to get back to work. Unless you need anything else?" Yanka asks.

I shake my head and wave her on. As soon as I turn to go into my office, my phone rings.

It's Lawrence Palillo.

"What do you want?" I snap.

"Dmitry," he says, sounding happier than I've heard him in months. "I hoped I would catch you. I have good news."

I frown. If Lawrence is in on this deception with his daughter, then he's a remarkable actor.

"What is that?"

"I have your money with interest," he says. "For the inconvenience. I will hand it over the moment I know Courtney is free. When do you want to—"

I hang up on him and it's only with Herculean restraint that I don't hurl my phone against the hallway wall.

How did Lawrence come up with the money? And how convenient that it happened the day after I began questioning his daughter's loyalty.

This was a scam from the beginning. A plot to overthrow me from the inside.

Lawrence Palillo pimped his daughter out to me so she could distract me and tear down my Bratva.

Not on my fucking watch.

21

COURTNEY

The days after learning about Sadie being shot are long and filled with torment.

Was this my fault?

Should I have told her the truth?

Unanswerable questions fill my head, along with worry for my father, myself, and my unborn baby.

What will Dmitry do to me?

He has made it no secret what he does with those who are disloyal to him. If he truly believes I've betrayed him, will he kill me?

Would he kill our child?

I try my best to go about my days as normally as I can, in hopes I can prove to him I haven't done anything wrong, but that proves impossible. On top of the normal nausea, discomfort, and hormonal fluctuations of pregnancy, I've been crying nonstop, barely eating, and barely sleeping. It isn't healthy for me or the baby. Needless to say, it makes going to school pure misery even when I force myself to keep at it. Once I'm kicked out of this house, I have to have something to go back to.

So, finally, after three days, I decide to sneak out of the house to go see Sadie.

Dmitry threatened Dad if I visit her, but I have to. I have to know if Sadie is really okay and what she was doing in that Mafia hangout. I have to know if she was really trying to spy on the Bratva. I also need to know if she's actually at the hospital.

The officer said she was expected to make a full recovery, but I haven't heard any information since. Dmitry certainly isn't going to keep me updated.

What if he already sent someone to take her out as punishment?

Even worse: what if she died, and no one has told me?

The thought sinks in my stomach like a stone, and my resolve hardens. I have to do this.

Where are we going? Tati signs.

I go into her room for the first time in several days, and Tati doesn't hesitate to follow me. I bundle her in her coat, a scarf, and a matching hat, and she helps me tie my scarf in a bow around my neck. She trusts me, despite my disappearing act. Besides, she's eager for any excuse to leave the house.

To get those foam rollers your physical therapist mentioned. My sign language has become much better over the last few months. Tati hardly even makes fun of me for it anymore. *They're at the hospital waiting for us.*

Tati follows me out of the house without further questions.

I just need to get there and return home before Dmitry finds out we are gone.

Sadie is out of the ICU, but it takes the nurse at the desk several minutes to tell me where Sadie is. She has to call over a few different nurses, and then they have to speak with the head nurse.

As they shuffle around the desk, moving papers and checking the computer, I grow increasingly more agitated, wondering if Sadie is here, if she's alive ... Or maybe the nurses are trying to find someone to break the news to me?

Finally, the nurse smiles and waves me over to the desk. The knot of tension in my chest doesn't ease until she tells me Sadie is being held in a private room on the third floor.

"Sadie Hatch?" I ask, certain this has to be a mistake. Sadie doesn't have the funds for something like that. "Are you sure?"

She nods and gives me the room number.

How did Sadie afford a private room? Last time I talked to her about it, she didn't even have health insurance. However, when I knock on the door and push it open, Sadie is propped up in bed.

Her blonde hair is pulled up in a messy bun that looks more like a nest than hair, but her cheeks are rosy, and she smiles when she sees me.

"Courtney!" There is relief in her voice, as though she was the one worried about me.

"Are you okay?" I rush towards the bed, tears burning the back of my throat. "I wanted to come sooner, but—"

"I was sleeping for days," she says, waving me away. "You would have just been sitting here talking to no one. I'm glad you're here now."

Tati looks confused, but I have her sit down in the recliner, and she complies, watching me closely.

"This is Tati. *Tati, this is Sadie*," I say, introducing them quickly before moving on to more pressing matters. "What is going on?"

Sadie lifts an arm to gesture around the lavish room. It looks more like a hotel room than a hospital, frankly, with the nice furniture, huge TV, and other high-end trappings. There's even art on the walls. "I'm receiving the royal treatment; that is what is going on."

"How?"

She shrugs. "I have no fucking idea." Then she slaps a hand over her mouth. "Sorry. I shouldn't say that in front of kids."

"You really shouldn't. She can't hear you, but she reads lips really well."

Sadie frowned. "Reads lips? Is she deaf?"

Tati nods behind me.

"See? She's good at reading lips."

Sadie's eyebrows lift, but I draw the conversation back on track. "Did someone else pay for this for you?"

"Apparently, but no one will say who."

Dmitry. I know it immediately. Who else could it be?

The Italians are too busy scrambling to recover from their attack to take care of a woman who was likely not even giving them very good information. I mean, what could Sadie have really known about Dmitry or the Bratva? I definitely didn't tell her anything useful.

"How did you end up here?" I ask.

"I was shot," she says, brows knit together. "Didn't they tell you that?"

I sigh. "I mean, how did you end up getting shot?"

The smile she has worn since I arrived falters slightly. "That's a longer story."

"I have time."

She bites her lower lip and then begins. "I guess it all started when you got kidnapped."

Immediately, I hold up a hand to stop her. "I was not *kidnapped*, Sadie."

"So you say." She stares at me, letting me know she doesn't buy my story, so I shake my head and motion for her to continue.

"Well, when you got kidnapped, I obviously called the police, but they didn't seem to think anything was wrong. I, however, know you very well and knew you were acting weird, so I went to that man's house."

"Dmitry's house," I correct her. "And I remember this part. I was there."

"Yeah, but what you don't know is that when I left, a man met me outside."

I frown. "Like, a guard?"

She shakes her head. "No, someone else. This guy who waved down my car when I was driving away from the house."

"And you stopped?" I ask, horrified. "Why on earth would you stop for a man waving on the side of the road? Do you have a death wish I don't know about?"

Her cheeks go pink. "Because he was in running clothes with no shirt on, and I thought there was a chance a porno scene was about to play out in real life." Her voice goes high-pitched and cartoony as she plays out the scene. "*Oh, you're out for a jog and got lost? Sure, I can give you a ride to the nearest gas station. Though, there's a storm coming in. We might get trapped on the side of the road with nothing but our bodies for warmth.*"

I bite back a laugh and wave her off. "She can read lips, remember?"

Sadie points over my shoulder, and I turn and see that Tati thankfully isn't paying attention anymore. She's playing with the remote and flipping through the channels.

"Well, anyway," she continues. "He didn't want to rub his body against mine, unfortunately. He wanted to pay me for information."

"What kind of information?"

"Information on Dmitry," she says. "I told him I wasn't interested, but he asked me my price, and I told him I wanted to help you. He agreed."

"Sadie," I groan. "I don't need help. I'm fine."

"Whatever," she says, clearly still not believing me. "So, I talked to them a few times, telling them what I knew about your situation, which wasn't much, thanks to you being so cryptic. They weren't thrilled with what I had to offer. And then there was a large boom and then shots going off like crazy ..."

I can tell by the way her story trails off that she doesn't really want to talk about it, and I can't blame her.

"Sadie, listen—" I start to say, hoping to convince her to walk away from this entire situation and forget it all. Before I can, however, there's another knock on the door.

I turn just as the large, red-haired Devon walks through the door.

He takes me in, but immediately his eyes turn to Sadie. She grins as he approaches, and I step aside just in time to have a clear view of their grotesque make-out session.

Tati's eyes are wide, and I rush over to block her view of the two love birds.

When they finish, Sadie giggles. "Sorry."

"I'm not!" Devon brags, puffing his chest. "I was afraid I'd never get to do that again."

"Again?" I ask. "Here?"

Sadie's face goes even pinker. "We may have done it ... once or twice before."

I hold up my hands to stop her. "That's enough. I'm happy for you, but I don't need to hear more."

"I just can't believe she got caught in that mess," Devon says, shaking his head. "What a freak accident."

Sadie glances up at me, her eyes serious, and I realize Devon doesn't know the whole story. He doesn't know that Sadie was there meeting with the Mafia, and clearly, Sadie would prefer it stay that way.

I respect her wishes.

Tati changes the channel and turns the volume up until we're all wincing against the sound. I grab the remote and turn it back down.

"Who is she?" Devon asks dumbly, noticing her for the first time.

"My kid," I say without really thinking about it.

Sadie's eyes go wide, and I scramble to correct myself. "Well, *a* kid. My boyfriend's kid."

Now I've labeled Tati as my child and Dmitry as my boyfriend, and neither of those things is true.

Though, they feel true.

I realize for the first time that I want them to be true.

Except I don't know if Dmitry feels the same way.

In fact, right now, I have a good reason to believe he doesn't like me at all. He even threatened my father to keep me from coming to the hospital although by now I'm almost certain he wouldn't hurt an innocent man. Yes, he punched him, but Dmitry doesn't kill indiscriminately. Right?

I look down at the small blonde girl beside me and wonder if I'm deluding myself. I wonder I'll be there if she grows up or if I'll be just another adult who leaves and never comes back.

Tati and I leave Sadie and Devon alone and head back to the house, but I can't stop myself from glancing back at her in the back seat and wondering what will happen to her and me and my unborn child.

The questions overwhelm me until I have to count the lines in the road to clear my head. Until I have to shove them out of my mind completely to avoid an emotional meltdown.

22

COURTNEY

Winter seems to come all at once. Somehow I make it through all my exams, even with the ongoing nausea and worry.

The golden hues of fall turn white and silver overnight, and suddenly, Tati is dragging me to the attic to look for Christmas decorations.

Yanka said everything would be up here!

It seems to me that Dmitry hired Yanka and the rest of his household help for the express purpose of doing things like decorating his house, but I can't deny Tati the pleasure of decorating a tree. Not when she has so few other pleasures. Not when this Christmas will be her first one without her parents.

Tati is too small to be of much help, so I end up carrying everything down from the attic in five trips. Then, there are several more trips down to the main floor sitting room where Tati wants to put the tree.

Right in front of the window, she signs, standing back and holding her hands up like a frame. She looks so old. So much more mature than any seven-year-old I've ever known before.

Maybe I only feel that way because I love her.

I knew I cared about Tati, but now that she's the only person in the house who is talking to me, my love for her has cemented in a way that I know will break my heart when I have to leave.

Dmitry didn't find out about our trip to the hospital. I didn't tell Tati not to tell him, but being the clever girl she is, I think she knew it was a secret anyway. Besides, we really did pick up the foam rollers her physical therapist mentioned, so it was only a half lie at worst.

Together, we fluff the branches and assemble the ten-foot tree in the front corner of the room. Then, we dig through boxes of bulbs and garland and strings with little red bells on them and with no restraint at all, we put everything we find on the tree.

It looks like Santa Claus and all his reindeer threw up on the thing.

Surely Dmitry won't mind our handiwork. Especially since Tati is so proud of it.

As soon as we're finished, he walks through the front door, and Tati runs to grab him.

He hasn't spoken to me in days, and I can barely even look at him.

It hurts too much. Seeing the way he glowers at me, seeing the anger in his face when I want to see something else entirely.

Considering our arrangement, I half expected him to still come to my room in the night. And though it would kill me to be physically close to him without any of the feelings to match, it would be something. It would be better than existing in the same house without ever really seeing each other.

The day before, a doctor arrived to examine me and confirm the pregnancy. Dmitry didn't tell me he had scheduled anything, and he wasn't at the appointment, but the doctor informed me he would be caring for me as long as I was living in Dmitry's house. He instructed me how to best care for myself and the growing baby, and it gave me hope that, on some level, Dmitry still cares.

However, when he walks into the sitting room without even a glance in my direction, the hope withers and dies.

He smiles at Tati and tells her what a beautiful job she did on the tree, but when Tati points to me and tells him how much I helped, Dmitry just nods and stares at nothing. Like I'm not even here.

Tati hugs Dmitry and then runs over to hug me again just because. She pulls away and gives me a lopsided grin. *Thank you, Courtney.*

I kiss the top of her head and can't help but smile as she runs up the stairs with a string of bells to hang them from the back of her headboard.

As soon as she's gone, Dmitry turns to leave.

"Wait." The word is strangled and small, and I worry he didn't hear it. But then he stops and turns back to me, his eyes focused on a point over my shoulder. I swallow back my nerves. "I ordered most of Tati's Christmas gifts while I was still in class, but now that I'm on break, I want to go out and get her something else."

Dmitry nods. "Okay."

"A pair of dance shoes," I offer without him needing to ask. "She seems to really enjoy it, and I thought she'd enjoy having a pair like mine."

He nods again, his jaw clenching. "Okay."

We stand in silence, a sea of emotion swirling between us, threatening to crash down on me any second. I sigh. "So, can I go or not?"

Finally, he looks up at me, and his eyes are blue and piercing. It feels freezing hot, like when you bury your hands in the snow. My entire body gets chills. "Our contract is over, Courtney. You can go wherever you'd like."

I can't say anything. My throat closes, and I can only stand there, frozen and mute as he walks up the stairs and leaves me alone.

When I finally make it up to my room, I feel like I've been in a car accident. My body is sore and my mind is a jumble. I don't want to be here if I'm not wanted. But then again ... I want to be here. With Tati. With him. With them. I don't understand why he hasn't thrown me out directly, but I'm guessing it has to do with Tati. While it's humiliating that he's only kept me around as a glorified babysitter, rather than because of any feelings he has for me ...

I'm still not ready to leave.

When I get upstairs, I grab my phone and call my dad. If our deal is over, then I can call him whenever I want.

The phone rings for almost a minute before his voice mail picks up. I hang up without leaving a message. The lump in my throat is impossible to talk around anyway.

I dress in jeans, knee-high boots, and a white knit sweater. My body is on autopilot as confused thoughts swirl around my head. They only grow more confused when someone knocks faintly on my door.

I answer it, expecting it to be Tati, but it's Dmitry. He's standing a breath away, the woodsy smell of his cologne overwhelming me. I should take a step back, but I can't.

I miss him.

"You can go wherever you want, but I'm sending a guard along with you," he says coldly. "Don't wander away from him."

Before I can ask any questions, Dmitry turns and walks down the hallway. Just before he disappears into his office, I see his shoulders heave with a deep breath, and his hand tugs through his hair.

Just as he said, a guard follows me outside and opens the car door for me. He asks where I want to go and doesn't seem at all concerned when I say I want to return to the mall, the sight of Tati's near-kidnapping.

I don't know if the guard is present to protect me or to spy on me for Dmitry. His tone wasn't as commanding as usual. He sounded worried. I don't know if it's about his business—the Italians, maybe? Surely he can't be worried about me.

I push aside the thoughts as we get to the mall, focusing on Tati instead.

Dmitry's soldier remains close by but discreet throughout my shopping trip, until I walk into the fifth or sixth store of the day.

There is an audible sigh behind me, but I don't care. I need to find the perfect shoes for Tati.

She wants a pair just like mine, but mine are several years old. I can't find the same pair, but I want to get as close as possible. So far, nothing has been good enough, but I hope the high-end sporting goods store will at least have something they can order for me.

There is a small section of dancewear in the back, and I'm scouring the shoe racks for anything that might work when my phone rings. For a moment, I'm disappointed when I see it isn't Dmitry, but then I realize it's my father.

"Courtney!" he says jovially when I answer the phone.

"Are you okay?" I ask with a frown, confused by how happy he sounds.

"Better than okay," he says. "Didn't Dmitry tell you the good news? I came up with the money."

"The money? Dmitry's money?"

"The very same," he says. "Your deal with him is done. When are you coming home?"

The information is more than I'm prepared to process, so I stumble over my answer. "Oh. Wow. Well, um—" I trail off.

I'm not sure. Now it feels like it was less Dmitry kicking me out and more like he was honoring our deal. Like … maybe he's not done with me, even though it sure felt like it. But maybe … maybe there's still hope …

I'd been counting down to this very moment, but I had months left. Months where I expected to get closer to Dmitry. Where I expected him to begin to return my feelings for him.

"Court?" Dad asks, sounding more concerned this time. "Is everything okay?"

Now, our time is up.

"Yeah, fine," I lie. "Sorry, I'm distracted."

"Well," he prods. "When are you coming home, kid?"

The question feels like ice in my veins. "Well, things are a little crazy right now. I have to make arrangements and plan to move my stuff."

"Stuff?" he asks. "You only went with one duffel bag."

"I know, but I've … accumulated things." Dmitry gave me clothes and books and jewelry. I assume they're all mine to keep, though now that I'm thinking about it, I don't know if I want them anymore. They would only be reminders. "I just need to work out the details. It might be better to wait until after Christmas."

"After Christmas?" I can't miss the disappointment in his voice. "Are you sure everything is okay? You sound upset."

"No, no," I insist. "I'm fine, really."

The store shelves don't have anything I'd want to buy for Tati, and I'm too distracted to bother asking them to order something. I'd rather just do more shopping online.

I step out of the store, the soldier trailing behind me.

"If you're sure ... " my dad says. "I'm just ready to see you. These last few months have been—"

His words are drowned out by a deafening bang.

The phone falls from my hand, and I drop to the floor instinctively, shocked.

I'm still wondering what the sound was when I realize everyone around me is running and screaming. People are scooping up their children and sprinting in every direction, and it still takes me a few stunned seconds before I find my legs and stand up.

I spin, searching for the soldier, and that's when I see him lying on the floor behind me.

A gunshot wound to his temple.

Blood is still spreading out around him in a puddle, and I take a stumbling step backwards, horrified. That's when I feel the barrel of a gun pressed against my spine.

The next words are hot against my ear. "Come with me if you want to live."

I jolt in surprise and a hand grips my arm. Hard.

"Don't struggle, or I'll shoot."

I want to fight. I want to scream and run and flail my arms.

But I can't.

It isn't only my life I'd be risking, but my baby's.

So, I turn at the shooter's command and walk out of the mall, a gun pressed to my spine.

23

DMITRY

The soldier was supposed to text me an update once every hour.

I didn't put a guard on Courtney because she was my prisoner, but because, as a member of my house, she was in danger.

The Italians have grown into a serious threat, and as angry as I was with her, the thought of sending her unarmed into the world was one I couldn't bear.

When the third hour passes with no text and no response to any of my messages, alarm bells begin to ring.

I direct Pasha to figure out why I can't get in touch with the soldier or Courtney, and just as he returns to tell me the news, my phone rings. It's Lawrence.

Any other time, I would have dismissed the call, but this time, I answer it.

"Hello?"

"It's Courtney," Lawrence says, sounding more upset than I've ever heard him. "I called her, and then there was a gunshot and screaming. She didn't pick up the phone again. I have no idea what happened but—"

I pull the phone from my ear and nod for Pasha to speak.

"A shooting," he confirms. "It's hitting the news now. Our guy is dead."

"Shit." I pick up the phone. "I'll call you back, Lawrence." I hang up as he's babbling something frantic.

"Where is Courtney?" I ask Pasha, grabbing my keys and the leather jacket from the back of my chair. Pasha didn't say Courtney was dead, only that our guy was. I pray that means she's still alive.

"No one has heard from her," Pasha says.

I take a deep breath. That's better than dead. It means there's still a chance I can find her.

"Have the nanny keep an eye on Tati and don't let anyone in or out of those house until further notice."

"I want to come with you," Pasha says. "I want to help."

"You'll help by staying here and protecting my house."

He lets out a frustrated heave but nods, and then I'm running. Down the stairs, out of the house, and to the car.

The drive to the mall is a blur of trees and cars, as I swerve through traffic and blow through red lights.

By the time I get to the mall, I don't care about the police presence. I screech to a stop just outside the barrier they've erected and rush to the first officer I see. It just so happens to be the same officer who came to deliver the news of Sadie's shooting.

"I wondered if I'd see you here," he says smugly. "Come to confess?"

I glare at him. "I'm here to find Courtney."

A flicker of alarm crosses his features. "Was Courtney at the mall today?"

"With the guard," I confirm. "He was supposed to be watching her."

"Shit." He grabs his walkie and turns away to speak into it, sharing the news.

"So, I assume you don't know where she is?" I ask, hoping I'm wrong.

"We have a dead body and no gunmen," he says sharply. "I was a bit distracted." Then, he tilts his head to the side. "How did you find out about this so quickly?"

"I just fucking told you!" I snap tersely. "My girlfriend and a guard were here."

"But Courtney is gone and the guard is dead," he says, raising a suspicious brow. "So, who told you about the shooting?"

I take a step towards him until we are toe-to-toe. "It's on the news, and she isn't answering her phone. Call me a genius, but I put two and two together."

The officer narrows his eyes. "Would you be willing to speak with one of our detectives? I'm sure we have some more questions for you."

"I'm sure you do," I growled. "Unfortunately, I'm going to be a little too busy looking for my girlfriend to participate in this massive waste of time."

I call every connection I've ever had. Every ally I've ever depended on.

No one knows anything about Courtney.

"I'll alert my men to be on the lookout, but I can't make any promises. The Italians are after us the same as you." Akio is an older man, closer to my father's age than mine, and he has never enjoyed the political side of being a mob boss. It was why he and my father got along so well. My father tossed Akio whatever scraps were available and joined his fights when necessary, and Akio stayed out of Tsezar Bratva business.

I, unfortunately, have not maintained the same symbiotic relationship with him.

I thank him and sigh, pinching the bridge of my nose.

I can hear my men moving in the main room, waiting for me to address them, but I don't know what to say. Aside from suspecting the Italians, I have no leads. No idea where Courtney could be.

Usually, situations like this involve a ransom note, but I'm empty-handed and desperate.

When I walk into the room, their hushed voices go silent altogether, and I feel all eyes on me.

"We've been attacked," I say, stating the obvious. "A guard has been killed and one of our own has been taken."

There is a rumble of discontent that moved through the room. Vadik is freshly out of the hospital and still sporting a cast after being attacked by the Italians, and he steps forward. "Sorry, but since when is Courtney one of our own? According to Rurik, she's a slave."

Rurik.

He was beaten and released days ago, and he's maintained a low profile since then. I didn't even bother to message him for this meeting. I'll reach out to him if I need him, but until then, I want him to know what it feels like to be on the outside, to be at the bottom of the totem pole.

But the damage is done, and the seed has been planted in the minds of the men before me. Courtney isn't exactly one of our own, but that doesn't change the way I feel about her.

It occurs to me that it's even possible this entire attack was a scheme put in place by her and the Italians working in unison ... though, I don't truly think so. Not really.

I can't imagine her agreeing to a guard being killed. I can't imagine her being so callous towards human life.

Courtney isn't like me.

"She's not a slave," I say, trying to find the words for what Courtney is to me. So many possibilities. Lies, shades of gray, deferments, and promises of future explanation. But I settle on the truth. "She's carrying the heir to this Bratva—my child. And when this is done, I will marry her. She will be your leader just as I am, and you will be pledged to protect her, just as you are pledged to protect me. What I'm asking is for your pledge to begin now. What I'm asking is for you to search for her the same way you would search for me."

Vadik's eyes are wide in surprise, but as I finish, he bows his head and steps back into the ranks of the rest of the Bratva.

My men agree wordlessly. Without any further complaint, they divide into groups and scour the city in search of her.

I want to join them, but I have to get home. I have Tati to think about.

She doesn't know Courtney is missing, but she knows Courtney is not home when she should be.

Home. Where she belongs.

Will she come back? Tati asks, bottom lip trembling. *Did you kick her out?*

No, I didn't, I say, telling her the truth. *I'm looking for her and will bring her home as soon as I can.*

She squeezes her eyes shut, tears rolling down her chubby cheeks. *Take me with you. She'll listen to me. I know she will.*

I smooth a hand down her shiny blonde hair and kiss her forehead. *I can't, sweetheart, but I'll be sure to tell her how much you miss her when I see her.*

Tati nods slowly, but then her lip begins to tremble with renewed force, and she bursts into tears. I try to lift her face, but she won't respond to my touch. She buries her face in the blankets, and when I leave her room, I feel useless. Helpless.

Without really thinking, I pick up my phone.

Lawrence answers on the first ring.

I give him a brief update on Courtney's situation, telling him what little I know. "I have my men searching everywhere, but I don't know anything yet. I don't know where she's or if she's alive or if I will ever find her, and I'm ... I'm ... "

"In love with her."

The man's words catch me off guard, and I shake my head. "Excuse me?"

"You love her," he says. "And she loves you, too."

"Lawrence, your daughter is missing. Now is not the time for this."

"But it is," he says, sniffling, letting me know he's crying. "I told Courtney she could come home earlier, and she resisted. She didn't want to leave you. Despite everything, my daughter loves you, and I can tell by the fact that you sound more out of sorts than I've ever heard you that you love her, too. That's why you will find her. That's why I'm not more upset. Because I know you will do everything in your power to bring her back to all of us."

I want to argue with him, but I don't have the energy to lie.

I do love Courtney.

I love her fire and determination. I love her kind heart and the way she doesn't flinch away from me in fear. The way she looks me in the eye and meets me where I am without judgment. Well, without too much judgment.

"I appreciate your faith, but I can't even hold a seven-year-old together right now. Courtney was better at dealing with her than I am. I'm out of my depth."

Lawrence sighs. "When Courtney's mom would leave, I'd give Courtney something of hers—a sweater or a necklace or something. It helped her feel close. Then, I'd tell her her mother would never leave without that item, and she'd come back for it as soon as she knew it was gone."

At first, I'm tempted not to take his advice. Courtney told me her dad deceived her. For years, he convinced her that her mother would come back when he knew she was gone for good.

I want to tell him I won't trick Tati like that.

Except, I'm not tricking her.

If all goes to plan, Courtney will be home. Soon.

She'll come back and live with us and be with us.

So, when I hang up, I go into Courtney's room and grab her cropped sweatshirt with the hood. I've watched her dance in it too many times to count and it smells exactly like her—sweet vanilla and spice.

When I give it to Tati, she clutches the sweater to her chest and then slips it on. The sleeves are laughably long, but because it's cropped, it actually hits just below her waist. She wraps her arms around herself in a hug, and I silently pray that I'll find her. That she will come home.

If she doesn't, I don't know what I'll do.

24

COURTNEY

The only thing I know is that it has been days.

Days of silence and meals slid under doors and silence. Endless silence.

No one will talk to me.

I can hear voices far in the distance and footsteps moving outside of my door, but otherwise, there is nothing.

No window, nothing to let me know how much time has passed, how many days I've been trapped here.

The only thing I can use to judge is the noise on the other side of the door.

For hours and hours at a time everything is silent. Is that night? I think so.

Then, the footsteps return. Voices return.

Daytime.

I count three cycles of that.

I also listen, pressing my ear to the crack in the door as hard as I can, hoping for something useful.

Half of the time the men are speaking in Italian, which tells me all I need to know about who is responsible for the murder of the guard and my kidnapping.

When they aren't speaking Italian, much of the information is useless. Discussion about which prisoners to feed, who to beat, and the change of the guards.

But no one beats me. Not yet.

Finally, during what I guess is the second day, I hear a guard with a deep baritone voice announce that "the Pig" is here. At first, I don't understand, thinking maybe they're talking about lunch.

Then: "Did he come with the lights and sirens or is he here to talk?"

"To talk," the baritone voice said. "No uniform. He needs to see all of the lieutenants."

The police.

The Italians have infiltrated the police. It doesn't do much to help me escape my cell, but it does explain why officers kept showing up at Dmitry's door. If they were working for the police, they could have been there to see who I was to Dmitry, to determine whether I was worth kidnapping.

Well, if that's the case, then they did a terrible job.

Dmitry doesn't care about me.

He was likely days away from kicking me out of his house altogether. He's probably relieved that I've been taken. Now, my father has paid his debts, and Dmitry doesn't have to worry about keeping me around any longer. He'll probably be thrilled to be able to finally have other women again. Although he probably had them while he was with me anyway.

I don't want to think this is true, but I can't stop my mind from wandering there. When there is no one to speak to and nothing to do aside from listen and think, the dark thoughts grow louder and louder until they push out the light.

Still, even if Dmitry isn't looking for me, even if he doesn't care ...

I still do.

If I ever get out of here, I want to have useful information, something that can help him take down the Italians and get the corrupt officers ousted. I want the days spent in my cell to be more than stolen. I want them to be worthwhile.

On what I think is the third day, a fight erupts just beyond my door.

I'm sleeping on the thin mat that passes for a bed in this place, tucked into a ball on my side, when a thud against my door jolts me awake.

I sit up and stare at the door, expecting someone to walk through it any second. Instead, there is yelling.

Everything is in Italian, so I don't understand a word.

I do, however, understand the sound of gunfire.

When the shot rings out, I drop to the floor and tip the flimsy bed onto its side and drag it to the far corner, close to the metal toilet. It won't offer much in the way of protection if anyone shoots into my room, but it's better than nothing.

The shot is followed by footsteps and more shouting, and then another flurry of shots.

I press my hands over my ears and make myself as small as possible, hoping to avoid any shots that might ricochet my way.

After what feels like hours but is probably only a couple minutes, the chaos quiets.

The yelling stops and the footsteps fade. Still, I stay hidden for a long time, too afraid to come out. Afraid any movement will alert them to my presence and draw unwanted attention my way.

Finally, I gather my courage and stand up. I tiptoe to the door and press my ear against the crack. As I do, the door shifts in the frame.

I look down and realize that in all of the gunfire, someone shot the lock off the door.

Fingers shaking, I reach for the handle and pull it open.

The hallway is empty, though there's a splatter of blood on the wall across from me. I blink several times, the vision transferring onto my brain, appearing against my eyelids each time I blink, and then I look away.

I try to focus on what is important: Where am I? Who is nearby? Can I escape?

To my right is a visible dead end, so I turn left, creeping along the hallway with my back pressed to the wall.

I have nothing to defend myself with aside from my two hands. Even then, I don't want to fight. Not while I'm pregnant.

So far, no one here has hurt me.

I slide down the wall, and I'm a few doors away from mine when I see another splash of blood. I look around and realize there is a very thin trail of it leading from my door down the hallway.

Going against all of my instincts, I follow it.

Finally, the blood turns right into a doorway, and I almost follow it inside when I realize the door is cracked open and there are voices coming from it. Immediately, I jump out of sight.

When I realize no one is charging into the hallway to apprehend me, I peek my head around the corner so I can see into the room.

There are two men standing up, facing away from me, and a third man on the floor at their feet.

Based on the blood trail leading to his body and his lack of movement, I assume he's dead.

"He was trying to go into her room," one of the men says. "I tried to stop him, and he shoved me."

"So you shot him?" the second man asks, shoving the first.

"He pulled his gun first."

They're arguing over the dead body as though they're debating who took the last slice of pie from the fridge. As though it's nothing.

"No one is supposed to touch her," the first man says. "That was the rule, and I was tasked with keeping watch over her. I had to do my job."

The second man groans and nods. "I can't believe we have all of this chaos over a woman."

"*His* woman," the first man says. "If we want Dmitry to respond to our commands, she can't be harmed. Not yet, anyway."

Not yet.

The words hang like a cloud over my head, threatening to dump rain on me at any second.

"If all of this is a ruse to lure him to the safe house, why does she have to be unharmed? Why can't we do what we want with her and then still offer her up?"

The first man shakes his head and sighs. "Because if the first plan doesn't work, he might want verification we haven't hurt her. For now, we have to cover our bases. We have to protect her until Dmitry Tsezar is dead."

My heart is lodged in my throat, and I can't breathe.

They're going to kill Dmitry and then me.

The instinct to run overtakes me, and I brace myself to try for an escape until a door further down the hallway bangs open.

Voices grow louder, and I can hear several sets of footsteps.

Too many for me to get past on my own.

I also can't keep standing out in the open. I now know they won't hurt me, but there are plenty of ways to hurt someone without leaving any evidence, and I don't want to give anyone a reason.

So, I tiptoe away from the door, avoiding the trail of blood, and then run back to my room as soon as I'm far enough away to go unheard.

The door will no longer lock, but I shut it behind me and then huddle behind the still-overturned mattress.

I have to get out of here. I have to warn Dmitry of their plan. Otherwise, they'll kill him.

∼

I don't have the chance.

Over the next few hours, there are constant voices in the hallway, not allowing any opportunity for me to escape. Then, my door flies open.

"*Che diavolo?*" the man shouts, studying the door and then the frame. When he sees the bullet hole bending the metal, he smirks. "You're lucky this hit the door and not you."

I'm too afraid for a witty comeback.

This man is the first person who has walked into my room and addressed me in four days. That can't be a good sign. It means something is about to happen.

"Are you slow?" the man asks, stalking towards me one slow, lumbering step at a time.

There is no one else with him, and I wonder if he's supposed to be here or if he simply noticed the door unlocked and helped himself.

"Or are you afraid?" he continues. "Perhaps both?"

I open my mouth to speak, but my tongue is dry and there is cotton in the back of my throat. I cough to clear it. "Neither. I'm thirsty."

His dark eyebrows rise in surprise, and then he smiles, showing off a silver tooth. "You are demanding. A woman in your position should not be making demands."

"I'm sorry," I say, batting my lashes, hoping I still remember what flirting looks like after four days of complete solitude. "I've never been in this position before, so you'll have to teach me the etiquette."

His lips part, his tongue darting out to swipe across his lower lip. "Rule number one: don't fight."

My heart is practically vibrating in my chest. If he doesn't want me to fight, it must mean he's about to do something I won't like.

"Fight?" I ask, tilting my head to the side, letting my now-greasy brown hair fall over my shoulder. "Do women usually fight you? I can't imagine that."

The man has thick black hair that sticks up untameably in every direction and a soft chin. He looks more like a puppet than a real person.

He moves closer to me, his eyes perusing my dirty, dingy appearance up and down. Then, he reaches out a slow hand to touch my elbow.

Everything inside of me wants to flinch away from him and run in the other direction, but I hold my ground. I smile up at him.

"Why are you here?" I ask, my voice buttery. My hand falls on his chest and drags downward over soft flesh. "Are you taking me somewhere?"

He looks down at where my hand is touching him, and I see the idea cross his mind. His head quirks back like he's checking the door. Then, he faces me, eyes narrowed. "Do you want me to take you somewhere?"

I shrug, mouth pulling up in a half smile. "It depends on where we're going."

He licks his lips and leans forward until we're sharing the same acrid air. His nostrils flare. "Wherever you want, *bella*."

I press onto my toes until our mouths are separated by only an inch. I can feel the hot exhale from his nose, and I want to whimper with disgust. "Tell me," I purr. "What is the plan?"

He turns his head to the side, and I think he's going to kiss me.

Then, all of a sudden, his hands are on my arms, and he's dragging me towards the door.

The world tilts, and I lose my footing, but the man's hold on me is tight enough that I don't need to walk anyway. He has me tucked under his arm like a spare jacket on a chilly day.

"Women are so fickle," he says, laughing and shaking his head. "Keep up that behavior, whore, and Dmitry might not want you back badly enough to go through with the plan."

I'm dragged to another room where two more Italian men join the first one in tying my hands and legs together.

When I try to speak, I'm threatened with a slap, and the men all laugh as they speak in Italian, gesturing to various parts of my bound body and making grotesque gestures.

By the time I'm carried out and loaded into a van, all I can do is hope that if Dmitry doesn't figure out the plan in time to save me and himself, that I'll die.

And not at the hands of these vile men.

25

DMITRY

In the last few days, I've barely slept. Barely eaten anything.

Every second has been spent pursuing leads, directing my men on areas to search, and trying to be there for Tati.

The longer Courtney has been gone, the more restless my niece has become, and the more she needs me to be there, to assure her that I'm not leaving, not going anywhere.

When the call comes through that my men have eyes on Courtney, and that she's being transported in an Italian SUV to an abandoned building on the outskirts of the city, I jump.

I don't ask questions. I don't investigate. I go.

The car waiting for me out front is an old police transport vehicle that the Bratva had outfitted a few years ago with bullet-resistant glass between the front and back seats. Usually, it's used to transport hostages, but I don't think twice when I see it waiting outside for me, back door propped open.

I hop in and slam the door shut behind me, mind racing. "Go." We take off, tires screeching.

For a moment, everything is fine. I stare out the window at the buildings racing past, trying to formulate some kind of plan.

I only grow nervous when I register that I don't recognize the guard behind the wheel. It isn't the person I commanded to call my men and direct them to meet me at the incineration plant.

Most of my top men are out working on the streets, so the lower recruits have been filling positions unfamiliar to them and to me.

Now, however, I want to know who he is.

I lean to my right to get a better look at the driver, and I realize with a sudden lurch in my chest that I don't know him, either.

I pat the pocket of my jeans for my phone but it isn't there.

I check my coat. Nothing.

Suddenly, I remember the strange guard posted in the entryway, handing me my jacket. I almost left the house without it at all, but he held it out and assisted me in slipping it on. He was rather handsy about it, but as with everything that I'm only just now paying attention to, I was too keyed up to notice. Too anxious to follow up on the lead, too desperate to find Courtney.

I was too rushed to notice that everyone around me was setting me up.

"Pull over," I command the driver.

The car doesn't slow, and the driver doesn't even turn to acknowledge my voice.

I've been trapped.

I allowed myself to become so caught up in finding Courtney that I forewent all of my security measures. People moved in and out of the house freely, bringing me information and following up on leads. Who knows how many enemies infiltrated my ranks without me noticing? How deeply they penetrated?

"Pull the car over now," I growl. The driver makes no move to obey my orders.

Wherever I'm being taken, there won't be a return trip. I know that.

Courtney might actually be there waiting for me, but this situation won't end well for either of us.

I have to get out.

I slide across the seat and try the doors, but they're useless. As I'm sliding back to center, my foot hits something under the seat, and I remember the toolbox.

After one of our transport vehicles broke down on the road with a hostage inside, I outfitted all the cars with basic maintenance supplies.

Usually, the supplies aren't kept in the back seat with the hostages, but once I push through my annoyance, I'm grateful for the fuck-up. If things go according to plan, it will save my life.

I lift the box quietly to my lap, careful not to let the tools bang around, and lift the lid.

Inside, there are jumper cables, flares, various oils and fluids, and a small tool belt wrapped up in the corner. I grab the tool belt and slip the ball peen hammer from its loop.

The glass partition is bullet resistant, but it can still break. If I can get off a few good swings in the same spot, the glass will shatter.

Even if it doesn't give right away, the driver will have to pull over and deal with me, so that will give me a chance to fight him off. I'd rather not show up to a gunfight with a hammer, but it doesn't appear that I have much of a choice.

I take a deep breath, lift my arm, and swing.

Just before my first blow connects, I see the driver glance back at me in the rearview mirror. His eyes widen.

"Hey!" he shouts, the car swerving as I crack the hammer across the glass.

It doesn't shatter, but a fine web of cracks radiates out from the center of the strike. I bring my arm up and swing again, aiming for the same spot.

The glass dents, and the driver pulls over.

The car soars over the bumps in the road and along the shoulder as he slams it to a stop. I jostle forward, falling into the glass, but quickly right myself and swing again.

Third time is the charm.

The hammer smashes through the glass, and I quickly shove my other arm through the hole, pushing the glass shards into the front seat to widen it. I can feel the jagged edges break the skin through the sleeve of my jacket, but I pay it no mind. A little blood is a small price to pay for not being delivered to my enemies like a trussed-up pig roast.

The car is still rolling forward, and the driver is scrambling for what I can only assume is his weapon.

I hurl my body through the hole in the glass and begin fighting for his gun. Shards of glass press through my coat and shirt, stabbing at my flesh, but I barely feel it.

The man opens his door and tries to run. I grab the collar of his shirt, jerking him back into the seat.

His hands fumble for his waist as he tries to get ahold of the gun, but I get to it first. The moment my hand is around the handle, the man stiffens.

"I don't know anything!" he says. "Don't shoot."

I pull the trigger.

The shot rings out in the car.

The man slumps forward against the steering wheel, and it takes me two good shoves to push him out onto the gravel along the road. Then, I shift the car into drive and take off, not bothering to check what the tires run over as I pull away.

Home is my first stop. Tatiana is my first priority.

When I get there, no one is around. The men I sent out this morning are still searching the city for Courtney. The others—all the men I should never have trusted—are gone.

I take the stairs two at a time and nearly sob with relief when I see Tati playing with her dollhouse. Her nanny looks startled to see me since I haven't been around as often the last few days.

I tell her not to alarm Tati and not to ask any questions, but that they both have to come with me, right away.

Where are we going? Tati asks as I load her into the back seat with a suitcase.

I'm taking you to see ... I hesitate, not sure what to call Lawrence Palillo. *Your grandpa.*

Tati frowns. She didn't grow up with any grandparents. My parents were dead when she was born, and her mother's parents weren't part of her life for a long time—not since she married my brother. So, Tati has never been familiar with the concept.

As we drive, I tell the nanny to translate for me, and assure Tati her grandfather will be very kind to her. By the time we pull up in front of the shop, she's excited.

When Lawrence sees my car pull up, he rushes out to get news on Courtney.

"I think I know where she is," I say as Tati jumps out of the car and wraps her arm around my leg. I smooth down her blonde hair. "But I need your help keeping Tati safe."

Lawrence smiles easily at the girl, hiding any sign of distress at Courtney's kidnapping. He waves and then speaks slowly so she can read his lips. "Courtney says you two are good friends."

Tati blinks and then nods, pinching her lips to keep from smiling.

"I'm Courtney's dad," he says, holding out a hand for her to shake.

"I told her you were Grandpa," I shrug. "Sorry."

Lawrence glances up at me, surprised, and then his eyes go misty. "No reason to apologize. Call me Grandpa, Tati."

Tati holds her thumb to her forehead, fingers splayed, and then arches her hand away from her head twice in an 'm' shape. When Lawrence does the same thing, she giggles and nods.

By the time I leave, Lawrence is letting Tati play with the ancient register behind his stand, and she's teaching him the signs for all the ordinary things around his shop—chair, light, car.

I want to stay with her, protect her, but I know the best thing I can do for Tati is end this fight with the Italians. If there is any hope of her having a normal life, I have to get Courtney back and somehow squash this feud.

The only person I can think to call is Akio.

"Twice in the same week," the Japanese says in lieu of a greeting. "You must be in trouble."

"You could say that. Can we meet?"

"When?" he asks.

"Now. Right now."

Akio sighs. "Come to my office."

I shift the car to park and kill the ignition. "I'm already there. I'll be up in a minute."

Akio is standing in the hallway when the guards let me inside. He beckons me into his office and closes the door behind me. We're alone, but I know there are guards listening intently outside the door in case I decide to do anything threatening.

Before Akio can even ask, I outline my morning. The information about Courtney, the setup, and my escape.

"I think the information is trustworthy, but I can't rely on my men. Not right now." It's a dangerous thing to admit to a rival. Akio has always been on good terms with my family, but relationships in the Mafia world are fickle. He could turn his back on me and attack me at my weakest in an instant.

The key is to be mutually beneficial.

"You can't take out the Italians with your men alone," I explain. "And I can't trust all of my men to support me. So, it makes sense for us to band together."

He drums his fingers on his stomach and leans back in his chair. "The Italians have been a constant burden to my dealings. Their reach is growing, and they show no sign of slowing down. They're becoming greedy."

"Together, we can shut them down," I say.

Akio holds up a hand. "Don't lure me in with talk of victory and vengeance. I don't need any help feeling powerful. Believe me, I hear enough praises from the women I fuck."

I raise an eyebrow, and Akio tilts his head to the side in a challenge. "I'm old, not dead, young Tsezar. One day, you will be old too, and you won't be so surprised by my appetite."

I have no interest in discussing Akio's sexual appetite, so I just nod. "Then what do you want? What do I need to do to convince you?"

He leans forward, fingertips drumming together. "Offer me something. Something I want but don't know I want yet."

"I will pay you for—"

"Money?" he scoffs in disgust. "Everyone wants money. Offer me something else. Bigger."

I exhale, the air coming out of my nose like dragon fire. "Stash houses."

Akio's eyes sparkle. "Plural?"

"Three of them," I nod. "In coveted territory along our border. They'll be yours for one year. At the end of that term, we'll renegotiate."

The man clicks his teeth together, studying me as he thinks. Then, he nods. "Fine. I agree to your terms."

I try not to show him how relieved I am, or how much I was depending on his help. "You'll offer up your men and help me plan this attack?"

"Yes."

"And you'll be loyal to me for the period of one year?" I ask.

"I don't like making promises of that kind," Akio says. "I don't blindly pledge my loyalty. However, if you will honor your end of the deal and bring no devastation of any kind down on me and mine, then I see no reason to renege on our agreement here today."

"I can agree to that."

We clasp hands, and for the first time in a long time, it feels like something has finally gone right.

So, with the details hammered out, we move into logistics.

The rest of that day and into the morning of the next, Akio and I, along with his trusted men and a few of my own—Pasha and Vadik—

work out a plan. To end the Italians' stranglehold on disputed territory.

To save Courtney.

By lunch the next day, we're ready to move.

26

COURTNEY

The building is something out of a dystopian novel.

Concrete walls, impossibly high ceilings, and sheer drop-offs into what looks like it was once a trash heap.

The chair I'm strapped to is a few feet from one of the drop-offs. Only a fence of corded wire guards the twenty-foot fall.

The man who drove me to the abandoned plant then dragged me inside, tied me to the chair, and left. There I sat for one hour, two, three. Too many to count.

Finally, someone came to walk me to a restroom, which, after days of solitude, I was conditioned to view as nice behavior.

Since then, though, I've been alone for several more hours and the gray walls are starting to press in on me. The ceiling appears to be dropping down, threatening to crush me into nothing. I know it's just a trick of my mind, but that knowledge doesn't remove the fear.

When I hear footsteps coming towards me, I'm not afraid. I'm relieved. I'm grateful for any distraction from the chaffing of the ties around my wrists and the flat gray of the walls and ceiling.

Then, a man turns the corner.

For a moment, hope burns in my chest.

I recognize him. I've seen him before. In Dmitry's house. In his office.

I never learned his name, but I know Dmitry trusts this man. And for one hopeful second, I think he's here to save me.

Then, he tilts his head to the side and smiles.

It's like watching a wild cat spot an antelope. Like seeing an owl hone in on a field mouse.

There is no kindness in his face. No warmth in his eyes. No friendship in his smile.

I shiver to my very core.

"Comfortable?" he asks with a grin, knowing full well I'm not.

"I've had better," I sneer.

His eyes narrow, but just as quickly as the emotion flickers across his face, it's gone. He sighs and nods to the two men behind him. "Untie her bindings."

As the men advance towards me, my heart is leaping out of my chest.

Does this mean Dmitry is here?

I'm so delirious that I don't realize I've said those words out loud until the man's face darkens. Even the illusion of friendliness fades, leaving behind only his hatred.

"I hope you do not think Dmitry is going to come save you," he says coldly. "Because he isn't. He may come with that thought in mind, but he will not succeed. Dmitry will die in this warehouse, and you will watch."

Bile rises in my throat, and I spit in the man's direction.

It lands woefully far from him, but that doesn't seem to ease his rage. Suddenly, he charges towards me.

The bindings are now off my hands, though my ankles are still tied to the chair legs.

I throw my hands up to protect myself, and the chair wobbles onto the back two legs.

I don't know exactly how close I'm to the edge, but it's definitely close enough to fear falling off, and I let out a yelp of both surprise and fear.

Then, the man slams his hands down on my thighs with crushing force, pushing the chair back onto all four legs. "If you think you're worth something because you allowed yourself to be impregnated by an arrogant fool of a don, I suggest you think again."

I inhale sharply. I didn't know anyone knew about the pregnancy.

Did Dmitry tell him? I wonder how many people know.

"Dmitry can't save you," he says. "And when you become fully mine, I'll show you how a real leader treats his slaves."

Fully mine.

The words ring inside of me like a bell, shaking me out of my complacency, out of my fear.

Suddenly, there is only anger. Rage.

I'm not a slave. Dmitry never treated me as one.

He loves me. I can see that now.

In his own way, Dmitry cares for me. It's difficult for him to show, but he tries.

And I love him too.

Despite everything, despite the complications of our arrangement and his dealings with my father, I love Dmitry.

Love him.

And I'll do whatever I can to be certain I don't become the property of another man.

The man smirks, his dark eyes dancing with enjoyment at my misery, and just as he begins to back away, I lunge forward.

My legs are still strapped to the chair, but I claw into the man's face for balance.

I drag my nails down his cheek and across his neck, holding onto him to keep from landing flat on my face.

He lets out a yell, and I open my mouth wide and dig my teeth into his face.

Warm blood fills my mouth, and I turn and spit it out.

At the same time, the guards grab ahold of me and pull me away from him.

The man's nostrils are flared and his eyes are wild as he stares at me, a hand pressed to his cheek.

"You fucking bitch," he spits. He shakes his head, top lip pulled back in a sneer. "You have no idea what a painful future you just created for yourself. Things could have been good between us. *Pleasurable.* Now, however, you will know only pain. Until you can learn to behave better, anyway."

I can feel spit and blood dribbling from the side of my mouth, and I spit again. Not at him this time, but on the floor. He looks down at the spot on the floor and then sighs. "Tie her up. Tight."

As his guards grab the ropes they just cut, the man moves towards me, fidgeting with the front of his pants.

It takes my adrenaline-fueled mind a second to recognize what he's doing, and I clamp my mouth shut and turn away.

"I'm going to show you what it means to be submissive," he growls between clenched teeth.

I squeeze my eyes closed.

"Rurik."

The man stops, and I peel open one eye to see what is going on.

The man turns to the sound of the voice.

Rurik. I recognize his name now. I heard Dmitry mention him several times.

"What is it?" Rurik asks impatiently.

The newcomer, a tall, skinny man with a shaved head and pale eyebrows, tilts his chin down as though afraid to deliver the news. "We've spotted him. He's approaching the site now. Alone."

Rurik zips his pants back up and grins. "Showtime, gentlemen."

He tips his head to the nearest guard. "Watch her."

The space clears out quickly, and I'm left alone with the guard.

I recognize him as well, though I don't know his name. He never worked as one of my guards or as a guard at the house, but I saw him come and go with the large groups of men Dmitry would occasionally have over. He always stayed near the back of the group, and now I understood why.

He was a traitor.

"Why did you betray him?" I ask, too curious to stay quiet. At this point, staying quiet won't save me anyway. I might as well get as many answers as I can.

He looks at me and then pulls his gaze away, and I think he's going to ignore me.

Just when I've given up hope of an answer, he sighs. "I didn't see it that way. At the time."

I frown. "But you do now?"

His hands fold in front of him and then he shifts them behind his back, making himself look even more like a soldier. "Are you really pregnant?"

"Yes." At first, I thought my pregnancy would save me. I thought it would keep me safe. Now, I know better. Rurik will do whatever he wishes with me, regardless.

The man's shoulders sag, and he turns towards me, the corners of his eyes pulled down in disappointment. "I was taught not to torture women and children. We take care of them."

I snort. "You people don't take care of anyone but yourselves."

"You don't see the whole picture. We're not monsters. Dmitry delivers money to the widows and orphaned children of the Bratva once a month," he says. "We offer them protection from their enemies, give them money to start over if they need to. We help more than we hurt. Not all men can say things like that."

I remember Dmitry driving around the city the night I left my father's shop with him. He left envelopes with women. All of the women seemed so happy to see him, so grateful, and I couldn't understand it at the time.

"He did that?"

The man nods. "Rurik said it made Dmitry weak, but now … "

His voice trails off, and I can see the regret swirling around his head like a physical cloud.

"It's not too late," I whisper. "You can help him. You can go back."

He shakes his head. "I can't. Not ever. I betrayed my Bratva."

"Dmitry could forgive you. I'll tell him what you told me. I'll help you—"

Suddenly, the man spins towards me, knife held out, and I yelp, thinking he means to hurt me.

Then, the ropes around my wrists loosen.

I lift my hands and roll my wrists as he drops to one knee to cut my ankles.

When I stand, my legs are shaky and blood rushes to my feet in painful pins and needles.

The man stands and stares down at the floor. When he looks up, his eyes are glassy and pained. "Run if you can. Don't try to fight. You'll only get in the way."

I furrow my brow. "What?"

"Dmitry is outnumbered," he continues. "It's unlikely he'll make it out. You either, for that matter, but I've cut your ties in case you find a chance. If you do, don't miss it. Run. Let Dmitry fight. Just try to get out."

"Come with me," I say. "Help me, and we could both get out."

I don't know why I so badly want to save the man, but I do. I don't even know his name, but I can see genuine kindness in his eyes.

He shakes his head and begins backing away from me, moving around a concrete pillar into the cement annex. "Just run."

He disappears around the cement, and I take a step to follow him, thinking he might know a way out. He might be able to lead me to a door. Maybe I could stick with him and convince Dmitry—if he survives—that the man deserves a pardon.

Then, I hear the shot.

And the thud.

I'm frozen in horror, praying what I think happened isn't what really happened. But all of my hoping is in vain when I see the blood begin to leak across the floor.

He killed himself.

The blood is slowly inching towards where I stand frozen when another man appears.

He glances in the direction of where the body is but doesn't respond, and I wish I could be that callous. That hardened.

It would be better than the ache I feel in my chest at the loss of the stranger.

This man is squarely built with a block head and meaty fingers he wraps around my arm. "You were supposed to be tied up," he says, mostly to himself. Then, he drags me forward. "Come with me."

I go with him and make a point not to turn and look at the body of the man behind me. Though, as I leave the room, I vow to him and myself that, if I find the opportunity, I'll run.

I'll fight.

The man leads me through narrow hallways that are all the same endless gray color until finally, we step through a door and into a cavernous room.

Pipes and rusted metal hang from the ceiling, and I can hear the distant ping of gunfire.

For a second, I think it's someone popping popcorn or some mechanical misfiring. But once I recognize the sound for what it is, it's unmistakable.

The man who came to alert Rurik said Dmitry had arrived alone. Then, why is there so much gunfire?

I want to believe Dmitry can handle Rurik and his men single-handedly, but I have to be honest with myself: it isn't likely.

I listen to the gunfire closely and try to decide where it's coming from. I intend to take the dead guard's advice, and when I do, I want to know which way to run to avoid being shot.

The guard to my right must take my concentration as a sign of fear. He chuckles to himself.

"Don't worry. This will all be over soon. Dmitry can't fight them all alone."

Having my own suspicions spoken aloud is depressing, and the little bit of hope that had sparked in my chest is extinguished.

The guard with me is large, and I think I can outrun him. I just have to wait for my opening, and then I'll dart behind the machinery and navigate to a door.

I understand my chances are slim, but they're all I have.

I'm taking a deep breath, preparing myself to escape, when there is the bang of a door and then frantic footsteps. I don't have time to move before Rurik rounds the corner.

The last time I saw him less than fifteen minutes ago, he wore a smug grin. Now, his eyes are wide, his forehead is sweaty, and he's frantic.

He sprints towards me, and I try to back away, to scramble out of the path he's cutting across the floor, but the guard grabs my shoulders and holds me in place.

My opportunity to escape is gone. It presented itself, and I hesitated.

Despair wraps around me like a thick blanket, stifling and suffocating as Rurik wrenches me out of the guard's hold and presses a gun to my forehead.

I don't even fight. I just squeeze my eyes closed and pray that dying doesn't hurt.

One second. Two. Three.

I count to nearly twenty before I crack one eye open and then the other.

I don't understand what is happening.

Rurik is breathing heavily beside me, his chest heaving and brushing against my arm with every inhale.

But he isn't pulling the trigger.

I turn my head slightly to try and see his face, but he jerks me forward again.

And that's when I see him. Rounding the corner ahead of me. Blood splattered across his shirt.

His blond hair gleams white in the fluorescent warehouse lights.

"Dmitry," I breathe.

Hope flares inside of me.

It might be my imagination, but I think I see the corners of his mouth pull up in the smallest of smiles.

27

DMITRY

Courtney whispers my name, and I take a long overdue sigh of relief.

She's still alive.

There's a gun pressed to her head, but for the time being, she's alive.

The confirmation is enough to make me smile. For a second.

Then, I see Rurik standing next to her, and my face twists into rage. Disbelief. Vengeance.

I knew I'd been betrayed when I showed up at the plant, as Akio and his men infiltrated in less obvious ways around the rest of the property, but I didn't know by whom.

Looking back, I should have expected Rurik. After the way he spoke to me in my office that day, I should have known something in our relationship had fractured.

But after Sevastian's betrayal by speaking with the FBI, I didn't want to believe that another one of my most trusted men could betray me. My own selfish denial might cost Courtney and our child their lives.

If it does, I'll never forgive myself.

Rurik's face is bloody and gouged, and I can see blood on Courtney's face. On her fingernails.

She attacked him. In spite of everything, I have to suppress a grin.

"Put down the gun," I say calmly, raising my own, aiming it at Rurik's chest.

He barks out a laugh. "I could say the same to you."

I hear footsteps behind me, and I know they're my allies. Akio's men took out the guards at the other entrances and then attacked Rurik's men from behind while they were focused on me. Rurik didn't see it coming.

I watched him run from the fight, and I knew wherever he was going, Courtney would be there waiting.

And here she is.

Here we are.

Rurik's men, Italians and some of my own men mixed together, stagger in from the wings. Akio's soldiers gather behind me.

We're two forces advancing on the battlefield, and I want to know who is going to take the first shot.

"Why?" I ask, partially to delay him and partially because I want to know.

"Because you're weak." The words are vile, spit at me with hatred and bitterness and years of resentment I'd never noticed. How did I miss something so obvious? "Your grandfather and father built this Bratva, and your cowardice is destroying it."

"How?" I ask. "Nothing has changed with our territory or inventory. We have allies, and we deal with our enemies."

"Nothing has changed?" Rurik says, shaking his head. "That's partially the problem. You aren't asserting our leadership, our dominance. You allow our enemies to attack us, to kill us. What kind of leader doesn't act?"

"The kind who doesn't want to start a war," I snap. "My father was constantly fighting and scraping. I didn't want things to be that way. I want peace."

Rurik tightens his arm around Courtney, but I can't look at her. If I look at her face—see the fear in her eyes—I'll pull the trigger. I'll kill Rurik on the spot, but it might not be enough to stop him from killing her too.

So, I keep my eyes on his face even as his expression morphs into blind fury.

"Your father told me he viewed me as a son," Rurik says. "Did you know that? Your father viewed me as a son, more so than you or your brother. And yet, I'm stuck as your lieutenant."

"My most trusted lieutenant—"

Rurik shakes his head, the hand with the gun waving around dangerously. I stop talking to keep him from accidentally pulling the trigger. "No, that was Sevastian. Remember him? The man you trusted most turned you in to the FBI. That should have taught you how poor your judgment is, but you refused to learn from your lesson. The moment Sevastian was gone, you brought this woman into your house."

Rurik turns away from me for a moment to look at Courtney, genuine hatred burning in his eyes. I push my rage into the back corner of my mind. I'll open it later. Not now.

Not yet.

"She brought nothing but trouble for you," he says. "It was so easy to take Tati from right under her nose and to convince her friend to spy for us."

My jaw clicks at the realization that Rurik was behind Tati's near-kidnapping.

"I tried to show you again and again that she couldn't be trusted, but you still welcomed her into your bed. Now, she's pregnant with a baby neither of you is ever going to meet." Rurik takes a deep breath and then turns to me, face red, screaming: "DO YOU SEE WHAT YOUR LACK OF LEADERSHIP HAS DONE?"

The room feels deathly quiet as the echoes of his yell fade.

Rurik clears his throat. "Then, you had me beaten for questioning her. After everything this bitch has done," he says, shaking Courtney. "You had *me* beaten for being disloyal. That's when I officially cut ties with you."

He laughs but it's a distant, disconnected sound. "Though, I suppose I actually cut ties with you when I killed your brother."

The world stops turning.

My heart stops beating.

Everything freezes and I take in Rurik. The amusement in his eyes. The joy he finds in my shock.

Rurik killed my brother.

"And his wife," he continues, smirking. "I nearly got the daughter, too, but children are resilient. She recovered."

"They were run off the road," I say, not truly believing it yet.

Rurik raises a hand and then points down at himself. "By me. Remember the mysterious car? Guess who … Your brother found out that I'd been asking around to see who was loyal to you. He planned to tell you, and I couldn't take the chance that that would be the one time you'd actually act on that kind of information. I couldn't risk you making an example of me and having me executed. So, I executed him before he could do the same to me."

Blood is pounding in my ears.

I don't want to shoot Rurik anymore; I want to rip his head off with my bare hands. I want to squeeze his neck until he turns blue. I want to feel the life drain out of him.

A gun is too impersonal.

"Fight me," I say, narrowing my eyes, breathing through my nose.

Rurik's brow raises. "Excuse me?"

"Fight me," I repeat more slowly. "Put down your gun, tell your men to stand down, and fight me."

Rurik rolls his eyes.

"Unless you're a coward."

Something in his expression crystallizes at that, and I know I have him. Rurik cares about appearances. He doesn't want to look weak in front of his men.

So, with one move, he shoves Courtney aside.

She drops to her knees and it takes everything inside of me not to rush over and help her up.

"Whoever wins takes everything," Rurik says.

I nod. "Do you want it in writing?"

"Not necessary," he says. "When it's all over, there will be no one left to dispute."

He's right. We'll fight to the death. At the end of this, only one of us will remain.

The circle of people surrounding us spreads out as Rurik and I move to the center of the large room.

Slowly, I divest myself of my weapons, revealing each gun, knife, and hidden blade before setting it on the ground and sliding it back towards Akio.

Rurik does the same.

I watch him carefully and count our weapons.

I know he has more.

"Is that all?" I ask.

He holds up his hands. "I'm clean."

This isn't a wrestling match. There is no bell, no cheering fans in the stands, no ring girls.

Just Rurik and myself, pacing in half circles across the concrete floor, growing steadily closer to one another with each pass.

He takes the first swing.

Just a lazy swipe of his arm across the air. I reach out and grab his wrist, jerking him forward slightly.

As he falls, I draw my knee up.

He dodges, and my knee misses his chin by millimeters.

Adrenaline pulses through me, blurring the edges of my vision as though I'm high. Rurik is crystal clear, though.

I lunge forward with a right hook, and he dodges. This happens again and again until I finally lunge forward and then swing my weight, kicking out at him with my back leg.

My boot connects with his thigh, and he winces. I take the opportunity to shuffle forward again and land a one-two hit to his cheek and his jaw.

Faster than I think should be possible, Rurik returns the blows with a left knee that lands dangerously close to the center of my legs and a right kick to the leg. My knee buckles, and Rurik brings down a fist to the top of my head.

I roll away from him over my shoulder and rise to my feet, blinking to clear my starry vision.

The fighting goes on like that until my arms feel heavy and sweat drips in my brow.

Rurik and I trained together. We learned to fight together.

We've been in many similar sparring matches over the years, except those were for practice.

If we knew then what we know now, we never would have trained together.

Rurik knows all of my moves. And I know his.

I know that he isn't afraid to play dirty. He isn't afraid to break the rules to get what he wants. Which is why I keep a close eye on him as we move, waiting for him to pull a dirty trick from up his sleeve.

Courtney stands in an open space between Akio's men and Rurik's men. I can feel nerves rolling off her like a physical heat, but I try to push them aside.

If I can focus now, then this will all be over.

My mind is half on Courtney when Rurik suddenly lunges forward and kicks my legs out from under my feet.

I'm on the floor before I realize it, and Rurik jumps over me.

His fist comes down again and again and all I can do is lift my arms to guard my face.

Rurik's punches become more and more brutal, and when he rears back to get even more power, I thrust my hips up, knocking him off balance.

He tumbles to his left, landing on his shoulder, and that's when I see the knife.

It slips from his hiding place inside his shirtsleeve and clatters across the floor a foot or so away. Right next to his hand.

Rurik's eyes widen in surprise, but he wastes no time lunging for the blade.

I scramble to my knees and try to push myself to my feet, but Rurik's right elbow collides with my jaw before I can, and I fall to the side.

Up until this moment, the fight has been in anyone's favor. The odds have shifted back and forth with every volley of blows.

Now, however, I know I will lose.

I'm off-balance, falling onto my back on the floor, and Rurik has a knife.

He will carve me up like a Jack-o-lantern before I can even regain my balance.

In the haze of the moment, I turn to look at Courtney one last time. To express in the half second I have left that I love her. That I'm sorry. That I should have trusted her.

Except, when I look over, she isn't there.

Just then, Rurik's body blocks my vision.

His knee lands in my stomach, and I groan, and there's nothing I can do.

I see the knife flash in the bright overhead lights, and I wait for the impact.

Suddenly, out of nowhere, a leg comes shooting in from my right.

It's Courtney. She's screaming a string of curses I'm too overwhelmed to understand, but her foot connects with Rurik's hand and the knife goes flying.

It clatters across the floor, and Rurik and I both dive for it. I grab his shirt, dragging him back across the concrete floor, and crawl over him, more determined than ever to end this.

When my hand closes around the hilt, I grip it until my knuckles are white, until I'm not sure if I'll ever be able to open my hand again.

Then, I roll onto my back.

Rurik is over me in an instant, but I don't give him even a second to understand how severely the scales have been tipped.

If he can play dirty, so can I.

I slash my hand up and over and blood sprays out like rain. Rurik tries to scream, but instead, he coughs up more blood.

28

COURTNEY

Cutting someone's neck is harder than I would have imagined.

Dmitry slices the knife across Rurik's neck, and he's clearly mortally injured, but it takes several more wrenches of the blade before Rurik finally stops trying to crawl away, before he finally lies still.

As soon as it's over, I expect Dmitry to order everyone around, to claim his position as their leader.

Instead, he turns towards the men who sided with Rurik and watches them carefully.

I don't understand. Dmitry won. He killed Rurik. So why the hesitation?

I've stayed away from him long enough and suddenly, I can't bear it another second. I step around the blood and wrap an arm around Dmitry.

His face is bruised and swollen. He's sweaty and breathing heavily and covered in blood.

But he's Dmitry.

My Dmitry.

He tucks an arm around my back and continues looking towards Rurik's men.

"Well?" he asks with a shrug. "Does it count?"

Does it count? Of course it counts. It has to count. Right?

"Oh," I say, realizing the problem. I helped him. For a moment, I'm embarrassed and maybe even ashamed, but as the absurdity of the situation washes over me, I'm furious. "Oh."

Everyone is watching me, and I can't believe there is any question about the legitimacy of who won that fight. I can't believe anyone would stand here and defend Rurik after what he did.

"You have to be fucking kidding me," I say, pushing away from Dmitry to stand in front of him, arms crossed over my chest. I point down to where Rurik is still bleeding out on the floor. "This piece of shit tried to cheat to win, and you want to debate whether it was fine for me to step in or not? You're all pathetic."

"Courtney," Dmitry says quietly. He reaches for my arm, but I give him my hand instead. I turn to him, eyes misty because he's alive. We're both alive. Somehow.

"I'm going to be this man's wife." I don't know where the words come from, but I know they're true and loud and undeniable. Dmitry blinks, stunned, and then his swollen mouth quirks into a slight smile. With what I know is his blessing, I turn back to Rurik's men. "I'm going to be the—the First Lady of the Tsezar Bratva—"

"Queen," Dmitry whispers, squeezing my fingers. "You'll be queen."

I like the sound of that. "I'm going to be the queen of the Tsezar Bratva, and unless you want both mine and my husband's wrath, I suggest you choose the correct leader to follow. And since your original one is dead, there is really only one choice."

Someone in the crowd mumbles something about the threat of my wrath, and I can't see who the scoffer is, but I point to Rurik again. "Two guards had to pull me off Rurik to keep me from ripping his face off, and my feet were tied to a chair. So perhaps you don't want to see my wrath."

Immediately, the room goes quiet, and I feel Dmitry standing close behind me. His warmth leaks into my skin, and I realize all at once how much I missed him.

How much I missed his body pressed against mine.

I lean back against his chest, my head resting on his shoulder, and he wraps his arm around me, laying his hand over my belly.

"So," he says. "Tell me: does it count?"

The men look at one another, searching for who the naysayer will be, but no one steps forward.

Finally, a middle-aged Japanese man behind us clears his throat. "If Dmitry hadn't cheated, Rurik would have won by cheating. So, I say it's fair. The wrong cancels the wrong."

The men around him nod in agreement, and I can tell he's a leader of some kind. I've never seen him before, but I smile, and he nods, his expression stoic.

Slowly, the rest of the circle nods, and as everyone reaches agreement, they begin to leave.

Dmitry and I stay standing in the middle of the room as it clears out, person by person.

After a few minutes, we're alone.

I just declared myself as his wife in front of an entire room full of people, so I'm not sure why I'm nervous, but I am. My palms are clammy, and my heart races as I turn around in his arms and look up into his eyes.

He's going to have bruises across the better part of his face but even through all of the black and blue welts, I can tell he's beautiful.

"I'm sorry," I say, staring at his chest to avoid the fire I feel in my stomach when I look in his eyes.

His finger hooks under my chin, and he lifts my face to his. "Why?"

I take a deep breath, trying to steady myself. "For—everything, I guess. I'm sorry you had to come here to save me, and I'm sorry I interfered in the fight. That could have ruined everything for both of us if they hadn't agreed."

"I would have died if you hadn't interfered," he says plainly.

I shake my head, unwilling to accept that possibility. "No, you would have found a way out. I should have waited and then you would have looked as powerful as you are in the face of your men. Now, they probably think I'm some power-crazed woman. I shouldn't have challenged your abilities that way, and I—"

"You saved my life," he says slowly. "Screw what anyone else thinks, Courtney."

My name on his lips is like a beautiful song, and I close my eyes and allow myself to be carried away in the melody.

"If you meant what you said ... " He drags his finger down my neck, over my collarbone, and around my side to my hip, making me aware of every nerve-ending in my entire body. "Well, if you meant it, then I want you to be powerful. I want my men to respect you and see how dangerous you can be."

"And what did I say?" I ask, curious if I actually blacked out and dreamt part of it.

Dmitry's large hand pressed into my lower back, pulling me firmly against him. "You declared yourself my queen."

"Oh right," I say. "That."

He circles his hips against me. "Did you mean it?"

I want to say that it was just for show, just to save our lives. I'm not ready to lay myself bare in front of him just yet.

But I can't stop myself.

"I meant it." I nod, biting my lower lip. "I really meant it."

Suddenly, his mouth is on mine.

I'm so surprised by the move that I flinch and let out a yelp, but in an instant, I'm sinking into his kiss. His lips are soft and warm, his tongue swirling into my mouth. I breathe him in and sag against him.

When he pulls away, I keep my eyes closed, hoping he'll come back. I'm not ready to be done kissing him.

I don't know if I'll ever be done.

"Courtney," he says gently.

I open my eyes, and then step back.

His blue eyes are pure fire looking into mine, and I'm afraid I'll be burned.

"If you are to be my queen, I have to insist that you never put yourself in this kind of danger again."

"I didn't have much of a choice," I snap. "I was kidnapped, if you remember."

"Just promise me," Dmitry says, leaning down to nip at my lower lip.

"What if I don't?" I say, trying to hide my smile.

He swipes his tongue across his top lip and arches a brow at me. "Then I'll have to punish you."

My heart leaps at the thought. "What kind of punishment?"

Dmitry rolls his eyes upwards in thought while his hand caresses down my back. When he reaches my backside, he slaps his hand against me. "Maybe a spanking would be in order."

"And that would be my punishment?" My lips pucker in pleasure. "Maybe I'll have to put myself in danger again soon. I might like that."

Dmitry smacks me again and growls. "Let's go home."

Dmitry drove himself to the warehouse, but as we're leaving, his face is starting to swell up in concerning ways, and I offer to drive.

"Okay, you're really trying to emasculate me now," he says as he tosses me the keys.

"That's my secret plan."

As I drive, Dmitry tells me about Tati staying with my father.

"He didn't mind taking care of a little girl?" I ask.

Dmitry shakes his head. "In fact, he seemed really excited about it."

My father raised me on his own, but I always assumed I was a fluke. Aside from me, he's never been good with kids. He's never been interested in them, either. He always complains when people sit in the waiting room of the shop with their kids.

"They get things all sticky," he says.

Tati is a special girl, though.

She's mature for her age, probably because she has been through more than most people experience in their entire lives.

She's an easy person to love, and it warms my heart that my father might come to love her, too.

Halfway home, Dmitry closes his eyes and lays his head back against the headrest. He squeezes my fingers and I smile, knowing he trusts me as I drive us home.

29

DMITRY

Courtney is still trembling when we pull up in front of her father's shop.

I'm not sure what to say to her. About my life. About the dangers she will face.

At the warehouse, she announced herself as my queen, but I don't know whether she really meant it or not. It could have been because, out of kindness, she couldn't stand the idea of seeing me torn apart by Rurik's men because of her interference.

Lawrence Palillo runs out of the shop before the car is even in park. I stay in the car to towel off as much of the blood as I can off my face. I watch through the windshield as he wraps Courtney in a hug, his face buried in her hair, and whispers words I can't hear into her ears.

I can tell by the shaking of Courtney's shoulders that she's crying.

When I've cleaned up as best I can, I step out of the car. Tati sees me and beams, but when she notices my injuries, her jaw drops.

Are you okay?

I give her the biggest smile I can muster. *Just a bruise. I'll be fine. Don't worry about me.*

She nods hesitantly, not sure whether to believe me.

Did you have fun? I ask Tati, trying to keep things light with her. I don't want her to know how close we all were to dying.

She tells me how she and Lawrence colored, ate candy, and watched television. *I even taught him a few dance moves. He isn't very good, though.*

"I'm sure we would all love to see those moves," I say and sign simultaneously. Courtney and Lawrence turn to us, and I twirl my finger at him. "Tati says she taught you to dance."

Courtney gasps in amused surprise and wipes at her eyes. "I tried to get you to dance with me for years, and you always refused."

Lawrence's cheeks go pink. "I've grown soft in my old age."

Tati spins past me and hugs Courtney's legs. Courtney scoops her up into her arms where they rub noses and giggle, and I can't believe I ever lived without the two of them in my life.

The reality that I might have to return to that life once again is only compounded when Lawrence walks over to me, envelope in hand. He presses it into my palm before I can refuse.

"This is yours," he says.

"Lawrence," I start, shaking my head, trying to push it away. "I don't want—"

"I don't want there to be any imbalance between us," he says, silencing me the way few men have ever been able to. "I made a deal, and I intend to stick to it. If the deal changes from this point on, then that's fine with me."

We both glance back at Courtney and Tati, both too lost in one another to pay any attention to us, and then I shake Lawrence's hand.

There won't be any further dealings between my Bratva and his shop, regardless of what happens between myself and Courtney.

Perhaps, I too have gone soft.

When we get home for the night, Tati is exhausted after a fun time with "Grandpa Larry," and we put her to sleep after a bath and several books.

As soon as Tati is out of the equation, Courtney and I slip back into silence.

There's so much to say that it feels overwhelming. I'm not sure where to start.

So, I simply start.

"Your father paid me what he owed," I say. "I tried to refuse it, but he's a proud man."

She folds her legs underneath her on the couch. "Not unlike another man I know."

I smirk and run a hand through my hair. She isn't wrong.

"You're officially free now." I say. "You can leave if you want. Go stay with your father. Go back to your dorm. You can do whatever you want."

"Whatever I want," she echoes, forehead wrinkled in thought.

I hope my desires aren't written as plainly on my face as they feel in my heart. Unlike any other woman I've ever been with, I want whatever Courtney wants. If she wants to be with me, I'll be the happiest man in the world. If she doesn't ... well, I'll try to accept it.

I stare at the log burning in the fireplace to give myself something to focus on while Courtney thinks, and I'm so distracted that I don't realize Courtney is moving towards me until the cushion I'm on sinks slightly.

I turn and see her crawling towards me on her hands and knees, caramel eyes liquid in the flow of the flames.

"I know what I want," she says, crawling over me and settling on my lap, her legs on either side of my waist.

My heart feels like it's swelling in my chest, and I'm afraid it will expand too much for my chest. I'm afraid it might burst.

"You do?" I ask, wrapping my hands around her waist, keeping her close to me.

She dips her head low, her dark hair fanning around us like a curtain. It's still damp from her shower and smells like vanilla, and I could live in it. Her lips brush across mine, teasing me with an achingly soft kiss before pulling away and pressing her forehead to mine.

"I want *you*, Dmitry," she breathes.

The words send a current through me, and I tangle my hands in her hair and pull her to me. Her mouth crashes over mine, and I hold the contact as I shift her sideways and lay her down across the couch.

She's wearing an oversized T-shirt and a pair of leggings, and I peel her clothes off delicately, as though they're the most expensive lingerie.

I lavish her body in kisses and bites and caresses, tasting every inch of her because I can.

Because she wants to be here.

Because she isn't mine; we belong to each other.

I whisper her name over and over again as I push inside of her, as she wraps her legs around my back and moans her pleasure.

Just as her moans reach a crescendo, I slip my hand between us and circle my finger over her center.

Courtney falls apart.

Every inch of her shakes and trembles, and I wrap my arms around her and press inside of her with gentle persistence until it's over.

"Oh my God," she says in a lazy, unbelievably sexy laugh, one arm thrown haphazardly over her face. Then, suddenly, she peers up at me, eyes narrowed, and grins. "My turn."

She pushes me to an upright position on the couch and presses my thighs apart.

When her mouth slides over me, I tip my head back and shudder.

Using her mouth and her tongue and her hands, Courtney pushes me to the edge of oblivion. And then she pulls back.

Over and over again, she toys with me, enjoying the control. Enjoying the power.

Finally, though, I can't stand it anymore.

I grab a fistful of her hair and drag her gently up onto my lap. She's grinning, proud of herself, as I fumble to get inside of her, desperate in a way I've never felt before.

Then, she slides down my length and rolls her hips against mine.

Courtney bucks and teases and grinds onto me until my vision blurs, and nothing exists beyond her. Beyond our bodies together.

I wrap an arm around her and pump into her faster and faster, growing more needy, more frantic with each thrust.

Until I fall.

Courtney smooths her hands in gentle strokes down my chest and back. She hugs my neck and kisses my cheeks as the most intense orgasm of my life moves through me.

When we're done, I cradle her in my arms and carry her upstairs, our clothes forgotten in the sitting room.

The night is spent wrapped up in one another until we're both too tired to move.

No matter how late you stay up making insane, acrobatic love to your girlfriend, there is no such thing as "sleeping in" when an excited seven-year-old wants to see Santa.

Courtney and I both wake up to the sound of Tati knocking on the door. Before we can even answer, she throws it open and jumps into our bed.

I tighten the sheet around my waist and Courtney clutches it to her chest, suppressing a surprised laugh. *What is it, sweet girl?*

Santa is at the mall, she says. *Can we go? Please, please?*

I turn to Courtney, worried how she'll feel about it. The last two times we went to the mall ended in disaster. It might be too soon for her to risk it again.

But when she looks at me, I don't see any fear. There is a steely determination as she says, *It's up to Uncle Dmitry. Whatever he wants to do.*

"Uncle Dmitry" can't refuse Tati anything, so I relent and half an hour after waking up, we're standing in line at the mall.

If Courtney is nervous at all, she doesn't show it. She holds Tati's hand and smiles at me, and it feels like we're any other normal family waiting in line.

When Tati gets to go up to see Santa, Courtney follows behind her to interpret, but as soon as Tati signs to the jolly old man, he signs back to her, asking if she's been a good girl all year. Misty-eyed, Courtney climbs down to stand next to me, watching Tati intently.

"You're really good with her," I say, wrapping an arm around her waist.

She lays her head on my shoulder. "So are you. I know you weren't expecting to be a father figure, but you've been amazing with her. So patient and gentle."

I kiss Courtney's temple, and we watch as Tati climbs down from Santa's lap, hugs both elves, and then meets up with us just outside the fence.

Well, what did you ask for? I ask, kneeling down in front of her. Part of me doesn't want to know. Tati has lost so much this year, and I'm afraid she'll want something we can't give her.

It's a secret, she admonishes with a playful slap on my arm. *If I tell, it won't come true.*

Those are birthday wishes, Courtney says, tweaking the end of her nose. *You can tell what you asked Santa for.*

Tati narrows her eyes, debating whether Courtney can be trusted. Then, she leans close, hands close to her chest. *I want to go to school. With other kids.*

I'm so stunned, I don't know what to think. Courtney reacts first.

School? Courtney asks.

Tati looks at Courtney as though she's crazy. *Yes. Like other kids my age. I know you guys said I have to get better. Well. I'm better. And I'm bored at home. And watching you guys kiss is gross.*

This time, I can't keep myself from laughing. "So much for being the adults in the room," I rib Courtney, and she grins.

Sure, Tati. If you're the only kid on the planet who wants to go to school as a Christmas present, you got it.

Tati beams. *And I want a life-size unicorn too!*

Courtney pulls her into a tickle hug until Tati can barely breathe from laughter, and I can't imagine a better way to spend a weekend.

We have each been through so much, but when we're all together, it feels as though our wounds are healed. As though we are slowly healing one another. And I know Courtney has played a huge part in that.

Without her, I'm not sure where Tati and I would be, and it makes me love her all the more.

Snuggled on the couch we made love on the night before, Courtney and I talk in the light of the fire and the Christmas tree.

About everything and nothing.

I've never been so at ease in a person's company before, so relaxed.

My life has always been striving and fighting and working to keep control and power. With Courtney, I can forget all of that.

Almost.

"I arranged for you to be my beneficiary." I say it casually, as though it's obvious, but I feel Courtney stiffen in my arms.

I smooth my hands down her arms to try and relax her but it's useless. She spins around to face me. "Why? I mean ... we just ... why?"

I kiss her lips. "I want you and Tati to always be cared for. No matter what happens to me."

"Nothing is going to happen to you," she says.

"It might."

She squeezes her eyes closed and shakes her head. I want to protect Courtney, but I can't let her be in denial about my life. About what it could mean for us.

"It might," I repeat, nuzzling my face against her neck. "And if something does happen to me, I want to make sure you and Tati will have everything you need. I don't want you to be left to fend for yourself."

"Like those widows you give money to?"

Her words surprise me. "Who told you that?"

"Rurik's man." She lays her palm on my chest. "That night you brought me home with you, you were delivering money to Bratva widows and their children."

I swallow. I didn't know anyone knew about that. I didn't even tell Sevastian. When I first introduced the idea to my father, he called it weakness. He said a real man would make sure his family was protected in case of his death. Therefore, it wasn't our responsibility to care for the families.

I didn't agree. So, I worked the money into the budget in small ways, ensuring the money came from places where no one would notice or question it.

I've been doing it that way for years.

"They're part of the family, too," I say simply. "Their children don't deserve to starve."

Suddenly, Courtney's mouth is on mine, warm and soft. Her kiss goes from gentle to heated in a second, and I wrap my arm around her waist, drawing her against me.

Her dancer's body is toned and limber, and I'm already thinking of all the things I'm going to do to her when she pulls away, breathless.

"I don't deserve you." Her words are so quiet I can barely hear them. She says it again. "I don't deserve you."

I grab her chin and lift her face to mine, forcing her to look into my eyes. "You're more than worthy of every good thing."

I can see in her face that she doesn't believe me, and I wonder how many years it will take me to convince Courtney that she doesn't have to earn my love. That she doesn't have to earn anyone's love.

She's already deserving.

"You make me feel like a better man, Courtney. You make me feel like I can be a father to Tatiana. Your fire and determination and kindness inspire me to lead the way I always wanted to, instead of the way my father dictated. You make me a better person and if that isn't deserving of love and protection, then I don't know what is."

Her eyes are glassy, tears beginning to spill over onto her cheeks, and I lean forward and kiss the trails away.

When my lips work their way back to her mouth, she's pliant and eager. After a few minutes, she grabs my hand and leads me up the stairs. Despite the little sleep we got the night before, Courtney and I don't even make it to the bed before we're naked and devouring one another.

Then, I carry her to the shower where I lather her up only to get her dirty again.

When I lay her down in bed in the early hours of the morning, she's weary, but she draws me over her and takes me in again, sheltering me in the warmth of her body and the love of her heart.

I'm not sure how we'll ever get a good night's sleep again.

Before the sun is even up, there's another knock on our bedroom door. Moments later, the weight of an excited seven-year-old crashes over us.

When I open my eyes enough to look at her, Tati is wide-eyed and frantic, signing the same thing over and over again: *It's Christmas! Today is Christmas!*

I kiss Courtney and hold her hand as we follow Tati down the stairs to celebrate our first Christmas together as a family.

30

COURTNEY

18 months later

The sand is warm, and I stretch out across it languidly.

The last year has been one of the busiest of my life. Between having a baby, going to school, and starting my own dance studio, I've never been pulled in so many directions before.

I've also never been happier.

Dmitry, of course, insists that I don't need to work. Olivia is still only nine months old and Tati is nearing nine, meaning she has more and more questions about what happened to her parents and some of her memories from the accident have begun to surface. Our kids need me, and he's more than happy to provide for all of us.

But the dancing isn't about money; it's about me.

Having an hour a few days a week where I can turn my mom brain off and focus on my body, my health, my happiness—it's priceless. And Dmitry supports it every step of the way.

I teach a few kids—Tati included—for a few sessions every week in the dance study Dmitry had installed for me. We put on performances for the parents and, one day, when I'm out of school, maybe, I'll have time for more classes and be a proper dance studio. We could even enter competitions.

That's a distant dream, though. Right now, I want to focus on my kids and Dmitry.

Just as the thought crosses my mind, a plastic shovel whacks me in the side of the head.

"Ouch." I sit up and Tati has her hand over her mouth, hiding a laugh.

Sorry. I didn't mean to hit you. She points to Olivia, who has crawled over to the beach bag and is squirting sunscreen all over the sand.

I jump up and drag her away from the bag, kicking and screaming. I had a solid three minutes of relaxing, which is more than I usually get at the beach when I'm alone with the girls.

When Dmitry comes on our little field trips with us, he likes to run with Tati in the surf and hoists Olivia onto his shoulders. More importantly for my entertainment, he walks around with no shirt on, allowing me to lie back and admire his muscles which ripple almost as much as the ocean.

He's busy today, though. He has been for weeks.

I don't begrudge him his work, but I miss him. The lease agreement he had with Akio and his Yakuza ended six months ago, and they have been fighting over the stash houses ever since.

Dmitry managed to reclaim two of them, but the third is more deeply in contested territory, and he's having a hard time negotiating it back, which has led to a lot of late nights for him.

I just pray it will be resolved before he winds up in another bloody feud. I don't want Dmitry to miss a second of Olivia's childhood. She's too precious and growing way too fast.

He's trying to cut back on the illegal dealings. He and Pasha have been moving towards starting a legitimate import/export business to bring in money and disentangle the Bratva from some of their seedier business ventures. I know he's doing it for me, and I appreciate it.

Still, I miss him.

Where is Daddy? Tati asks, raising a hand to her forehead and squinting up at the house.

No one told her to call Dmitry 'Daddy.' She made the choice on her own. Every time she says it, my heart melts a little.

Working, but he'll be home tonight.

She frowns, and I pinch her cheek. *Are you ready to go inside and get a snack? I'm hungry.*

Her eyes widen. *Ice-cream cones? I want the one with caramel in the middle.*

I wrinkle my nose like I'm thinking, but when Tati presses her hands together in a plea, lower lip pouted out, she knows I'm putty in her hands. I relent and gather up Olivia and the towel while she runs up the hill to the back deck of the house.

I'm too busy brushing sand from Olivia's chubby thighs to notice the figure standing just inside the sliding glass door until I'm on the deck.

Tati is wrapped around his legs, leaving wet stains on pants and sand all over the floor, but Dmitry just kisses the top of her head and sends her into the kitchen. When he turns and sees me, his face splits into a smile.

At home, he turns into *my* Dmitry.

Not the Bratva leader or the boss. My boyfriend. My partner. The man I love.

It's the smile he reserves only for me, and it makes me weak in the knees every time I see it.

"Tati insisted you told her she could have an ice-cream cone for a snack," he says, taking Olivia from me and kissing her cheek.

"She gave me the puppy-dog eyes."

He smiles and shakes his head. "You never stood a chance."

"What are you doing home early?" I ask, slipping out of my sandals and wrapping my towel around my waist.

Dmitry grabs the towel and throws it on the ground, raising sexy eyebrows at me in my bathing suit.

My body has changed since having Olivia, but a healthy diet and regular dance classes have helped me feel more confident. Dmitry's obvious appreciation of my post-baby body also makes it easier to feel sexy.

"Courtney?" I hear my dad's voice coming from the front hall, and I frown.

"I didn't know my dad was coming by today." I reach down and wrap the towel around myself again, swatting away Dmitry's hand when he playfully tries to disrobe me again.

Dmitry shrugs like he had no idea either.

"Back here, Dad."

As soon as he walks into the room, Tati is jumping into his arms.

He grimaces at her wet bathing suit, sand-covered legs, and ice-cream covered face for only a second before gladly accepting her hug and kissing her temple.

Missed you, he signs with one hand.

Sign language hasn't come as easily to him, but he's trying really hard, and Tati doesn't mind.

"What are you doing here?" I ask.

Like Dmitry, my father is strangely evasive. He mumbles something about it not being a crime to come visit his grandkids on a Saturday and then allows himself to be dragged back to the playroom by Tati.

"We won't see him for a while," Dmitry jokes. "Tati will have him hostage back there for hours."

He once again kisses Olivia and then turns, handing her off to the nanny who has been waiting suspiciously in the wings.

"What is going on?" I narrow my eyes and do my best to make a serious face, but as soon as the nanny is gone with Olivia, Dmitry yanks my towel off with one smooth pull and slides his arms around my waist.

"My father is here," I whisper as he kisses me.

Dmitry trails his kisses across my jaw and down my neck. "He'll be occupied for hours, remember?"

"That does not mean I want to have sex with you in our living room," I hiss, eyes fluttering closed as he bites my collarbone.

"Then let's go out to the deck," he says, pulling the door open and pushing me outside, never once taking his hands off my body.

I stumble back and cling to him so I won't trip. "So our neighbors can watch us. Good idea."

A low laugh rumbles through him, and I feel the vibrations in all the right places. "It will be the best show they've ever seen."

With every press of his lips on my skin and every caress of his hands, my head is getting more and more fuzzy. If I let him continue, I really will strip down and let him do unspeakable things to me in full view of everyone else on the beach.

With every ounce of self-restraint in my body, I push him away.

"I wasn't really going to take you out here." Dmitry gives me a wicked smile. "Unless you wanted to, of course."

I want to, I sign, not trusting my voice. I clear my throat. "You are dangerous."

He winks at me and then reaches for my hand, walking me towards the low glass railing that looks out over the beach and the water.

"You're home early," I say, stating the obvious. "Is it good news or bad news?"

"Good news."

"Did you take care of everything with Akio?" I ask hopefully.

He gives me a small smile and nods. "I think so. He gave me the third house."

"He gave it to you?" I ask. "No questions asked?"

Dmitry shrugs. "He was tired of fighting, and I have more men than he does. I kept things fair, though."

After six months of back and forth fighting, it's hard to imagine it could end so easily, but I'm so relieved Dmitry will be around more that I don't say anything.

"I don't want to talk about that, though," Dmitry says, mirroring my exact thoughts. He twines his fingers through mine and pulls me closer to him.

I feel naked in my swimsuit since he's still in his work clothes. His jeans are dark, resting low on his hips, and his black shirt is tight in all the right places. It isn't a seasonally appropriate outfit, but I'm not about to tell him to change. He looks yummy.

I lay my palms gently on his chest and sigh, content just to be close to him. "This is nice."

He smiles. "How nice?"

"Really nice?" I say with a shrug. Dmitry answers with a soft roll of his hips against mine, and I hold up a finger to stop him. "Not that nice. I told you, I'm not giving our neighbors a free show."

He laughs and bends down to nip at my lower lip. "I'm sure we could arrange a payment system. It could be like pay-per-view. We'll advertise and gauge what the interest is. It could be another good side business for us both."

"It would certainly allow us to spend more time together," I say, rolling my eyes.

Dmitry nuzzles his stubble against my cheek, and I wrap my arms around his neck and bite his earlobe. "But I don't think they can afford us."

He growls and pulls away to peruse my body, and I suddenly wish I hadn't awoken the beast. Dmitry can make me drop my underwear with his normal ocean-blue eyes. So, his sex eyes are positively panty-melting.

"Later," I say, looking out towards the water to regain my composure. "Keep thinking what you're thinking, and we'll pick this up later."

He takes a deep breath. "When later?"

"Later," I shrug. "Whenever you want. We have plenty of time."

"How much time?" he asks.

I turn to him, brow furrowed. "All the time in the world. What do you mean?"

He rubs his lips together nervously, and suddenly I'm afraid, though I can't say why.

"Not too long ago, I remember when we only had six months," he says quietly. "I remember thinking you were going to leave, and I honestly didn't know what I was going to do."

"You would have been fine without me," I say, swatting at him playfully even though my insides are molten. Something is happening, and I'm afraid I'm not ready for it.

Dmitry grabs my hand and brings my fingers to his lips, kissing each fingertip individually until I can't breathe. "No, I wouldn't have been. I would not have been fine without you, Courtney."

I blink up at him, unable to find any words, playful or otherwise.

"You and the girls are the only people I've ever thought I couldn't live without. And that thought scares the shit out of me," he admits. "The idea that my happiness is so dependent on you being here with me. On you not giving up on me because I'm moody and violent and distant. My happiness hinges on coming home to you every day and lying down next to you every night. My life revolves around seeing the sweet smiles of our girls and knowing that you and I have all the time in the world."

I smooth a hand over his chest. "My happiness depends on those things, too. Don't worry. You have me, Dmitry. As long as you want me, you have me."

Before the words are even out of my mouth, Dmitry pulls away from me. I reach for him until I realize what he's doing.

He pulls something from his back pocket and drops down to his knee, and my vision goes fuzzy. My heart is hammering inside my chest, and I'm nearly convinced this is a dream. A wonderful, wonderful dream.

"I want you forever, Courtney," he continues, unable to keep himself from smiling that gorgeous smile he saves just for me. "Will you marry me?"

I grab his face and kiss him, too excited and shaky for words. It's a long, deep kiss that seems to go on and on. I never want it to end.

Dmitry laughs and pulls away from me. "Is that a yes?"

I kiss him again in case the kiss-to-English translation isn't perfect.

When he pulls away again, he's beaming. Actually shining from the inside out.

I nearly forgot about the ring, so when he slips the huge rock on my finger, I gasp. "Yes!"

"Oh, *now* you answer," he teases, pulling me against his chest. "Do you like it?"

"I love it." I lower my hand and look up at him. "I love you."

He kisses me, and I don't know how long it lasts, but it ends when the sliding glass door opens and Tati runs out, my dad holding Olivia just behind her.

"Are congratulations in order?" my dad asks.

I nod, tears brimming, and he hoots, bouncing Olivia gently in celebration.

Tati is confused because she thought we were already married, and she's way more excited about going back to the beach than opening a bottle of champagne. So, Dmitry and I vow to celebrate properly later when my dad is gone and the girls are asleep.

For now, we're happy to run in the sand and splash in the ocean with our family.

31

COURTNEY

Four Months Later

"He's going to lose his mind when he sees you," Sadie says, laying my train over my shoulders and adjusting my hair underneath.

She's pinned half of my hair up into a braid that wraps around the crown of my head and left the other half to tumble down over my shoulder in shampoo-commercial waves.

"I feel like I'm setting the bar too high. I'll never look this good again," I say.

"Dmitry would disagree," Sadie says, raising an eyebrow. "When you take off that dress tonight, it will be the best moment of his entire life."

I laugh. She's probably right. Dmitry tried to seriously suggest we just skip the reception and go straight to the honeymoon. He wanted to carry me down the aisle and straight to our bedroom.

He also wanted *that* to be the honeymoon.

"We can travel as much as you want later," he said. "I just want you and your body for one uninterrupted week."

I disagreed only because I thought one uninterrupted week of Dmitry's naked body would kill me.

"Are you ready?" Sadie asks, standing back. "Because I'm done primping. You are perfect."

"I think so." I squeeze my eyes closed and take a deep breath. "I can't believe this is really happening."

Sadie gives me a hug and then leaves to track down Devon. He and my dad are on babysitting duty until the wedding starts, and Sadie is desperate to see her boyfriend around children. They're even taking the girls for one night of the honeymoon to give my dad a break because Sadie wants to see what kind of father Devon would be.

She hasn't specifically said so, but I know things between them are getting really serious. Devon didn't make the best first (or second or third) impression on me, but I'm trying to like him more. He's important to Sadie and seems to make her really happy.

I give myself one more look in the mirror and then leave to find the photographer. The ceremony is intimate—just our family and friends on the beach—but I wanted to document it properly.

When I open the door, however, there are two bodies blocking my way.

I yelp in surprise and stumble back. Immediately, a warm, familiar hand is around my wrist, and Dmitry pulls me back to standing.

I go to thank him before I remember it's our wedding day and wrap my arms around myself. "You aren't supposed to see me before the wedding. It's bad—"

The words die on my lips when I finally look over and see the second body in the doorway.

My mother.

"Hi, sweetheart," she says with a small smile.

I blink at her, unsure what to think.

Sadie told me my mother had come into town when everyone thought I was kidnapped or missing, but after a day or two of no news, she left like always.

My mother grows bored quickly. She can't stay in the same place for very long, which is why I long ago gave up on keeping track of her. Even if I'd wanted to send her a wedding invitation, I didn't know where to send it.

Dmitry grabs my shoulders and leans forward. "I know you didn't invite her, but I thought it was important that she be here. If I was wrong, I'll personally escort her off the premises, but I just think you should consider how you would feel years from now if your mother wasn't at your wedding."

His voice is low, but I know my mother can still hear him. Her eyes go soft, forehead wrinkled, and I realize that—even though it makes no biological sense—she has the same puppy-dog face as Tatiana.

Unfortunately, it has the same devastating effect on my heart.

The ice in my chest thaws slightly, and I kiss Dmitry and agree to speak to my mom.

"I only have a few minutes," I tell her, stepping into a side hallway just off the kitchen.

"I know," she says, standing back to admire me. "You look beautiful, sweetheart."

I smile but don't know what to say, and my mother sighs. Her dark hair is the same shade as mine, though she has been dying hers for years to keep away the grays, and she tucks it behind her ear nervously.

"I know I haven't always been around when you needed me, but when Dmitry reached out to me, I knew I had to come," she says. "I've never been the best mom to you, but I hope you know I still love you."

I cross my arms, unwilling to give her even an inch. I want her to spill her guts to me before I make my decision.

"That Dmitry is a catch," she says. "Handsome and thoughtful enough to try and make today perfect for you. Hold onto him."

"I will."

She swallows and folds her hands in front of her. "Well, I don't have anything else to say. Just that I'm sorry, and I hope you'll let me stay. I want to see my daughter get married."

Before Tati and Olivia, I might have turned my mother away. I might have refused to let her attend my wedding day.

But now, I can't help but think how devastated I'd be if one of my girls experienced a big life moment without me. Even though my mother missing out on my life has been entirely her fault, I don't want her to ever be able to blame me for keeping her away. So, I nod.

"You can stay, but keep away from my girls. I don't want you confusing them." The words catch in my throat, and I swallow back tears. "I only want to introduce them to you if I know you're going to stick around."

My mother nods, understanding.

We don't make any plans for the future. There are no promises for our relationship to change or for her to be around more, but for today, she's here, and I have to admit, it isn't the worst thing in the world.

∽

The wedding is a blur of happiness mixed with adorable cameos by our girls.

Tati is the ring bearer in a frilly white princess dress she picked out herself, and she pulls Olivia in a wagon behind her. Olivia is supposed to be the flower girl, but she's much more content playing in the basket of flowers than throwing them in the aisle.

They're perfect.

The breeze off the ocean makes Dmitry's hair stick up at strange angles and it whips at my dress and veil until I finally take the veil off and hand it to Sadie to hold. Seagulls squawk loudly from the shoreline and the neighbor's kids scream as they boogie-board next door to us, interrupting the minister a few times.

It's all perfect.

Every single second is perfect, and when Dmitry bends me back in a kiss to the whoops and cheers of our family and friends, I've never been so happy in all my life.

I convinced Dmitry to have a reception, but he vetoed the idea of a dance and dinner. Our guests are invited back to the house for cake and coffee before men from the Bratva politely yet firmly escort them out.

Do I have to go? Tati asks, her eyes wide and blinking.

No puppy-dog eyes, Dmitry warns her before kissing her forehead. *You are going to have so much fun with Sadie and Devon.*

"I bought so much candy you won't even believe it," Devon says, enunciating so Tati can read his lips.

That's enough to assuage Tati's worries, and Sadie does her best to assuage mine.

"Olivia will be fine," she says. "I've babysat before."

"Not all night, though," I say.

"The nanny will be there, too," Sadie reminds me. "Don't worry."

As Sadie and Devon load up the girls, I do my best not to fret, though it's difficult. It's the first time I'll be away from Olivia for more than just one night.

Dmitry lets me stand on the porch and wave until the car is no longer visible, but then he wraps his arm around my waist and drags me inside like a caveman.

"You aren't worried at all?" I ask as he kisses my neck and chest, his hands exploring the curves of my body.

"Maybe a little," he admits. "But I'm way more turned on than I am worried."

I gasp, trying my best to hide my amusement. "That is horrible."

"It's honest," he says, searching my side for the zipper. "I want to get this dress off you and hear you scream my name. If that makes me a bad father, then so be it. Tonight, I'll be a bad father."

I want to reprimand him, but at that moment, he finds the zipper and a rush of cold air hits my body as he peels the dress down.

I didn't need to wear a bra with the dress, so with one tug, I'm left standing in a white thong and my lacy garter. Dmitry growls and drops to his knees in front of me.

His hands caress my thighs and then he drags his teeth down the inside of my leg until they catch on the garter. He tugs it off and tosses it to the side like a dog throwing a bone. Then, he focuses his attention between my legs.

I curl my fingers in his hair as he pushes my panties aside and flicks his tongue over me. He sucks and plays and massages until my legs are trembling, and I'm not sure I'll be able to stand much longer.

"Dmitry."

He groans. "Like that," he says against me. "I want you to say my name like that."

I laugh and just as I do, he wraps his lips around my center, and pleasure blooms inside of me. If Dmitry's arm wasn't pressed to my stomach, pinning me to the wall, I'd fall flat on my face.

He caresses me with soft kisses until the trembling fades, and then he stands up, pressing his body into mine until we are flush. Until there is nothing but him.

"My legs are JELL-O, and we're still in the entryway," I say, pointing to the door.

Dmitry grins and scoops me into his arms. "Good thing you're light enough for me to carry."

He carries me up the stairs and throws me back on our bed.

I don't even have time to sit up before he grabs my hips, rolls me onto my stomach, and then pulls me to the edge of the bed.

I arch my back and shimmy my hips from side to side. Dmitry moans and unzips his pants.

"You shouldn't do things like that," he says, snapping the waistband of my thong against my skin. "Not unless you want our first time as husband and wife to be really, *really* rough."

I look back over my shoulder, and Dmitry's blue eyes are black. Despite the sunset streaming through the open window, his pupils are dilated, and his eyes are pinned on my body, consuming me.

When he looks into my eyes, I lick my lips and arch my back even further, allowing him all the access he wants. "I like it rough."

The animal rips through him in a growl, and Dmitry positions himself at my opening, his pants around his knees, and slides inside in one stroke.

I gasp, but he doesn't slow down. Doesn't ease it in. Doesn't allow me time to adjust.

Just like I wanted, Dmitry is rough.

He claws at my hips, dragging my body onto him again and again until I'm certain I'll break. He drills into me faster and harder and it still isn't enough.

"More, please," I say, gripping the comforter. "Dmitry."

"Fuck." His hands have a bruising grip on my hips, and somehow, he finds the energy to speed up. To give me more.

Another orgasm tears through me, and I bury my face in the comforter. Immediately, Dmitry wraps his hands in my hair and lifts my face so my words are no longer muffled.

"God. Dmitry. Yes. Yes."

When my trembling finally stills, Dmitry slides out of me and rolls my limp body over. When he crawls over me, I kiss his forehead, then his lips, and then his neck. I bite his earlobe as he slides into me again, and the pace is less crushing.

It's soft and easy, and I plant my hands on his lower back and roll myself over him.

"Oh damn," he moans. His breath is hot on my neck, and I want to show him how much I love him.

I want to show him how much he means to me.

So, I make love to him. With every roll of my hips and caress of my body against his, I tell him.

I hook my legs around his thighs and draw myself up to him. I grab handfuls of his hair and moan into his ear.

I give Dmitry everything I have left, and when he finally comes, he's looking in my eyes.

His forehead wrinkles, and his eyes flutter closed for a second, but when they open, he stares at me. He brushes his blue eyes across my skin as he empties himself inside of me, and I know this is the most intimate thing I've ever done.

I know Dmitry is telling me the same thing I've been trying to tell him.

I love you.

32

DMITRY

Six months later

The house is quiet. Everyone has been asleep for hours, but I can't seem to settle.

Courtney has noticed my foul mood, but she hasn't said anything. I can only tell because she's gentler with me. Still kind and loving, but nervous, as though I'm a wild animal she adopted as a pet, and I've suddenly grown large enough to eat her.

I hate that she's nervous to talk to me, but I'm not sure how to get out of my funk.

Everything seemed to change at once when she and I got together.

I've shifted towards more legitimate businesses and away from some of the violence of my old Bratva lifestyle. And suddenly, I'm not just worried about myself and the bottom line. I'm terrified every second of where the next attack will come from and if it will harm my family.

I should be happier than ever with Olivia walking and Tati excelling in school and proving so resilient despite the trauma in her past. I should look at my gorgeous wife, who is running her own business and working towards her dreams of being a clinical psychologist, and feel nothing but joy. But I can't keep the dread at bay.

The Yakuza have completely disappeared from the city.

Akio has stopped returning my calls, and for all I know, he's dead.

The fact that he agreed to return the final stash house to me without a full-on bloodbath was always suspicious, but now I can't help but think I've underestimated him. His silence has settled over me like a dense fog, and I'm having a hard time finding my way out.

Especially since I can't just track someone down and torture them for information the way I would have before.

Well, I could, but I know Courtney wouldn't like it, and I'm trying to respect her wishes. Especially since things are already tense between us. There's no need to add another issue.

I hear Olivia cry from her nursery down the hall. I wait, hoping she'll settle herself down, but after a minute, I walk into the hallway.

Courtney is already there, along with the live-in nanny.

She's thinner than ever—Courtney, not the nanny. And she looks as tired as I feel.

The nanny, Barbara, must see it, too, because she offers to take care of Olivia and tries to push Courtney back into the bedroom. Courtney allows her to comfort Olivia, but she doesn't go to bed. She comes to me.

Even though the first six months of our marriage haven't been sunshine and roses like I hoped, Courtney still wraps her arms around my waist and buries her face in my chest. I kiss the top of her head.

"Why aren't you asleep?" I whisper.

"Why aren't you?"

I sigh, unable to give her an answer, and we both just stand there for a moment. I'm debating whether I should force Courtney into the bedroom with the threat of punishing her if she disobeys. It has been a while since we've done any role-playing and maybe that would tire her out enough that she'd get some sleep. However, before I can, Tati's door opens.

She squints against the bright hallway lights and presses a palm to her forehead. When she looks around and sees us, she jumps in surprise.

Courtney extracts herself from my hold and kneels down in front of Tati. *What is it?*

My head, Tati says, face twisted in pain.

Another headache? Courtney asks.

She nods and lets Courtney fold her into her arms.

Tati has been getting migraines for a few months. Nothing seems to help, so we rub her shoulders, offer heating pads, and keep the lights dim until they pass.

Go to your room, and I'll be in with a heating pad, Courtney says.

Tati listens and shuffles back to bed.

"They're becoming more frequent." Courtney pinches the bridge of her nose like she has a headache of her own. "We should take her to another doctor."

I lay a hand on her shoulder, offering a small amount of comfort. "I'm sure she's just growing."

"All kids grow. Not all kids get crippling migraines," she snaps. I can see immediately that she regrets it and opens her mouth to apologize, but I hold up a hand to stop her.

"No, I'll do it. Olivia is asleep, and you two both look exhausted," I say to Barbara and Courtney. "Get some rest. I'll sit with Tati tonight."

Courtney tries to argue, but I pull her into a hug and smile at the nanny. "Thank you. We appreciate it."

"It's my job," Barbara says, waving us off as she goes to get a heating pad.

As soon as she's gone, Courtney turns on me, her cheeks red. "I don't like the nanny."

"What?" I ask. "Barbara has been a lifesaver."

"*We* should be taking care of the girls," she says, gesturing between the two of us. "You and I. Not a hired helper. I feel like you're always too busy to help, and I can't do it on my own anymore."

"Which is exactly why we have Barbara. Because we can't do it alone."

"*I* can't do it alone," she says. "You've been focused on work for months now. I thought now that the stash house arrangement was sorted out, things would be better. But there is always something."

I look around, not wanting Barbara to hear us arguing, and then pull Courtney into my office. I pull the door closed, and she's like a caged tiger, pacing back and forth across the floor.

"You knew what you were signing up for," I say, trying to hide the panic in my voice. "I told you this life would be messy."

"I know you did," Courtney says, taking a deep breath. "I just thought we were signing up to do it together. I didn't think I'd be left to manage everything on my own. Do you know it has been two weeks since you've touched me?"

"We just touched in the hallway."

"Sex," she clarifies, though I already knew what she meant. "Do you still want me? Because I don't know anymore. I feel like your head is always somewhere else, and I'm not sure how to make you stay with me."

Her words break my heart, but if I crack open, there is no way of knowing what will spill out. I clench my jaw. "I'm here with you right now."

Courtney's eyes turn down in sadness, and I step forward and wrap my hands around her waist. I press a kiss to her neck.

"I'm here with you now," I repeat. I put as much feeling, as much meaning as I can into the words.

But I'm afraid. Afraid it won't be enough.

She's hesitant at first, but her body softens in my hands. She arches herself against me, and when our lips meet, I know she's as hungry for me as I am for her.

It has been too long.

I turn her around and lift her up on the edge of my desk. Courtney wraps her legs around my waist, and I moan into her mouth.

My hand is sliding down her stomach, headed for the warmth between her legs, when there's a knock on the door.

She pushes me away and wipes a hand across the back of her mouth, and I growl out, "Come in."

I expect it to be Barbara or Tati, but instead, it's Pasha.

"What in the hell?" I ask. "It's the middle of the night."

He winces. "Sorry, but she called you back. You told me to tell you when she called."

"She?" I ask.

Pasha nods, confirming the question I didn't ask.

"Elena?" Courtney asks.

I turn to her, my lower lip pinched between my teeth. "Please don't wait up for me. It may be a while."

I see the disappointment on her face, but I can't ignore this meeting. I have to go, and she knows that.

Pasha steps into the hallway, and I kiss Courtney once and then follow him out. As the door is closing, I think I hear Courtney whisper a teary "I love you," but I'm not sure, and for some reason, I don't open the door to check.

I knock on the door and wait.

I'm standing on the porch alone in the dim yellow glow of a porch light. My men wanted to come, but I told them to stay behind. I don't want anyone with me. Not for this.

When I see Elena for the first time, I want to be alone.

The door opens only a crack, and I see one eye staring out at me. "It's late."

"You called me," I remind her. "I wasn't sure this opportunity would ever come again if I didn't answer."

She stares at me for another second before opening the door.

She looks older than expected. Gray is threaded through her hair now and there are fine lines around her eyes and mouth. She's solidly middle-aged. It doesn't help that her face is pulled down in a permanent scowl.

"Come in."

The house is dark and smells like cigarette smoke, but it's clean. Pictures of Rurik hang from the walls of the hallway, and I try not to look at them.

I have no regrets over what happened. He tried to kill me, and I defended myself. Still, I'm sorry for Elena. For what she lost.

She and Rurik had been together since they were teenagers and were married for almost as long. I can't imagine what kind of mess I'd be if something happened to Courtney.

"What do you want?" she asks as she takes her seat in a recliner in the sitting room.

She doesn't offer me a seat, but I sit on the edge of the sofa and reach into my pocket for the envelope. I hold it out to her, but she doesn't reach for it.

"What is that?"

"What you're owed," I say. "Think of it like social security."

She shakes her head. "That isn't mine."

"It's Rurik's. As a widow of the Bratva, you're entitled to a small sum of money every month. I would have brought it right away, but you refused to accept any of my calls."

Rurik was a traitor. A liar and deceiver from the start. Still, I feel honor-bound to carry on the custom. To take care of Elena the way I hope someone would take care of Courtney and the girls.

"Because I didn't want to talk to the man who murdered my husband," she spits.

"We don't have to talk," I say simply. "Truly, I'd rather not. I'm just here to give you this and then I'll go home."

"Keep your money and go home."

I drop the envelope on the table. "Fine."

"You should have never come."

At first, I think she means it was a waste of time, but there is something new in her voice. Another layer of emotion beyond pure hatred.

There is … *amusement*?

The hair on the back of my neck stands up, and I stare at her.

She stares back for several seconds before her mouth pulls up at the corners into a hideous smile, like a witch, like something out of a horribly twisted nightmare. "You should have stayed home, Dmitry. You should have been there to protect your precious girls."

The world stops turning.

It feels like an anvil has landed on my head, crushing me into the ground.

Seconds turn to horrified hours as the meaning of her words washes over me.

This is a setup.

My family is in danger.

∼

There's no time for anything else as I sprint from her house and back to the car.

I call Courtney over and over again on my way home, but there is no answer. I call the guards on duty, but they don't answer, either. I call Pasha and leave a message for him to get men to my house now, but he lives further away than I am right now. I know I'll beat him there, and I'm terrified at what I might find.

I screech into the driveway, and I'm out of the car before it even comes to a halt. The front door is cracked open. I can barely breathe as I run up the stairs.

Everything looks so normal—just as I left it—but dread creeps into my bones like a chill.

All the doors upstairs are closed except for the nursery, so I take a deep breath, draw my weapon, and tiptoe towards her room. I push the door open slowly.

It takes my eyes a second to adjust, but when they do, I see Tati sleeping in the baby crib.

She's too large for the small bed, her little body curled into a ball, and she doesn't move as the light from the hallway washes over her, but I can see that her little chest is still moving. She's alive.

Then, I see a larger figure on the floor, and when I realize it's Courtney, bound and gagged and unconscious, I take a large step forward, instinctively wanting to drop to my knees and check on her.

"Ah-ah," a deep, familiar voice warns.

My blood runs cold, and I turn to see the large shadowy figure of Devon sitting in the rocking chair in the corner. Olivia is sleeping peacefully in his arms.

Courtney never liked Devon. She told me over and over again that he made her uncomfortable, but he was dating her best friend, so she tried to forgive him. And I tried to be open-minded since Courtney wanted us all to get along.

Now, I wish I'd listened to her.

"You don't want to wake them up," Devon says, a devilish smile on his face. "They're sleeping so peacefully."

"What did you do to them?" I growl, nostrils flared.

He rolls his eyes. "A little sleep aid. They'll be fine. Don't worry."

I point my gun at his head, and he holds Olivia closer to him. "How confident are you in your aim?"

I slide my finger away from the trigger. Not confident enough for that.

"That's what I thought," he says.

"Why are you doing this?" I ask. "Has this been your plan all along?"

Devon looks down at Olivia and smiles as though he cares for her. As though he isn't a monster. "How did you enjoy your visit with my mother?"

I frown, confused by his question. But when he looks up at me, it becomes clear.

He has the same thick nose as Elena. And the same mean slant to his eyes as Rurik.

How did I not see it before?

"My father was always a planner," Devon says. "He had a plan for his life, and he knew I'd play a part in that. Of course, I'm sure he thought he would be alive when he revealed his secret son, but plans change."

"What do you want?" My hands are fists at my side. "Why are you doing this?"

Devon waves a flippant, casual hand. "To take what you have. Isn't that fair? Wouldn't that make us even? You took everything I had, after all."

Courtney's foot slides out, and her head turns ever so slightly. Enough to let me know she's alive and trying to wake up. God only knows what kind of drugs this fucking monster dumped into her system.

"That one is a fighter," Devon says. "Always has been. A real stubborn bitch. It took all of my strength to knock her out."

Fire roars in my chest, and all I see is red. "I'll fucking kill you for touching her. I will rip your—"

"Tut, tut," he says, wagging a finger at me. "You should not threaten the man who has your family. Their lives are in my hands now."

I take a deep breath. "I'll give you money."

Devon bobs his head back and forth like he's thinking. "Nah, I'm okay. You know, I think I'll make more money elsewhere. These three will fetch a healthy price from an interested bidder."

This time, no amount of deep breaths in the world can ease my rage.

Just as I lunge forward, ready to snatch my baby from his arms and strangle him until he turns blue, Yakuza soldiers run through the door behind me and grab my arms.

I scream, not worrying any more about waking up Tati or Olivia. I just want to save them.

I thrash and fight, but then I feel a cold poke in my arm.

Whatever they've injected me with warms my bicep and works quickly.

I lose the ability to stand as my legs turn to mush, but I crawl across the floor, reaching for Devon's foot. I won't stop until I kill him.

He lifts his foot and brings it down hard on my hand.

I can't even scream in pain.

I've been betrayed again and this time, my family's lives are the ones at stake. I try to say Courtney's name, but my lips move around silent words.

Everything goes black.

Dmitry and Courtney's story concludes in **DAYBREAK,** *available now*.
Click the link below to start reading!
www.amazon.com/DAYBREAK

MAILING LIST

Sign up to my mailing list!
New subscribers receive a FREE steamy bad boy romance novel.

Click the link below to join.
https://readerlinks.com/l/1057996

ALSO BY NICOLE FOX

Kornilov Bratva Duet

Married to the Don (Book 1)

Til Death Do Us Part (Book 2)

Volkov Bratva

Broken Vows (Book 1)

Broken Hope (Book 2)

Broken Sins *(standalone)*

Heirs to the Bratva Empire

Can be read in any order

Kostya

Maksim

Andrei

Tsezar Bratva

Nightfall (Book 1)

Daybreak (Book 2)

Russian Crime Brotherhood

Can be read in any order

Owned by the Mob Boss

Unprotected with the Mob Boss

Knocked Up by the Mob Boss

Sold to the Mob Boss

Stolen by the Mob Boss

Trapped with the Mob Boss

Other Standalones

Vin: A Mafia Romance

Box Sets

Bratva Mob Bosses (Russian Crime Brotherhood Books 1-6)

Tsezar Bratva (Tsezar Bratva Duet Books 1-2)

Printed in Great Britain
by Amazon